TENERIFE!

Books by Elsinck:

- Tenerife!
- Murder by Fax
- Confession of a Hired Killer

TENERIFE!

by

ELSINCK

translated from the Dutch by H.G. Smittenaar

NEW AMSTERDAM PUBLISHING, Inc.

ISBN 1 881164 51 9

Printing History:
1st Dutch printing: September, 1990
2nd Dutch printing: April, 1991

1st American edition: 1992

Cover Design: Studio Combo (Netherlands)
Typography: Monica S. Rozier

TENERIFE!

The train of thought of an obsessed person always runs on a single track.

For information about sado-masochism, the author wants to thank Ingrid Harms, whose article on the subject appeared in a special insert of Vrij Nederland (Free Holland) of May 13, 1989.

1. Madrid, Wednesday, February 22, 1989

Although the man had been dead for several minutes, killed by a final blow to the neck, the murderer worked on the face of the victim with fists protected by leather bands, studded with iron points. He looked at the result as an artist might look at an almost finished painting, still on the easel. The black leather blindfold, befouled with blood, hung around the victim's neck. The whip had transformed the naked torso into a mass of raw meat. The chains around the wrists had bitten deep into the flesh. Like a marionette after a performance, the body swayed from the hooks that had been installed in the door frame.

The room was horrible. Old, dirty and neglected. It stank of the unwashed bodies that had slept, copulated and masturbated on the bed. The cracked washbasin was yellow from urine and the grubby towel, full of holes, had not been clean for some time. Brown and black spots in the ceiling were silent witnesses to the many leakages from higher floors. The wall paper was unable to hide the cracks in the wall. Two large greasy spots accentuated the head end of the rusty double bed on which a ragged blanket formed the only protection against damp and cold. Undetermined spots were visible on the wall, parallel to the bed, in the vicinity where genitals might have been positioned. Behind the half closed curtain was a window with a view of nothingness. It was drafty during the cold Madrid winter and it could not be opened during the hot summer. Through the window a small rectangular courtyard was visible, like a high concrete pipe with a view of three square yards of sky. A concrete tube, of rooms not much better than this, if not worse. People lived here. One could smell them and hear them. Sounds ricocheted against the four forbidding walls. There was singing, talking and above all, shouting. There was boozing and eating, defecating and pissing. Trash was thrown down from every floor and from a number of pipes dripped liquids and solids onto the courtyard where the Sanitation Department had long since given up all hope. Children with old faces played among the rubbish. The landlords of these rattraps rolled in luxury at the Costa's and waved Golden Credit Cards. From one of the windows the balmy voice of Julio Iglesias wafted a song about hope and love. "Quizas, quizas, quizas," sounded through the room where the corpse hung. From hooks originally destined to support a child's swing. Whereby belonged the voices of children. Hooks, not normally found twisted into the door frames of decrepit Madrid hotel rooms. A room where happiness was reduced to the number of hours a visitor could afford.

It was not a place to die. Or perhaps it was?

The murderer took the leather bands off his hands and cleaned them under the tap. Then he lovingly took the hand-braided whip, which he had been able to obtain in England, and removed the last blood stains with the discolored towel. The leather ball-gag, which had been in the victim's mouth, was removed and carefully cleaned. A black leather brief case was on the small table. He opened it and removed a bottle of colorless oil. With a soft cloth he rubbed the oil into the leather. With another cloth he rubbed it out. He carefully placed his devices in the compartments made in the foam rubber with which the briefcase was lined, as a technician would carefully place delicate tools. With the same precision lavished on the storing of his torture instruments, he had prepared the punishment and the killing of his victim. The tracking, determining the place and the time had all gone according to plan. He had even spoken to him. Right in the street. Asked directions. He had wanted to see his eyes. The eyes that had seen everything. The flames, the destruction from which screams sounded to heaven. The same screaming he heard every night as if he had been there himself. Which woke him, sweating. The pictures in the newspapers that did not go away, that never faded. They had left an imprint in his mind that would never leave. He looked at the soulless body without any feeling. After twelve years, he had his revenge. The scenes from the past had reoccurred more frequently during recent years. There had been a time that it was less, even bearable. There had even been a period when it seemed as if it had been forgotten. Not just the flames, but also the image of his naked mother in the winter of 1945. And Frau Vollmer. The hate, the desolation, the hunger and the degradations. Naked in the snow, the woman whom he had loved, who had read to him before going to sleep, who had taken him in her arms. Everything had become vague during the period of career building. Uncle Jan and Aunt Marie who were waiting for him at the station in May, 1945. He did not know them and they did not know him, but there they were, she with arms outspread, like his mother, and he with a kindly laugh. Next day immediately into a 'plus-four'. He felt himself quiet grown-up, how proud and also how sad. But Uncle Jan had arranged for a bicycle with blocks on the pedals and Aunt Marie had made the most wonderful chocolate milk. The years that followed took care of a gradual numbing and the new impressions and events completed the process. But after that disastrous day, everything had returned. The images, the feeling of being deserted by everything and everybody. Slowly, like a cancer, but more often and more intense.

He is now fifty years old and often thinks he is going mad, feeling the need for revenge, just revenge. Perhaps Frau Vollmer was dead, or a pitiful old grandmother in a village, somewhere in Bavaria. Who knows. Nobody there will ever know who, or what, Frau Vollmer was. *He* knew. But Frau Vollmer had disappeared, perhaps with another name.

The thoughts drove him crazy, the endless film which was continually projected on his inner brain, every day again. And the flames were so real. Uncle Jan and Aunt Marie ... flames ... revenge!

He did not feel anything while he looked at the soulless body. He washed his hands, as a surgeon after an operation. He took a clean towel from the briefcase and dried himself. Again he donned the cheap clothes which had been hung over a chair and looked at himself in the peeling mirror over the dirty sink. He walked around the room, checking for anything he might have forgotten. From a compartment in the briefcase he pulled an envelope. He opened it and looked at the contents. A beautiful postcard, high gloss. Aloud, he read the text to himself:

"ESPANA-HUNGRIA: 1-1."

He put the card back in the envelope, placed the chair in front of the body in the rigging and put the envelope against the backrest of the chair. He looked at the arrangement with an approving look, took the bundle, wrapped in gray paper and tied with rope, closed the briefcase and left the room.

As he left the establishment, the owner said pleasantly:

"Buenos noches, Señor Van Kleef!"

He walked down the street and in a portico he removed the poor pants and torn jacket he had put on over his own, neat clothes. After that, as he passed a dumpster, he threw the old clothes and the gray bundle among the trash. At the end of the street he hailed a taxi, entered and was driven to the center of Madrid. A long distance from the Hotel Monte Carlo, he got out and walked the rest of the way.

At the reception he asked for the key to room 327. He longed for a bath, clean clothes and a good meal.

Next morning he hastily scanned the Spanish newspapers. Nothing about the murder in the cheap hotel. With a smile he folded the papers and returned to his breakfast.

His plane would leave in two hours.

*2. *Polderkerk, Friday, February 24, 1989*

A merciless, cold wind blew across the flat lands of the new province. Where not long ago the sea had reigned and the treacherous waves made life miserable for fishermen, towns and villages dotted a well planned and symmetric landscape. Everything was young and new. The land, the houses and the dikes. Farms were placed squarely on sharply delineated acres that showed no difference from the designs that had once covered drawing tables. All disorder was avoided and nothing unplanned was allowed. Trees grew where architects had planned them to grow, according to sort, number and height. Everything had been planned, nothing had been left to chance. Everything in the new village was straight and dull and the shopping center, with its artificial ambiance and never ending background music, lacked warmth. Warmth cannot be drawn up or designed. The houses, where people lived, had been grouped in courtyards, squares, or long, impersonal streets. Little gardens in front and little gardens behind. With different fences and gates and divisions. The little garden with the gnome next to that with the ecological wilderness. The handmade windmill with the plastic wings, next to the little garden with the artificial rocks. Street after street, square after square. The only individuality shown was evidenced by the different gardens and many styles of front doors that had replaced the unimaginative straight doors. All styles together. From smoothly sanded farmer's doors to doors which reminded one of an English pub. All different, all individuals, all people who wanted to show some originality. People who created their own little palaces in a land where the wind mercilessly roared. The Dutch had conquered the sea, but the wind remained. It was unconquerable.

Jacques Meyer lived in one of the houses. Alone. That is how he liked it. If you were alone you could not be bothered. You were able to do what you wanted and did not have to explain yourself, or be responsible to anyone. Nobody was going to put your things were you could not find them. Nobody was going to tell you what to eat, how to spend your day, or move your chair. Nobody was going to dirty things, or leave them dirty, or put a jam spoon in the butter and the butter knife in the jam. Everything in his house had its place and its function. That could not be changed. His books were placed according to type, by author and with millimetric precision on the shelves. Unsullied and regularly dusted. A pair of black gloves were ready in case he wanted to look up something, or read. Whenever he drank or ate something, a coaster, a place mat, or a napkin was used. The flowers were made of silk, because real flowers created a mess. Every morning he dusted and vacuumed. The furniture all had its own place and when he had finished watching television, he wiped the knob after he shut it off. The alarm clock rang at a quarter past seven and breakfast was at nine; lunch was at one and dinner at six. The routine did not vary.

He lived on the interest of a moderate capital that had been invested, painstakingly and carefully, in Netherlands Treasury Bonds. In addition a small pension from Organization 40-45.* He was frugal and thus never short.

At a quarter past seven the alarm clock startled him awake from a deep sleep. That was unusual and he had to get used to it for a moment. Usually he was awake, with his mind churning at full capacity, making the ringing of the alarm clock superfluous. But this night had passed without complications. It was as if a load had been lifted. A cheerful mood came over him. Today he could tackle the entire world. A rare feeling for him, to be enjoyed to the fullest.

"Monique will be here tonight," was his first thought. They had now known each other for about seven months. Sometimes he thought that he would like to live with her. Monique was a companion he did not want to loose, but he lacked the courage to commit himself. She was independent, had an important job with an insurance company. Last year she had been nominated as a candidate for 'Businesswoman of the Year'. Independent, cool and calculating, she maintained herself in a world usually reserved for men. She had presence, knew exactly what she wanted and how something should be done. She never forgot that in her position she could not afford any mistakes. When she prepared a strategy, or chaired a meeting, everything would be planned meticulously in advance. No detail was neglected and there was nobody in the organization who could hope to equal her ready knowledge of the business, irritating men who jealously wanted her position. She knew it and it reinforced her inner resolve to remain a winner. She was the boss and they'd better know it and those who could not accept that would be better advised to look for another job. Really, his arrangement with Monique was ideal. They both led their own lives but shared a number of mutual interests. She could relax when they were together.

After his daily ritual of vacuuming and dusting and straightening, he was ready for breakfast. Exactly nine o'clock. After a shower of at least twenty minutes, he carefully selected the clothes to be worn that day. Everything was arranged according to color and season. Everything had its own place, drawer, or hook. Shoes that looked like new formed a perfect row on the bottom shelf. Every pair of socks had been assembled in the same manner and could be found in the therefore designated drawer. Ties hung without wrinkles from a special rack and shirts were arranged in three stacks in the designated compartments. After some consideration he selected a pair of trousers and a shirt and held them against the light to verify the color combination. Then he chose tie and jacket and began to dress. In the hall he put on his winter coat and checked to see if everything was accounted for. Keys, money. When he felt for his wallet in an inside pocket, he felt the passport.

"Damn, almost forgot," he said aloud.

He went to the kitchen and placed the passport on the counter. He removed his overcoat and jacket, removed the gold cufflinks from his shirt sleeves, rolled the sleeves up and lit the gas. Slowly the passport burned as he held it over the flame. Slowly the letters carbonized, one by one.

First the V, then the A, then the N, then the K, then the L, then the E and another E and finally the F.

When the passport had been burned he removed the ashes with a small hand vacuum cleaner and wiped all traces away with a small rag, which has been placed, folded to a perfect square, on the counter.

A little later he closed the front door behind him and felt the cold wind lash his face.

---

* An organization to help victims of WWII.

3. Madrid, Friday Morning, February 24, 1989

The owner of the cheap hotel in the Calle Magellanes in Madrid, dirty hands waving in the air, maintained his innocence. From under the few, greased-down hairs sweat dripped down his unshaven face. The bleached shirt, bulging over the trousers, showed sweat spots in the arm pits and along the back. This morning, the maid who changed the sheets once a week, had been screaming from room 17. He had run upstairs and discovered the naked corpse, with protruding eyes, hanging from the chains. He was used to a lot, drug overdoses, suicide, but this tableau was enough to make even him throw up in the wash basin. Although used to take care of his own business, without bothering the police, this was too much. He phoned. Photos had been taken, the room had been scrupulously searched and several specialists were now trying to localize some finger prints. The mutilated body had been removed more than an hour ago and was probably already on ice, or on the marble dissecting table of the morgue.

Bewildered, Captain Cortez-Carreras of the Madrid Policia Nacional looked around. His eyes sparkled fire when he looked at the untrustworthy face of the owner of this pest hole.

"Did you not see the man enter?"

"No, Señor Capitan, I swear to you by all the Saints!"

"But you are sure that this is not the man who rented the room?"

"Seguro, seguro, Señor Capitan, it was a foreigner, I am certain."

"All right, we know," he looked again at the smutty hotel register and read:

"Van Kleef, Number 20, Gentlemen's Canal, Amsterdam."

"No passport number?"

"I probably forgot. I have a lot of work."

"About what age did you say?"

"Fifty, fifty five, but I didn't get a good look at him in the dark."

"Moustache, beard, glasses?"

"No clean shaven really ... now that you mention it, he was always clean shaven."

"It happens," Cortez could not resist to say. "Color hair?"

"I told you, I usually saw him at night ... not too much hair, anyway. A little bald on top and gray here," he pointed at his temples.

"What did he wear?"

"I don't notice those things, the usual, a long coat, black, or gray. I mean, it is rather dark."

"There isn't a lot of light here. Did he speak Spanish?"

"Un poco, Señor Capitan, but I didn't talk to him much."

"Otherwise anything peculiar?"

"Now that you mention it, Please don't misunderstand me, Señor Capitan, you know, I have been inside a few times, and ..."

"Yes, I know."

"And you know, I definitely don't want any more problems. I have my own business now and everything is above board, I pay my taxes on time, you can check that with the Hacienda. You saw, I register all guests."

"Yes, yes, I know, come to the point," Cortez said impatiently.

"Well, you know, I am of course used to a certain type of public, you understand; I know that this isn't exactly a four star hotel, so you watch things. How shall I say, he looked so ordinary, like everybody around here, you know. I mean, different than you, Señor Capitan. You are a caballero, but he was just, you know. But what I noticed was a very expensive watch. I know a little about that, if I say so myself."

"Yes, we know," said Cortez with some emphasis.

"Well that was a bit strange, I mean, the regular clothes and the expensive watch. Also his face was more, eh, senoral, more gentleman than his clothes."

Thinking, Cortez looked in the distance and said: "Si, si."

"But I didn't see him that often, I told you, he usually came at night."

"But he rented the room for three days?"

"Yes, but I don't think that he slept here."

"What? You waited this long to tell me? He had rented a room for three days but didn't sleep here?"

"Well, eh, yes, I don't know for sure, but I think so."

"Why?"

"He used to come around seven at night and leave again around eleven."

"And he didn't come back at night?"

"I don't know. Everybody has a key to the front door. I am not here at night. But I never heard anything during the day, I mean, it isn't all that big here, usually you hear something, but it was always quiet."

"So the murdered man could have entered at night without your knowing?"

"Si, Señor Capitan, that is very possible."

"Has anyone entered the room during the three days? A cleaning woman, a maid?"

As he asked it, Cortez realized how ridiculous the question was in such a pigsty.

"No, Señor Capitan, absolutamente ni una persona."

"I am taking you to Headquarters to help make a composite of the face. You better have a good memory."

"But I hardly saw him," said the hotel owner and raised his arms to the heavens.

"Well, I should think hard, if I were you," Cortez said abruptly. He turned his back on the man to indicate that, for the moment, the conversation was terminated.

"Find anything?" he asked the Lab people.

"I think the fingerprints of Columbus are still here, it has been at least that long since it has been cleaned," was the despairing answer.

"Finish up and seal the premises when you leave. I am going back to the station and will call you from there."

When Cortez reached the street, the owner was waiting. For the visit to the station he had put on a clean shirt.

The policeman at the wheel maneuvered expertly through the Madrid traffic. It was cold. Behind the fogged over windows of the many bars and restaurants, people drank hot chocolate and ate portions of *churros*. Near the government buildings a group of demonstrators was trying to keep warm by jogging in a circle, while chanting slogans. A little later they entered the protected parking lot of the police station and after the driver had found a parking place, he opened the door for his superior. Cortez entered and the hotel owner followed, shivering with cold. After delivering the man to the police artist, Cortez went to his room. Through the opened door he yelled for his assistant, Adjutant Pablo Ramos, who entered almost immediately.

"Urgente," barked Cortez. "First, a telex to Amsterdam, attention Commissaris Bakkenist. Request information regarding this person, description to follow."

He gave the name and address of the guest from the hotel register.

"Next, check all hotel registers for the twentieth, the twenty first and the twenty second. See if Van Kleef has stayed anywhere else. Plane arrivals and car rentals. In short, the normal procedure.

I want to know something by 6 o'clock tonight. Have Pepe assist you."

"You want me to pull him off that counterfeit case?" asked Pablo Ramos.

"Yes, that can wait and don't forget to check missing persons for the last three days."

"Found nothing that can help us?" asked Ramos.

"Nothing, no papers, no jewelry, not even any clothes. It looks as if he went upstairs naked."

After Ramos had left, Capitan Cortez called his friend Pedro Portales of the Federacion Espanola. After having passed the usual information about mutual friends, family and daily concerns, Pedro asked:

"Well, James Bond, why did you call me?"

"I know that as President of the Federacion you must know everything about soccer, because that is why they pay you the enormous salary. I am working on a murder and I want you to tell me what you know about a soccer match Espana-Hungria with a 1-1 result. When was that played and where?"

Pedro Portals had a memory like a steel trap and said, without hesitation "Let's see, that game was played in 1977, the 27th of March, and that was in Alicante in the Rico Perez Stadium."

"You amaze me every time, Pedro! Please, what can you tell me about that game?"

"What do you want to know?"

"Was there something special about the game? Riots, quarrels with coaches, tainted money, secret payments, strange happenings?"

"No, not as far as I can remember. You didn't have the rash of vandalism at that time. It was a bad game on our part, but that was all, just an exhibition game. Nothing to help you, I think. But if you'd like, I can research it further."

"That would please me very much, call me if you find anything."

Cortez replaced the telephone, stared into the distance, remembered the glossy post card he had found on the chair and murmured: "Alicante ... March, 27 ... 1977 ..."

The date seemed to mean something, but he lost the thought almost immediately.

4. Amsterdam, Friday Afternoon, February 24, 1989

Commissaris Bakkenist was in his room at Headquarters of the Amsterdam Police at the Marnixstraat when a constable entered with a paper in his hands.

"Seems to be urgent, sir, fax from Madrid." He left the room after having placed the paper on the desk.

Bakkenist had the habit to look for the name of the sender first and then at the contents. He smiled when he saw the name Cortez. They knew each other personally. Their first professional acquaintance came about during the investigation of widespread drug distribution from Mallorca, via Barcelona and, of course, to Amsterdam. He thought about that with satisfaction. It had been a perfect example of European cooperation. It had started with a detective from Scotland Yard who lived on the vacation island and who had first stumbled on the case. The gang was now behind bars in England, Spain and Florida. Even the big boys and that was unique. During that period the friendship between him and Cortez had started. Cortez was a dedicated sea-sailor and so was he. Only last summer his Spanish friend had been able to rent a seagoing boat for a reasonable price for the Bakkenist couple and together, each in his own boat, they had 'done' the Spanish Coast. Jaime Cortez had led them to the most breathtaking spots and bays on the Iberian peninsula and, blissful memory, the best and cheapest restaurants.

He read the fax and pushed the intercom. A little later Inspector De Berg entered. Bakkenist gave him the fax and after De Berg had absorbed the contents, he said:

"Want me to follow up, sir? Shouldn't take long."

"I think it may be for nothing, but take Freriks with you, just to be sure."

"OK, sir, we'll be back soon." De Berg was ready to leave.

"Also check if a passport with that name has been reported stolen, or lost."

"Of course, sir, I planned to do so. You'll have an answer within the hour."

He was one of the better ones, Arie De Berg, no blabbing, but action. 'Yes, sir. OK, sir'. Abrupt, decisive and straight for the goal and a quick arrest. Of course, most suspects were no more than small heaps of human sadness. Abandoned children, it happened more and more, sometimes no older than twelve, or thirteen, stealing, robbing, selling themselves. Abandoned by parents who couldn't face the responsibility any longer, or were too selfish. People for whom, even in the Netherlands, the last doors had closed. Never before had there been so much freedom, wealth and health in this part of the world and it seemed as if entire groups couldn't handle it. And they watched them pass through. Everyday again. Twenty four hours a day. The hopeless, the disappointed and the disillusioned. A long line of human beings that, one way or another, had missed the boat. But also the cheats, the chiselers, the heartless. Because in his long career he had learned that it was well to remember that at least fifteen percent of mankind was just plain bad.

While he sat thinking, staring at the wall, the phone rang and a moment later he heard the familiar spanglish of Jaime Cortez.

"Buenos tardes, comisario Baakkenieste!"

"Ah, el Capitan, how are you?"

"Bien, very good, everything good with the familia?"

"Very well, thank you."

After a few jokes and teases about each other's seaman's skills of last summer, Cortez came to business.

"You received my fax?"

"Yes, we are working on it. I hope to have something in about an hour."

"I called because I have some additional information."

"Tell me, what is going on there in Madrid?"

Cortez gave a complete report about the events of the day. How the man had been found, the description of the hotel owner and the mysterious postcard with the corpse and the date of the soccer match. He also said that the suspicion that the man hadn't slept in the fleabag hotel was correct. He had stayed in one of the better Madrid hotels under the name 'Van Kleef'. The receptionist had been able to give an accurate description of the man. They still didn't know who the victim was, but they were sure he was a Spaniard. After Bakkenist had listened to the complete story, he said:

"You're dealing with a madman, they cannot be predicted. What I want to know, are you sure that it was a Dutchman?"

"I am certain, now. Look, the passport could have been stolen, but according to the receptionist he bought a Dutch newspaper everyday."

"How long are you going to be in the office?"

"As long as you want, otherwise you can call me at home."

About forty five minutes later De Berg entered, trailed by Freriks.

"And?" asked Bakkenist, hopefully.

"Nothing, of course, sir. They had never heard the name at 20, Gentlemen's Canal."

"And the passport?"

"Pinched, on February 19, at about ten thirty near the Central Station. Here is the report of the duty officer."

Bakkenist read it and asked:

"Did you speak to the real Mr. Van Kleef?"

"Just now, by telephone. Had nothing to add. Left the Central Station, knocked on the head, woke a few hours later in the hospital and passport gone."

"Perpetrators?"

"Take your pick."

"Has a doctor looked at the wound?"

"Yes, and that's what doesn't make sense, sir, it's in the report, it's difficult to say what caused unconsciousness."

"Have a talk with that doctor."

"All done."

That's De Berg, he should have known.

"What did he say?"

"They found traces of a sort of oil, mainly used for leather. The weapon therefore was probably made of leather. Not in the shape of a stick, but more like a ball. The perpetrator must have known where to hit, because a few centimeters lower and it would have been murder."

"So, an experienced person?"

"Probably, yes."

A little later Bakkenist reported to his friend and colleague that he had little to report. The next morning he received a complete description and a photo composition of the suspect. After having looked at the documents he tiredly placed them on his desk.

There were at least one and a half million Dutchman who looked like that.

5. Poldérkerk, Friday Evening, February 24, 1989

The wind had died down and the polder was shrouded in an impenetrable fog. It was not too cold for the time of year. It had really hardly been winter at all, this year. Temperatures were far above average. It still had not been below freezing and the watery ice rinks looked abandoned and neglected. The tall poles for the lights that were to illuminate the fun and games on the ice stood forlorn in puddles of water and the small stalls intended for the sale of hot drinks and food looked just sad. The seats, where children were supposed to tie on skates, stood around in useless stacks. Winter had not come and it looked like it would not come. People whispered about the ozone layer and the pollution from nuclear reactors. Farmers complained about the wet grounds and predicted a spoiled potato harvest and so-called experts warned of an unbelievable insect infestation during the spring.

When Meyer looked out of the window, the fog made it almost impossible to see the gate of the little garden. He had called, but Monique had already left the house. That meant that she was on the way. In spite of the fog and the warning to drivers to be careful and only to make necessary trips. She was coming, that was certain. Around eight o'clock he heard her car stop in front of the house, he looked out of the window and could just see the vague outline of her white BMW. He walked to the front door and opened it before she could ring the bell.

"I was worried with this fog, I was afraid you wouldn't come. I tried to call," he said while he kissed her on both cheeks.

"I always come, you should know that."

He helped her out of her coat and together they walked into the living room. She fell onto one of the leather couches and said:

"Wonderful, that's what I needed."

He went to the wine rack, chose a bottle and said:

"A Fleurie 81, what do you think?"

"Delicious! And then my master is going to tell me how he liked his little trip to Spain."

"Real interesting, it is a fascinating city, just a little cold."

He talked while he uncorked the bottle, placed coasters on the table, put a napkin around the neck of the bottle, took glasses from the cupboard and poured for both of them.

"In retrospect, I saw little of Madrid. The first day I went to the Prado. Unbelievable what is there. Room after room of Jeroen Bosch, Goya, Murillo, Rembrandt. Then a day to the Escorial, but that is not enough. You want to see too much in a day and after a couple of hours in a museum, you really don't see anything anymore. It is too much. I should go there for much longer. The town is so big, it is one big monument and what you notice at once is that the Spaniards nurture their history. In the Rijksmuseum here you mostly see Americans, the average Dutchman has never seen the Nightwatch. He only knows that Van Gogh was a painter and his paintings are now worth millions, but he won't go to the Van Gogh Museum, or the Kroller-Muller Museum."

"Well, don't be so somber, I don't think it is all that bad."

"No, it is. Did you know that a Dutchman, compared to people from southern countries, is the least knowledgeable about his history and art treasures? The French, the Spanish, the Italians, they know what they have and go and see it, they are proud of their history."

This was his pet subject, she knew, and she really couldn't totally disagree with him. She loved Holland and the Dutch, but there was a farm mentality, the lack of a healthy national pride that she sometimes detested. There was so much in this country to be proud of, but the Dutch remained stolid and were afraid and suspicious of boasting.

Here everything was different. She loved being here with him, after a week of macho colleagues, preening men, unwilling insurers and stubborn clients. She loved it, it had become a part of her life she could not do without. But now she longed for his bedroom where she could forget everything. He knew what she wanted and could bring her to the peaks of excitement. He could exercise his power and she could be his slave.

He turned the light down lower, lit two candles which had been prepared and approached her. She stretched backward onto the couch and spread her arms to embrace him. An unquenchable desire came over her when he placed his body next to hers.

"Careful darling, we have all night."

"Let's go to the bedroom, we can eat later."

The bedroom was large and modern with a king-size bed in the center. A black leather bedspread and black leather pillows covered the bed. A gleaming steel construction was attached to the bed which reminded one of a heaven with a black roof. A chain was attached to the metal beams that connected the four posts. Some whips and a *plumeau* hung from hooks on the wall. One wall was covered with mirrors and the adjustable, indirect lighting delivered a macabre twilight.

Slowly he undressed her and when she stood naked before him, he sat down on the bed and looked at her. She threw herself on her knees and began to undress him. With slavish attention she undid his shoelaces and removed his shoes. Then the socks, the trousers, the underpants and the rest. He stood up and went to a corner of the room. There was a coat rack with black clothes. He put on a pair of black leather trousers that stretched around his buttocks as a second skin. He put an abbreviated harness round his chest. He put a wide black belt with metal pins around his waist and covered his head with a black, leather cap. He chose one of the whips from the wall and sat down on a stool. Meanwhile she had pulled on some black stockings which reached halfway up her thighs. She next took a black leather garter belt and after putting it on, attached the stockings. She placed a collar around her neck. A harness was attached to the collar and the belts led under her breasts and could be tightened in the back. She turned her back to him and he pulled on the belts till it took her breath away.

"Tighter, much tighter," she gasped.

Next he put wide cuffs around her ankles and wrists. She walked to the bed and he hung her from the steel construction by her wrists. She was powerless but she enjoyed it. All daily cares seemed to flow away. She reached orgasm as if intoxicated. She had lost control. The feeling could not be compared to anything. It was like a drug. To be physically and psychologically abused and humiliated by him was all that she wanted. Something she would never tolerate in her work or in her relations with other. Just here, in her own protected world. He spread her legs and attached her ankles to the vertical poles. The small whip now hit for the first time. Just a little harder, every time. Then he stroked her neck and lightly stroked the genital area. The he hit her again, ten times, and she had to count the blows. As he hit her, she moaned with pain and pleasure. With a flat leather paddle he hit her buttocks until they were red. And always she had to count, every blow. The lashes showed on her back. Leisurely he wrapped her in rope, around the waist and through her legs, pulled it tight. She enjoyed the soft, feathery whip with the plumes that worked on her clitoris. He wanted her to beg for mercy, but she would not.

"Master, may I have an orgasm?" she begged. No she was not allowed. She would be allowed when he let her. A face formed vaguely on his retina. He recognized it. Frau Vollmer, Germany, 1945. Would it never leave? Would it always return? The scenes, everyday again. Frau Vollmer who begged for mercy, but that was impossible, it was another voice, he knew the voice. A darling voice. The voice of his mother, begging for mercy. Frau Vollmer wielded the whip until one begged for mercy, or until death ended all suffering. The naked woman in the snow, the last view of his mother. Oh, God, why did it have to return every time? Why did he now beat the only woman he loved? The last one on this godforsaken planet? He couldn't comprehend it. Everything had been lost, his parents, his little sister. Why did he humiliate her again and again, why did it give him pain as well as pleasure? He thought, no, he *knew* he was going mad.

After almost an hour they rested, exhausted, next to each other.

"How do you feel?"

"Fine."

"May I ask you something, but if you don't want to answer, that's all right."

"Go ahead, ask."

"Jacques, tell me, who is Frau Vollmer?"

6. Polderkerk, Friday Night, February 24, 1989

She felt his body stiffen, as in death. His eyes started to turn wild and sweat stood out over his face.

"What is it darling, don't you feel well?" she asked, worried.

His head moved in uncontrolled jerks from left to right and his powerless fists beat the mattress.

"My God, what have I said!?" she cried.

She jumped out of bed and ran to the wash basin where she put a towel under the cold tap. She put the wet towel on his forehead and only then saw the wild look in his eyes. Something was the matter with him that she did not understand. Their involvement had really been superficial. Suddenly she realized that she did not really know him. That had been her wish, she did not want to belong to a man completely, that she could not allow. Not after the experience and the bitter memories of two marriages that had both failed because of her wish to have a career, as well as a husband. Something that, despite many solemn vows and agreements, had proved to be impossible. With him it had always been strictly physical. It started with a classified ad in the Volkskrant (a newspaper):

> Dominant man, 50, wants to meet young woman with masochistic fantasies.

He had placed the ad. The nice, modest letter with enclosed photograph touched her. On her way to her first rendez-vous with him, she had been impressed with the stark reality of the new land. After she passed the old windmill, the last sentinel of her regular life, the long dike, which was both a protection from the sea and the main communication link between the old and the new, stretched out before her like the gateway to a secure haven. The unrelieved flatness was like another planet. Here she could create her second, secret world, so different from the small, gabled houses and the ubiquitous canals.

She had been aware of certain feelings since she was sixteen. Even then she fantasied about heroic women in leather and tight corsets. When she bought her first magazine about S&M she had been terribly excited. But she fought it, she wanted to be like everyone else, she did not want to be strange. She had been raised in a decent catholic household where such thoughts were not to be imagined. She married, twice even. Both times she had quickly felt hemmed in by frustration. Therefore she had, in the ensuing years, concentrated exclusively on her career and it occupied her day and night. The place she had chosen in society, forced her to be extremely careful with her sexual partners. The man from Antwerp, with whom she had been involved for some years, had never known her address, or her real name. For certain elements within the world of S&M she could be a heaven sent subject for blackmail. She had no illusions about that. That is how her agreement with Jacques Meyer had started. Just for physical pleasure, no more. But, against her will, she had begun to love this lonesome man.

Slowly the shivering diminished while she tenderly stroked his hair and looked him lovingly straight in the eyes.

"What is the matter with you?" she said softly.

"I don't know, I was afraid."

"Afraid, what for?"

"It's difficult, I can't tell you, sometimes I am afraid."

"But I am here, then there's nothing to be afraid of."

"You're darling, you really love me too much."

"But why be afraid, we are fine together."

"I will never force you, you know, you are always free to go."

"I know that, but there may come a time that I won't want to leave at all, anymore."

"How did you know the name?" he asked abruptly.

"What name?"

"You mentioned a name."

"Yes I mentioned a name and I'll never repeat it."

"But I want to know how you knew."

"Later, first we'll go downstairs and look at the food, then we'll eat and you'll soon feel like my master again."

They put on robes and went down the stairs. A little later they put the finishing touches to the minestrone and the lasagna. They were silent during the meal. Neither spoke. There was something that could not be discussed, something that should be avoided, but both knew it could no longer be avoided. There was an agreement between them, a 'deal' they called it seven months ago. But the conditions and circumstances had changed and the deal was no longer valid. They knew it and they felt it. Neither knew what to do.

When, after the meal, they were on the couch together, she said:

"You don't even know my address."

"No, perhaps I want to know sometime, but not yet."

"Tell me about yourself, who are you really, Jacques?"

"I could ask you the same," he answered.

"Then why don't you ask. Do you want me to tell you?"

"Yes, please."

"All right then. I was born in Noordwijk on January, 25, 1949."

"You just had a birthday."

"Yes, but that was still part of the previous deal. No presents, no commitments. My father was a GP, my mother was a housewife and I have an older sister and a brother younger than me. Enough about me, for now. Tell me something about yourself."

She felt his body tremble slightly, before he started to speak.

"I was born in Amsterdam on August 20, 1939. My father had a furniture store in the Langedijk and mother was a housewife. I also had a sister three years older than me."

"You said 'had', is your sister dead?"

"She died when she was nine."

"How terrible for you. And your parents?"

Again she felt his body tremble and she wondered if this was a smart idea for a conversation.

"My parents were relatively old when we were born and meanwhile both have died." he said, faltering, and his voice shook with emotion.

"If you rather not talk about it, you don't have to, darling."

"Yes, I know, I want to tell you, but I am just afraid that when you know everything about me, I'll lose you."

"Such nonsense."

"It is always been that way. It is all I can say about myself. I am afraid it will be so again."

He started to sweat and his eyes filled with tears.

"Darling, what is the matter with you. This cannot go on. Whatever it is, try to set it aside. Don't be afraid, I'll never leave you again. 'That's a deal' and you know that when this business woman says that, you can believe it."

"I know, but maybe you don't want to leave and they'll take you away."

"Who would want to take me away from you?"

"Frau Vollmer!" he screamed, witless.

"Who is Frau Vollmer, Jacques. Tell me, Jacques, who is Frau Vollmer!?"

She took him by the shoulders and shook him wildly back and forth. She felt as if something was choking him that had to come out.

"Come on, Jacques, tell me, I love you, I'll always love you, but throw that bitch Vollmer out. No matter who she is, or was, I am here!! Do you hear me!!!? I am here! Tell me about Frau Vollmer!"

Suddenly it looked as if he had regained his self-control, Quiet and calm. Only his eyes still had a slightly wild look in them. His mouth moved and he whispered:

"Frau Vollmer beat her to death."

"Who did she beat to death, Jacques, who?"

His eyes closed as if ready to sleep, while he murmured softly. She placed her ear against his lips and heard the same series of numbers, over and over again.

"... 89219 ... 89219 ... 89219 ..."

He fell into a deep sleep.

Although it was part of their routine that she would go home afterward, she stayed with him that night.

7. Madrid, Sunday, February 26 1989

Madrid is built on a number of low hills that form a plateau on both sides of the Manzanares river. To the north are extended neighborhoods with high-rise apartments, to the south are the steep banks of the river. The endless flatland around the city is arid, barren and without trees. The temperatures fluctuate violently and Madrid is not known for its wonderful climate. During the summer the city is covered with a thick layer of humid, suffocating air, saturated with the exhaust fumes from hundreds of thousands of cars and other waste products, resulting from an affluent society. The winters are bitter cold. An endless desert of streets, neighborhoods and high-rise buildings wherein more than five million people live, work and breed. As do many other, self-respecting cities in the modern world, Madrid also suffers from insoluble traffic problems. The ear-shattering noise created by the millions of automobiles continues day and night. Except on Sunday. On a cold day, every Madrilene stays indoors, unless there is a very compelling reason to leave the house. The greater part of the moveable tin will be parked, unused and in chaotic abandon, along the hundreds of thousands of miles of curb sides. Such a Sunday is a breather for the city. On such a day the beauty of Madrid, with its gorgeous buildings and magnificent art works, can briefly be appreciated.

The Rodriguez family lived in a roomy apartment in one of the better neighborhoods. The lobby of the building was finished in white marble. There was a doorman, to watch the comings and goings of the tenants and their guests, to accept the mail and to take care of the many small repairs around the building. Two large elevators provided access to the twenty-two floors. The interior of the apartment was typically Spanish. A lot of rooms, but all slightly on the small side. The most important room was the room designated for daily use. The kitchen. A long, comfortable sofa faced a permanently switched on television set, next to the refrigerator. The living room was hardly ever used. Except on special days, or to impress important visitors. The living room, with its gleaming furniture and plastic flowers looked more like the showroom of a furniture store, than a space in which people lived. An imposing wall combination wherein unread books looked expensive next to a statue of the Holy Mother. Vaguely Persian looking table cloths covered the highly polished tables, in turn covered by crystal vases wherein no flowers ever bloomed. The walls were covered with an expensive wallpaper, the colors of which, clashed with the colors of the carpet that covered the shiny, parquet floor.

Señora Rodriguez had been drifting from kitchen to living room and back again, Her children and grandchildren watched her tear-streaked face in silence. Nobody could think of anything cheerful, or hopeful, to say. It had all been said, all possibilities had been discussed and rejected. All family members, friends and acquaintances, all over Spain, had been contacted and all without result. The youngest grandchild was sleeping in a portable bassinet and Señora Rodriguez checked on it about every ten minutes. The child was the only one unaffected. This morning the oldest son had finally gone to the police, to report his father as missing. The inborn Spanish pride had made them wait four days. It would have been out of character to act sooner in such a case. Who knows, there might be another woman involved and that is something to hide from outsiders.

A shock went through the house when the buzzer of the front door suddenly broke the silence. As if paralyzed, unable to move a muscle, Señora Rodriguez stared in the direction of the front door. The baby woke from the sudden noise and started to cry. The oldest son walked toward the hall and lifted the receiver of the intercom.

"Si ... si ... yes, let them come up."

Back in the kitchen he said, resignedly:

"Two people from the police are on the way up."

"Santo Cristo!" cried the Señora. With a helpless gesture she slapped her palms together while walking into the hall to open the door of the living room wider. A little later Cortez and Ramos were perched uncomfortably on the edge of a hard bench in the showy room. The entire family had seated themselves in an attitude of expectation in front of them. A daughter, baby on the arm, stood in the door opening. Cortez looked down and cleared his throat. He had been hardened in his profession, at times he could be ruthless, but this was something that was almost too much for him. He never knew how to start this sort of conversation and, once started, could never find an appropriate way to end it. He could so well imagine the grief and sorrow he would be leaving behind in this shattered family, after he had given them his message. Again he cleared his throat, took a deep breath and said:

"I have bad news for you, Mrs. Rodriguez. Your husband has been found some days ago. He was dead."

Except for the gurgling noises of the baby, the room remained silent.

"An accident?" asked the son.

"No, I wish that were true, señor, your father was murdered."

"Murdered? Why!?"

"We don't know."

The bewilderment and horror was almost tangible. Nobody said a word. They had difficulty absorbing the horrible news.

"May I see him?'

"Señora Rodriguez, I believe you shouldn't."

In the car, on the way back to the station, Captain Cortez was deep in thought. Again he went over everything he had learned so far. No leads at all. Why kill the man? Why in that dirty, despicable place? A man with an unblemished record at Iberia Airlines and now the chief-controller at Barajas Airport near Madrid ...

He sighed deeply and said:

"We have chosen a rotten job."

Ramos agreed in silence.

*8. *Polderkerk, Monday, February 27, 1989*

After breakfast and after cleaning the kitchen, he went upstairs. He put on his old work clothes. For the past few weeks he had been busy with the installation of a special room upstairs. First the walls had been covered with a sound absorbing material. After that, the entire room, including the ceiling, had been covered with a soft, dark carpet. In the middle of the floor a thick-piled, white carpet covered a piece of foam rubber. The combination felt like a thin mattress. An Andreas Cross, made from two-by-fours, was anchored to one of the walls. A number of decorated, black leather cuffs, with heavy clasps, were attached at the height were wrists and ankles could be conveniently placed. The opposite wall was covered with shelves. The shelves had hooks attached to the outer edge and his attributes could be easily hung from the hooks. The items which could not be easily hung, were arranged on the shelves. Different types of instruments, carefully sorted, arranged and displayed. One shelf for various kind of hooks and clasps in all sizes. Another with ropes and leather strapping belts, neatly rolled up, or hung from appropriate hooks. Another with various lengths of chains in different thicknesses and strengths. A long shelf with belts, constraints, corsets, harnesses, hand cuffs, masks, etc. Another shelf was full of black leather items decorated with studs, rivets and nails. Hard to define items that could all be worn as some sort of restraint. For all parts of the body. From weights to be attached to a scrotum to clamps that would bite into the tender flesh of nipples. The "Sling" was placed in a corner. A steel frame with a jungle of leather belts, cuffs and anchor points. The place was dark and macabre. Satisfied he looked around and could not resist stroking and caressing the black leather. He spent the morning in cleaning, sorting and re-arranging his extensive collection of whips.

After lunch he got into his car and drove toward Amsterdam. He knew where he wanted to go, although he had never been there. After he rang the bell, a beautiful Thai boy of about seventeen, opened the door and let him in.

"I have an appointment with Mr. Roy," said Meyer.

"Mr. Roy is in his room," the boy answered in slightly accented English.

The room to which he was led was of an almost unearthly beauty. The basic color was blue in all its facets. All metal had been gilded. Thai Buddhas were placed in special niches. Chinese vases and screens were placed with refined elegance and highlighted by hidden spotlights. Crystal vases, filled with large amounts of carefully selected flowers were placed on the white grand piano and the glass tables.

Everything had been decorated with an incredibly decadent taste to achieve an atmosphere of sensitivity and old-world elegance. Meyer sat down on one of the three white sofas.

The surface of the table in the center was made of cut glass, supported by three enormous ivory tusks.

Roy, laboriously supported by his walking stick, entered and with a bored drawl said:

"Hello, my dear Jacques, you finally decided to pick up some nice toys from your Auntie Roy?"

A black codpiece was attached to his black leather pants. If the codpiece could be believed, he was enormously well endowed. His black silk shirt was open to the navel and showed a vulgar brooch, studded with diamonds, against his hairy chest. The brooch hung from a thick, gold chain. There was a hint of lipstick on his lips and his long nails were manicured and polished a bright red.

Meyer got up to shake hands, but Roy kissed him on both cheeks. He sat down on one of the benches and rested before lighting a fresh cigarette.

"Oh, my darling," his tone was quasi-seductive, "how wonderful of you to visit me."

"How are you, Roy?" asked Meyer.

"Well, so-so, you know. I sit down when I'm tired and keep going when I'm rested. Did you see my Thai demonstration model? Isn't he gorgeous?"

"You don't live with Dai anymore?"

"Oh, of course. Imagine! But don't you know? Dai is sick too."

Dai was Roy's regular lover and both had tested positive for AIDS.

"But we still enjoy life, you know. We watch the birdies in the garden. That can last years. Look darling, I remain optimistic, you know that. I don't mind the legs not working so well, as long as the mind keeps functioning. Don't you agree?"

A dry cough could not be controlled.

"But I won't tire you any further with my problems. Shall we go to my little shop of horrors, my darling?"

They descended a set of stairs to arrive in the large basement space of the old canal house. It was dark and humid. Here was his business. They called him the Pierre Cardin of S&M. Here one could find a collection that was the dream of every connoisseur. Soft, supple black leather clothes, masks, harnesses, restraints, chastity belts, belts, corsets and collars. On one side of the long, wide corridor were two cages with thick steel bars and heavy locks. Against the opposite wall there were whips of every kind, by the gross.

As they passed this display, Roy said:

"I'll spread-eagle you against the bars, tie you securely and then I can do with you what I want."

At the end of the corridor was a complete S&M space. The walls were covered with helmets, steel harnesses and scrotum weights.

"Would you believe it, my darling, there are guys who want to hang as much as a hundred pounds from their balls. Can you understand that? But what the hell! Whatever they want, Mama Roy will supply."

A glass case displayed nipple- and penis-enlargers, steel cock rings in all sizes, underwear of finely woven chain links, bras and panties lined with horsehair and padlocks in all sizes.

"Come, I'll show you the medical section," he said. Leaning on his inseparable walking stick, he slowly led the way. In this space was a gynecological examination chair, complete with stirrups, in order to facilitate the piercing of any body part. Meyer became excited at the sight of all these wonders. He knew he had created a marvelous playroom for Monique and himself, but there were so many possibilities he had never even thought about. The pillory, for instance, over in the corner. He could make one before he would show Monique the new playroom. Because she didn't know about it. It was going to be a surprise. A cozy corner was still to be installed, a small bar with stools, a sound system ... With a little luck, he might be finished by Friday.

An hour later he left Amsterdam with a trunk full of purchases.

9. Polderkerk, Friday Night, March 3, 1989

She could not rid herself of worry when she drove home in her white BMW. She loved Jacques, but what was the matter with him? He had shown her the new playroom, but she had been unable to make love there. It was too much, too obvious, too technical and too calculated. Perhaps her background called up different associations from his, at the sight of a cross. It was a game they played, a game they both enjoyed equally, no more and no less, but this was too absurd. Of course, she had not disappointed him, when he showed her everything. She had reacted enthusiastically and then, with female tact, she had led him to the bedroom. Much nicer. The playroom was really macabre, with dripping candles in bottles and the terrible music from the movie *9-1/2 weeks*. She also noticed that during their games he was a lot rougher, than ever before. That too, worried her. She enjoyed pain, it was the highest pleasure, but the ideal combination could only be established if her partner knew exactly how far he could go. There had to be limits. He was allowed to humiliate her, he was allowed to hit her and at the time it happened she thought it mean and she hated it, but it also gave her an immense kick. And that was the game. She could let go of all her emotions and lose all her inhibitions and afterward she would feel fantastic. She was always the submissive party and she asked for more and more. But he had to know the limit. And it seemed as if he went over that limit more and more, further and further. She felt the welts on her back as she leaned back in the car seat. The way he looked at her was also different. There was a definite change and, in retrospect, that had started a few weeks ago. She suddenly remembered all sorts of small incidents that had seemed unimportant at the time. What was the matter with him? Tears sprang in her eyes, because the feelings of love for him could not be denied. Why was she put together this way? Why was she unable to make love like normal people, straight up and down? What caused it? She had tried to save both her failed marriages with every possible effort, but they were both sexual disasters. Was she sick in the head? Abnormal? Did she need psychiatric care? Why this urge to crawl for her master? Especially since he was anything but a dominant figure in his daily life! On the contrary, he was always self-effacing, a bit of a teddy bear. What was the matter with him? Tonight again, that name, Vollmer! She heard him. Her attention had only been partially on the game. She had watched him, more than other nights. She had listened to him. She had played a part, only partly involved with the game she loved and needed. She had been unable to let herself go completely. She wanted to catch every word, but there was only that name. There was something desperate about him, something frightening.

When she entered Amsterdam around two thirty in the morning, instead of heading South, where she lived, she went to the center of town.

She parked in one of the few parking garages Amsterdam is able to boast and hailed a cab. She mentioned the name of a bar in a small street behind the Rembrandt Square. The trip was short. The doorman took her coat in the narrow lobby and she entered the smoky place. It was busy and people were stacked three-deep in front of the bar. She almost never came here anymore, but this time she had a reason. She knew the bartender, who was also a one-time friend of Jacques. Perhaps she could find out something about Jacques from him. She stood among the crowd in front of the bar and managed to get a stool after a short while. The bartender saw her and recognized her.

"So, Madam Director is going to tie one on, tonight," he joked.

"To be honest, Madam Director feels like it tonight!"

"Things that bad?"

"Ach, forget it, give me a double gin and tonic."

When he placed the drink in front of her he said, in a conspiratorial tone:

"Let it all hang out, darling, Harry will protect you tonight."

"To how many women have you given that line, today?"

"Nobody, because they're all here with their guy."

"Dirty old man."

"One does not discuss age in this establishment," he said as he turned to a new customer.

After about an hour it became a little less crowded and the bartender took some time to talk to her. She knew him from the time before Jacques, because she used to come here a lot with her second husband. She was light headed after the four double gins and tonic. But not too light headed to forget the reason for her visit.

"Harry, you used to be friends with Jacques, weren't you?"

"Oh yes, still am, I think, but I haven't seen him in years."

Her tongue felt thick and swollen and she had difficulty in making it do what she wanted.

"I want to know something."

"As long as you don't ask for my wallet, you can ask away." A regular joke, uttered at least a dozen times a night.

"Tell me something about Jacques."

"Great Scott. What do you want to know? It's been so long. I knew him, but we were never what you call bosom friends. He was a bit of a loner, hard to pin down."

"Do you know anything about his parents, his youth?"

"No, he never talked about that."

"Did you know his parents?"

"He had foster parents. But don't forget, it's been at least fifteen years since I saw him last. I was still married to Josie at the time."

"Do you remember the name of those people?"

"The foster parents? Jesus, who knows. I've been there just once, I think."

"Where did they live?"

"In the Sarphaty street ... no, wait, that's called something else, that's it: Sarphaty Park."

"Do you remember the number?"

"No, it was near the end, there was a dairy store on the corner."

"Try to remember the name."

The man stared vaguely across the bar and tried to remember.

"Perhaps it was Vollmer?"

"No," he said decisively. "It was a common name, there used to be a pianist at the time, with the same name. Damn, what was the name of that geyser?"

"A pianist, from Amsterdam?"

"No, no, on the radio, eh, I can't remember. It's on the tip of my tongue."

"Nero?"

"No, no, wait a minute, Peter Kellenbach. That was the name, those people were called Kellenbach!"

"Fantastic, you're a darling." She opened her purse and wrote the name in her notebook.

She offered Harry a drink and then he offered her a drink and when it was time to close the bar, they were both in a happy mood. Outside she realized that she was unable to drive and they hailed a cab. Harry opened the door for her and she said:

"When did you stop escorting single ladies?"

In the cab she really noticed how drunk she was, but she couldn't care less. Laughing they took the elevator to her floor, she turned a few dim lights on and started the record player. All slavish attitudes had disappeared. She took the initiative. She pressed her breasts and belly against him and felt his penis respond. Her hand slid down and slowly she opened his zipper. She took the erect member between her fingers and slowly she moved the foreskin back and forth. Abruptly she discarded her skirt and panties, fell back on the sofa and said:

"Take me, now!"

He fell on his knees in front of her, she spread her legs, took his hard penis in her hand and guided him inside her. Impatient and abandoned she moved her pelvis. She rubbed her clitoris with her sharp nails in rhythm with his movements. Then she rose slightly in order to observe the sliding movement of his penis in and out of her vagina. She wanted to know, no, she had to prove, that she was capable of normal sex.

When, with a shuddering motion, he lost his seed in her, she realized that she had felt nothing, it had left her untouched. No feeling, no emotion, no passion. She had not even been just horny. It was finished in a technical, almost clinical manner. Like a whore, according to the book.

*10. Amsterdam, Saturday, March 4, 1989

That morning Monique woke with a hangover. What had she done? She had cheated on him. She, the girl with the nice catholic upbringing and an important position with a renowned insurance company. Why had she taken such an idiotic risk? She loved Jacques. Instead of helping him, she went to bed with another man. She had practically raped the other. She had grabbed his genitals and then offered herself. Just an hour ago she had walked Harry to the elevator. He had kissed her on the cheek and mumbled something like "I'll call you, sometime." After that she had soaked in the tub for more than an hour. She was sorry and wanted to see Jacques. She wanted to hold his hand and she wanted to understand him better. Perhaps he was the man she had always searched for. But how could she combine that with her job, which totally absorbed her? There had to be a solution. Jacques was so different from the usual kind of men, she met on a daily basis. He was worth an effort. Her previous two husbands had held her back in her career. They had their own careers and that, to them, was more important. Two careers in the same household, that's asking for trouble. But Jacques was different. In addition, they were extremely compatible sexually. There was hardly any sex life with the other two.

She lifted the receiver of the telephone and hesitated for just one more moment. Then she dialed the number. She heard his voice and said:

"How are you?"

"Good, why do you ask?"

"Because, suddenly I wanted to know how you are."

"You never did that before."

"I know, but there's a first time for everything."

"What a nice surprise."

"You mean that?"

"Most certainly, it was not part of our deal, remember?"

"We can change that, true?"

"Are you doing anything special tonight?"

"Yes, but I can cancel it," she said gladly.

"It's not all that important?"

"In a way, but you're more important. Where will we eat tonight?"

"Is that an invitation?"

"You want me to send a formal invitation?"

"Business woman!"

"What time?"

"You say."

"Seven o'clock at my place?"

"Your place? I don't even know your address."

After she gave him the address, she said:

"Don't forget your toothbrush."

"You think I'll need it?"

"You never know."

"Bye."

"Bye."

She replaced the receiver and felt happy and relieved. Her original appointment for that evening was partly business and partly social. She called the party at home and made her excuses for cancelling the appointment. The remaining time she spent on business she had taken home from the office and originally was scheduled for the next day. But the next day too, Sunday, she wanted to keep free for Jacques. She wanted a Sunday like everybody else. Tea in bed and coffee around eleven, followed by brunch somewhere. And no business at all during the day. She felt she was entitled.

She took a shower at six, made her face and selected one of her favorite dresses. At exactly seven o'clock he rang the bell. So typical of Jacques, so punctual! She pushed the intercom, heard his name and pushed the door opener. She walked toward the elevator and waited for the doors to open. He emerged with an enormous bouquet of roses. She embraced him, kissed him and took him by the arm.

"Enter the holy of holies," she said and embraced him again.

"What is the matter with you, today?"

"Nothing, I'm just happy, happy to have you here." She pressed herself against him.

"Watch out for your flowers."

"Oh yes, flowers from you, how beautiful."

She looked at the bouquet and felt loved and flattered. She was used to receiving flowers on the job. But those flowers meant little. Regular business exchanges, small bribes. She took the bouquet to the kitchen and selected a crystal vase while he looked around the apartment.

She came back to the living area, placed the flowers on the marble top of the dining room table and asked: "What do you think of my space? Do you like it?"

Impressed by the rich architecture and furnishing, neither of which had come cheap, he only managed to say:

"She calls it space."

The apartment covered almost 2,500 square feet, with large balconies in the front and in the back. The dominant color was pearl gray, combined with accents in either black or white, whereby all objects, such as the flowers, or a collection of fine porcelain, were highlighted in a most attractive manner. An enormous sofa, covered with a silk-like material, matched perfectly with the heavy Chinese carpet and a fireplace bordered in white marble. Modern, expensive book cases covered two of the walls and some original, modern paintings were tastefully spaced around the remaining walls. When he looked at the names on the paintings he knew there was a small fortune hanging there. She noticed that he was somewhat overwhelmed by the luxury and tried to put him at ease.

"My father bought the paintings in the fifties. He was an art collector and made the right kind of investments."

"I can see that, they're magnificent."

How he envied people who could be proud of a past, and could talk about it. A father who was an art collector. How rich was your life already with those kind of presents. What a nice way to start a life. Roots! His roots had been severed in the winter of 1945. With an effort he resisted the somber thoughts and said:

"What have you planned?"

"I reserved a table in a wonderful Indian Restaurant and that will be our first stop."

Two happy people together. Two people who went out in old Amsterdam, came home around one in the morning and then, just as casually, went happily to bed and to sleep. Together.

11. Polderkerk, Friday Night, March 10, 1989

They were close to each other in the large bed in the dark bedroom. Still enjoying the wonderful tiredness and the satisfied feeling. He had been a darling. The aggression she had noticed during the last few weeks and which worried her so, had completely disappeared. He did not try to convince her to play their game in the horrible room with the cross. Here, in this bed, in this room. That was enough for her. There was no time for love in the other room, everything was geared for results. A sinister laboratory where one could only experiment with orgasm, with her as a guinea pig on a cross. She had accepted herself. She had accepted the fact that she was different. But she would not allow escalation. It was a game. It had to remain a game. A game in which she could act like a whore, could be provocative, could be a slave. When, after the lengthy and prolonged foreplay, he came into her, she would tremble, shake and almost pass out with lust and pleasure. She loved him. They had not said anything for some time, when she broke the silence.

"I loved it, last Saturday and Sunday," she said. "We have to do that more often, my darling. What do you think?"

"Is that possible, with your work?"

"You leave that to me, just tell me if you'd like it."

"I loved it. It must have been twenty years since my last time on an excursion boat."

"Amsterdam is beautiful, don't you think?"

"Fantastic, and on such a Sunday it is more beautiful than ever."

"Shall we do that more often?"

"Every Sunday in the boat?"

"Come on, you know better, I mean every week-end at my place and Friday nights here."

"Yes, but ..."

"Don't start again about my job. Be a little aggressive, Jacques Meyer! I just want to know if you would like it. Don't be so self-effacing. After all, you have certain rights over me, by now."

"If you think it will work."

"Damn you, Jacques, I told you to leave that to me. Or don't you want to?"

"I would like nothing better."

"Then let's do it. Darling, we are so good together, let's enjoy it. You're already fifty and I'm forty. Time flies."

"Yes, but you have such an important job and who am I?"

"What has that to do with it?"

"Everything! Sooner or later I will have to meet your friends and relations, or we meet them by accident and then what'll you say?"

"You look very presentable, you dress well, you have taste. Who's going to ask who you are? Nobody cares."

"Do you know what I have done in my life?"

"No, I don't."

"I was just a simple government employee. A faceless white collar worker. One of thousands who worked for the city."

She turned on her side, supported her head on her hand and rubbed his chest.

"What do you live on, Jacques?"

"An inheritance."

"Is that enough?"

"For me, yes. Enough anyway, not to have to do the nine-to-five routine anymore. I didn't like it and it's pointless."

"Well, how many can say that? I know whole tribes who would love to change places with you. Don't you get bored?"

"You have any idea how boring an office is, day after day?"

"Did you never have the urge to do something you really wanted?"

"It never occurred to me. I wasn't in that sort of situation."

"How was the situation?"

"I'll tell you sometime, but not now."

"Why not?"

"I don't know. But not now."

"Little Jacques Meyer, I want to know everything about you and if you don't tell me yourself, I'll try to find out some other way."

"Maybe that's better."

Instinctively she felt that she had to drop the subject. She said:

"Are you happy with me?"

He kissed her forehead and did not answer.

"Why don't you answer?"

"You shouldn't *beschrieje*."

"What does that mean?"

"It's Yiddish, it means you shouldn't tempt fate."

Suddenly it dawned on her. That was it! His scared face when she asked, a few weeks ago, about Frau Vollmer. The number he kept repeating and the death of his parents and little sister. Something horrible had happened in the life of this man. She would help him. He had become a part of her life. A very important part.

"Let's agree that you come to my place every Saturday, around seven. Any work I have to do over the week-end will then be finished and we'll have all of Saturday night and all day Sunday together. We can go to the movies, a museum, or whatever. Does that interest you?"

"You bet!"

"On the rare occasions that I have something to do on Saturday night, you'll come anyway and then you wait for your baby with a nice glass of wine and a nice prick."

Playfully she squeezed his crotch.

"I'll give you a key and if you feel like stopping by during the week, you just come. Even if I am not home, I'll just find you in bed. That sounds like heaven to me."

She rolled herself on top of him and started to kiss him enthusiastically. He tried to get himself away from under her and said:

"Do you mind if I say something?"

"Yes, I do. Just keep your mouth shut and love me."

The words would not pass his lips. He was trapped. He was committed and he was afraid. Always he had been careful. Always afraid for the inevitable parting. The parting would come. It had happened too often. Every time. He tried to insulate himself from the pain by not giving of himself. By keeping to himself, as much as possible. Always that caveat. Again and again. Oh, God, he did not want to lose her. Not again. Not now. But he had to finish his task. It was an almost impossible combination, but it had to be done.

*12. *Amsterdam, Monday Night, March 13, 1989*

Meyer parked his car behind the Central Station in Amsterdam. It was a drizzly night. It had been raining for days and now it had changed to a penetrating drizzle that soaked everything. From the trunk he took his heavy English whip with the stiff laced handle and the solid monkey's fist at the end. He wrapped the whip end around his hand and held the handle in a reverse grip. This way the handle was as dangerous and as deadly as a cosh, or a lead pipe. Lovingly he caressed the beautiful leather lacings that gleamed from the special neat's foot oil he used for upkeep.

The plan, which he had carefully thought out and which, for years now, had lived a life of its own in the back of his head, was going to be executed and completed. He had prepared for it with the same minute attention to detail that had become a part of his day-to-day existence. The names of his victims had been easily located from the many newspaper articles at the time. It had been more difficult to track down the current addresses. He had found the means to discover what he wanted. He knew who they were, where they lived and where they worked. He had no idea what they looked like, but that would be solved when he reached the areas of operation. In Madrid it had been a simple matter to call the airport, ask when the person in question was scheduled to come off duty and then he just waited near the house for him to arrive. The nameplate on the door had given him the necessary confirmation. In five days he would drive to Frankfurt and from there, via Lufthansa, to Barcelona. Last time he had travelled via Brussels. The border check for motorists belonging to the EEC was non-existent. Even if he was asked, he would show his own passport. The second passport was just for the stay in Spain. That's why he did not want to start his trips from Holland. It was too easy to check the passenger lists at Schiphol Airport. The plan had slowly, but surely taken form until it became an obsession. He had undergone a familiarity process that had reduced the horrible facts of his deeds to unimportant details. The vision that he had formed, based on vague suppositions, had grown to the imagined size of an abscess and had been accepted as the only truth. Punishment had to be meted out. There was no other way. And if nobody wanted to take the responsibility, then he would have to take matters in his own hands. The revenge which fed on his sorrow, left him no way out. He was unable to fight the impulse. The nightmares which woke him nightly, drenched in perspiration, formed the final spur. Perhaps Frau Vollmer had escaped her just punishment. Perhaps, or maybe not. He did not know, but this time justice would be done.

He walked to the station and entered. The Paris train was expected in about five minutes. He went trough the long underground corridor and took the stairs to the platform. The majority of the travellers, arriving from Paris at this hour, would be business people and that was an advantage. Most of them were his age and almost all of them carried their passport. When the train came in, he stepped back and surveyed the alighting passengers from a distance. Suddenly he joined the crowds and walked outside. He noticed those that took cabs and those that started to cross the huge square in front of the station. Three walked in the direction of the Royal Palace. Two of them, both dressed in green Loden coats, obviously belonged together so they would not be considered. The third, dressed in a raincoat, turned left and crossed the bridge toward the Henrik Canal. He then turned right and stopped at the edge of the curb to let traffic pass. He reached the divider in the middle of the roadway and then walked on until he stopped in front of the Victoria Hotel. Meyer was less than sixty feet away and watched carefully. The man talked to the doorman and then entered. Meyer felt a slight whiff of despair. For a moment he contemplated following the man into the hotel, find out the room number somehow and attack him in his room. Almost immediately he rejected the idea. Somebody might notice him and might be able to describe him later. It was too dangerous. Also, how was he supposed to get upstairs without anybody noticing? Disappointed and angry, he turned around and walked in the direction of his car. Suddenly he spotted one of the two men in the Loden coats. The man walked in the direction he needed, away from crowds. At once he changed his plan and started to follow him. Perhaps the night would not be a loss, after all. The man crossed the road and walked toward the Criers Tower. Meyer was now less than thirty feet behind him. The fact that the man walked in the direction he did, bolstered his self-confidence, because he knew this part of Amsterdam like his back pocket. Every twisted street and every alley was known to him. He took the whip, which had been hidden under his coat, into his right hand and arranged it to his satisfaction. It was quiet in the streets and he knew that whoever was still around, would not get involved with anything. As they approached the corner, Meyer increased his speed. He took one more look around and did not see anybody, except his intended victim. Satisfied, he bunched his muscles and just before the man could round the corner, he hit him. The heavy handle landed on his head and with a soft burp the man collapsed.

The briefcase fell on the pavement, Meyer grabbed it and disappeared along the dark canals. Quickly he walked the length of the first canal, turned into an alley and went in the direction of the Central Station. Via the pedestrian tunnel underneath the station he soon reached his car. In the car he carefully cleaned the heavy English whip with a black cloth from the glove compartment. Then he opened the briefcase and, without touching anything, looked at the content. In one of the compartments, against the lid, he saw the little black book. He had been lucky. Carefully he removed the passport, opened it and looked at the picture. He saw a man, about fifty, fifty-three years old, grey on the temples and with horn-rimmed glasses. The name was on page 4: Kranedonk, Henry John. Satisfied he put the passport in an inside pocket and carefully wiped the briefcase.

As he was ready to start the engine, he saw two man close to the car, looking at him. Before he realized what happened, one of them had opened the driver's door and hit him in the face, momentarily stunning him. In that same instance, the other man opened the other door and grabbed the briefcase and the whip from the passenger's side.

Before he realized it they ran toward the back of the station and disappeared.

When he had himself once again under control he noticed that the briefcase and the whip had disappeared.

"God damn, the bastards," he cursed angrily.

On the way home he rethought the entire incident. In retrospect the incident wasn't too bad, at all. He'd lost his expensive whip and that was too bad, but, if on the other hand, the briefcase was ever found, it could never lead to him. His victim had not seen him, he was sure of that. And if those two guys were ever caught, they would also, automatically be charged with the attack on the owner of the briefcase. He hoped they'd be caught. It would make things easier for him.

Satisfied he drove to Polderkerk, parked the car in front of the house and went in. A little later he drank a glass of cold milk with a cheese sandwich. He went to bed around two in the morning.

13. Amsterdam, Monday Night, March 13, 1989

The two police constables, patrolling the pedestrian tunnel underneath the Central Station, observed two men with greasy hair and dirty clothes. One carried an expensive leather briefcase and the other carried a beautiful leather whip.

"Typical business people, Kees," one constable remarked to the other and winked.

"Captains of Industry, no doubt about it," replied the other, while they increased their pace.

"I bet their car and driver is waiting for them."

"No, they just got off on the wrong side of the train. They're looking for the Royal Waiting Room."

Meanwhile they had overtaken the two and when they were right behind the suspects, one of the constables said:

"Good evening gentlemen, how's business tonight?"

Startled the two turned around, saw the constables and tried to run away. Before they could take a single step, however, they were firmly taken by the arm.

"Not so hasty, gentlemen, the driver will wait."

"Wadda ye want from us?" One of the men tried to struggle away from the constable.

"Just a little conversation, gentlemen, nothing to get excited about."

"Yeah, I know all about your conversations," said the man with the whip.

"Well, well, now I recognize you! An old acquaintance. My dear Abdul, do you live near the race track these days?"

"No, no, my boy," said the other constable. "It is *Mister* Abdul and he owns his own stable of Arabians these days. Isn't that so, sir?"

"Elegant briefcase," he continued, pointing at the item. "So smart, it's really you. Do you want us to look inside, or would you rather come to the station and avoid all the complications?"

"That's my briefcase and none of your business!"

"But I know that, my friends," calmed the constable, "I was just remarking on the fact to my colleague here: Look, I said, there is Mr. Abdul, the well-known horse trainer with his whip and his partner, carrying a Cartier briefcase full of important papers. How apt."

Decisively he took hold of the briefcase and opened it. Briefly he sorted through the contents.

"Look at this, Kees," he said, holding some of the papers up to the light. "The young gentleman has arrived in the world. His name is now Kranedonk and he has managed to obtain a law degree. My, my," he continued in the same sarcastic tone, "he's even become a partner with the well-known firm of Kranedonk & Melzer."

"Gee, Hans, no doubt the Inspector will speak harshly to us about inconveniencing such important people."

Quickly they hand cuffed the two men and led them away to the patrol car which was parked in front of the station.

* * *

"Goddamn," cursed the desk sergeant at the Station in the Warmoes Street. "It's only ten thirty and already three robberies. Perhaps the weather is changing."

"Well, in any case, John, it will keep you off the streets and out of the shopping malls," yelled a colleague from behind a typewriter.

"Otherwise you wife will just nag you," yelled another, trying to be funnier.

"Hell, with the schedule the way it is lately, I've forgotten what she looks like."

"Well, congratulations, man. It'll be like the first time, every time you go to bed."

"Easy for you to say, young bachelor person. I bet your housekeeper brings you breakfast in bed every morning, right? Are you paying rent in services?"

"Exactly," teased the young cop. "She even presses my uniform and shines my shoes. Look at that!" With a provocative gesture he placed both feet on the desk and looked complacently at his shiny boots.

"Now that you mention it, we noticed you've been looking rather fine lately. Right boys?" John looked around for agreement.

"As far as I know, she even gives him baths and rubdowns," remarked a voice from the corner.

"Look, I understand, you poor married bastards are going home after a long night and than the old lady is all over you with this complaint and that problem, before you even have a chance to hang your cap on the hook. I know! But this young gentleman goes home in a little while and there is nice cup of hot chocolate waiting in the microwave and some home-made cakes, or whatever, ready on the table."

"And then you still have to serve the old lady, right?"

"No way, there's even a tiny little napkin to wipe the last delicious crumbs from my mouth," he continued unperturbed.

"Go away, you need the napkin for wiping in bed as well? Afterwards?" came the voice from behind the typewriter.

"Gentlemen, I do believe that is enough for tonight, don't you agree?" The voice of the lone female constable suddenly came clearly through the large room. She was all too familiar with this sort of teasing. It remained a men's world and she was used to it. In her heart she enjoyed it. Men were like children and you had to give children a chance to let off steam. This was rather mild. Some of the language she heard, she would be unable to repeat at home. But sometimes she grinned to herself about the inventive teasing that so belonged to the Amsterdam folklore. Cockneys, true cockneys, she decided, probably came closest to it.

"How nice for you, my boy, to be working with your mama," said the typist who had stopped typing.

"If you have nothing better to do, Ed, would you mind typing this up for me?" She gave him a number of handwritten pages.

"You're as bad as my wife," he said grumpily, but started the work.

"Three robberies and only just ten thirty," repeated the desk sergeant.

"Ten forty five," yelled someone.

"All right, ten forty five ...!"

At that moment the door opened and two constables entered, escorting the man with the briefcase and the one with whip.

"John, I want to present a lawyer and a jockey."

"Well, that's easy to see and even easier to smell. Room five is vacant. Specifically reserved for the better public," answered John.

They took the men to the interrogation room and started the preliminaries.

About five minutes later a new visitor arrived, dressed in a green Loden coat. He approached the desk sergeant and said:

"Good evening, sergeant, I have been attacked and robbed."

"And where did this happen, sir?"

"Close by, behind the station on the corner of ..."

"What time was that, sir?" interrupted the sergeant.

"I don't know exactly. I was hit on the head." he pointed at a head wound.

"One moment, sir." The sergeant walked away and returned quickly with a plain clothed officer.

"Please follow me."

In one of the interrogation rooms, the officer shook hands and introduced himself: "Gelder, detective branch."

"Kranedonk," said the man in the Loden coat. They sat down.

"Tell me, Mr. Kranedonk, what happened?"

"Well, I can tell you precious little. I just returned by train from Paris, with a colleague. I was walking along the Henrik Canal, where I was to stay with some friends. I live in Arnhem, but I have another appointment here in town, early in the morning. I remember hearing somebody behind me but that was all. When I came to, I was on the pavement at the corner and my briefcase had disappeared. That's all inspector."

"You saw nobody?"

"No, nobody, I cannot remember a thing."

"What was in the briefcase?" asked Van Gelder, looking at a piece of paper.

"Some money, business correspondence, contracts. I am an attorney."

"A lot of money?"

"Perhaps 500 in Dutch money and some French francs, but a number of very important papers. The reason I am here. I hope that maybe the papers can be recovered. They can keep the money, as long as I get the papers back. Perhaps they'll turn up, they are of no use to anybody else."

Gelder handed the man a form and a pen. He said:

"Would you be so kind as to fill this in? Then we'll see what we can do for you. Please give as complete a description as possible. I'll be right back. Would you like some coffee?"

"Please."

Gelder walked to the door and then turned around: "Don't you want a doctor to take a look, at your head?"

"I don't think so. It's just a swelling and I am not dizzy."

While he was still filling out the form, Gelder returned and placed the briefcase on the table.

"Sometimes we can work amazingly fast, Mr. Kranedonk," he said.

Surprised he looked at his possession, opened it, quickly scanned some papers and said:

"I'll be! How did you manage that so fast?"

"Our job, Mr. Kranedonk, has a lot to do with happenstance." He related the story of the two constables in the pedestrian tunnel under the Central Station.

"I don't suppose there is any use in you confronting the suspects, is there? You said you didn't see anybody."

"Yes, that's right. I am sorry, but I can't be of assistance in this matter."

"Do you mind one last question?" asked Gelder.

"But, of course, feel free."

"Did you carry a whip?"

The man started to laugh and said:

"But that's absurd. Why would I need a whip in Paris?"

"Sometimes people will do the craziest things, Mr. Kranedonk."

14. Sitges, Wednesday Morning, March 15, 1989

Matias Oliver had a round face with sparkling eyes that always seemed to enjoy life. His short figure gave the impression of overweight, but he was still reasonably muscled at sixty two years of age. He had been an avid sportsman, during his early career with the Spanish Air Force, and he still kept in training. Everyday he could be found on the tennis court near his hotel and at least once a week he spent a day on the golf course. For the last 37 years he had been married to a woman from a good Spanish family and he was one of the important people in the town of Sitges. Forty years ago, Sitges was no more than an unimportant fishing village with a population of less than 1,500 people. During those days the fishing boats were pulled up on the beach and the nets would cover the primitive boardwalk while the old women repaired them. Adolescents and small children were the only ones who played on the beach in the summer, or swam in the sea. Sunning, or tanning, was unknown. A brown skin was common. It was more important to find shade, when possible. The sun was there to ripen the fruit, but otherwise a bit of a nuisance.

Matias Oliver's grandfather had been a simple farmer with large land holdings, but hardly a peseta of income. By inheritance from father to son, the barren acres had eventually become the property of Matias. Extended woodlands, filled with conifers and rocks, where nothing would grow and where development was impossible, in a time when bulldozers and tractors were not readily available. And sand dunes, almost endless sand dunes, close to the coast, falling away towards wide, sandy beaches. What possible use could sand dunes be to a farmer? Far inland there were a few pieces of land that did bear some fruit and they provided the meager income for the family. Olive trees, that was the only cash crop worth mentioning. Every year the entire family would concentrate on picking the fruits, pressing them and then, finally, the oil could be sold for just enough money to keep total starvation away for another year. Everything was that way. Nothing was simple and nothing brought a living wage. There were a few almond trees. They required netting to be spread under them in order to catch all the nuts. Then the nuts had to be cracked and peeled. During September the family was almost totally deaf because of the indescribable noise of the mechanical nut cracker. A few more pesetas. A few vegetables and some chickens. A few eggs to be sold to the poor population of Sitges. Transport was by mule. A hard existence in a pitiless climate. Hard work and almost no income. Grandfather Oliver died in 1950 at the early age of 59 and left three sons and a daughter. The sons were already married and the daughter had entered a monastery. The inheritance was divided according to the age-old customs of Spain. The oldest son received the few pieces of productive ground. The second son the less productive ground and the youngest son received the worst ground. The ground consisted of rocks, dunes and sand and was located near the sea. The youngest son was the father of Matias.

In the early fifties the first campers from the North descended on the area. Pulled by underpowered Volkswagens, they soon made way for more sophisticated visitors who demanded bungalows, air-conditioned apartments. Matias' father had the right ground. Barren, but on the coast. The worst disadvantage suddenly became an advantage. Things progressed at break-neck speed. The fisher women threw away their nets and opened souvenir shops. And the landowners could ask whatever they wanted. Hotel Cristina was just one example of the economic improvements that had blessed the area. Matias Oliver was now the owner and he also owned some bungalows and a high-rise apartment complex. His father had given him the management of Oliver Enterprises just two years ago. This ended his career with Iberia Airlines, where he had worked after his demobilization from the Spanish Air Force.

After a game of tennis with the Chief of the Sitges police, Matias Oliver entered the Cristina Hotel at exactly 10 o'clock in the morning. Whitewash was being removed from the windows and the rust was being removed from the terrace furniture. Everything was being freshly painted, the swimming pool, after a thorough cleaning, was being filled with fresh water and a thousand other tasks, small and large, designed to wake the hotel from its long off-season hibernation, were being performed with feverish haste. The season was starting early this year. Just nine days untll Good Friday. Easter was on March 26 and 27. Bookings were not good. Just about thirty percent from previous years. The summer season looked troublesome as well. Everybody knew that Spain had become too expensive for mass tourism. For the same price an airplane would fly to resorts that were three, four times as far away and much cheaper. If the coming summer also was going to be sunny in the North of Europe, a severe recession had to be taken into account. An unusual experience after the years and years of continued economic growth.

After Matias had checked on the progress of the various projects, after he had given his opinion, direction, or correction to a score of workers, he retreated to his office. He interviewed a number of job seekers and then prepared himself for the daily battle with Travel Agencies and Tour Operators, who either wanted to cancel arrangements, or, in the best cases, wanted to severely curtail their obligations. Last fall, in a wave of optimism, they had reserved large blocks of hotel space. But now, after the publication of the brochures and a severe down-turn in the expected bookings, they were all trying to avoid red ink. Matias knew the game and he played it well. With the same sparkling eyes, that so enjoyed life, he refused decisively to lower his prices, or to forgive penalty clauses as proposed by his opponents. Everybody wanted to profit from the situation and it was now a matter of who could hang on the longest. After having taken care of the business of the day, he got into his car and drove leisurely along the Paseo Maritimo, along the Mediterranean, toward his apartment complex. Sitges still showed a deserted and desolated face to the public. The many boutiques and souvenir shops were still shuttered. A resort town in the off-season looks something like a ghost town. Everything was there: the bars, the restaurants, even the benches along the promenade. But there were no people. Everything was empty. A carnival in the rain. The crowds, the parties, the smell of suntan oil were yet to come. He liked the desolation. The expectant wait for the next season, the slow awakening, the high points in July and August and the slumber in the Fall until the last windows had once again been whitewashed and the last terrace table had been stored for another winter. The lack of continuity. He liked it.

He drove slowly in order not to miss a single sign of the awakening that was happening. From a distance he saw that Bar Ramon had taken all its beach chairs out of storage. Ramon himself was outside, a can of white paint in one hand and a brush in the other. He recognized the car, raised a hand and yelled:

"Buenos dias, Señor Oliver!"

Matias Oliver opened the window of the Mercedes and waved his hand enthusiastically. Despite the hundreds of thousands that would soon descend on Sitges, it had remained a small town and all the locals knew each other and all of them knew about each other. Just like forty years ago, when the first VW puffed into the village.

Ramon looked after the metallic blue Mercedes as it disappeared in the distance, dipped his brush in the paint and continued with his work.

*15 Sitges, Wednesday Morning, March 15, 1989

Except for one, all the benches along the promenade of Sitges were empty. An immaculately dressed gentleman with horn-rimmed glasses was seated on the single occupied bench across from the Bar Ramon. An unremarkable man. It could have been a business man with a little extra time before seeing his next client. It seemed that way, but the appearance was an illusion. He was reading a newspaper. Or rather, he pretended to read a newspaper. The newspaper was camouflage. Of all things, it was a German newspaper, a newspaper in the language he hated most. But there had been no other way. The stall where he had bought it, only had Spanish papers and just this one, foreign paper from the previous day. He did not want to buy a Spanish paper. In the first place because he didn't know enough about the language and secondly he did not want to be taken for a Spaniard. It would have entailed the risk that somebody would have sat next to him to start some kind of conversation. The last thing he needed. One never knew if his description would be given to the police, although that would be the most incredible coincidence. One did not readily associate a well-dressed gentleman with a violent crime. But an ounce of prevention was better than a pound of cure. Everything had been planned and figured down to the smallest detail. In Frankfurt, in the name of Kranedonk, he had purchased a round-trip ticket to Barcelona. He had crossed the border on his own passport. Therefore his name would not appear on the Lufthansa passenger records and there would be no problems with the customs. He knew that for a while now, the Spanish customs had abolished the practice of stamping passports for entry and exit, so there was no proof of his stay in Spain. Nobody knew where he was. Despite the fact that he had hardly any contacts with his neighbors, he had connected a number of lights at the house to timers. As far as anybody could tell, he was home. Monique had told him weeks ago that she would be in London for the week-end, on business. His disappearance would not be noted, even by her. He had left the car in front of the house and travelled to Frankfurt by train. The luggage had been stored in advance in a locker at the Central Station, because a man with a suitcase would stand out in Polderkerk. He had arrived on Monday and taken a room in a Barcelona hotel under the name of Kranedonk. Today marked the second time that he had taken the bus from Barcelona to Sitges. He did not rent a car. Perhaps in the coming days. He had not needed a car in Madrid, because there had been cabs everywhere and one more passenger in a city of millions would remain anonymous. That was different here. For instance, even if a room had been available out of season, it would have been too risky to stay in a local hotel. He would probably have been the only guest and would have been very easily tracked down. The surreptitious following of his next victim was a lot more difficult here, then in Madrid. From a terrace he had been able to spot the entrance to Hotel Cristina and he discovered that the owner drove a light blue Mercedes.

Twice he had been observed entering at ten in the morning and twice he had driven to the apartment complex in the late afternoon. The last time he had stayed there until 7:30PM. The work crews, who were preparing the empty buildings for the season, left for home around seven. The director closed and locked the service entrance after that. That was last night. He would check it again tonight. The distance between Hotel Cristina and the apartment complex was a little less than two miles. Walking distance. He had taken a close look at the service entrance, earlier today. A row of cypresses hid it from view. An ideal place for the first part of his plan. The time that the victim locked the door was also ideal. It was already dark by seven thirty. The building was extremely well suited for the execution of the punishment. There was light, there were dark curtains in front of the windows, that were almost all closed and every apartment had, of course, a bathroom.

Startled, he suddenly saw the blue Mercedes appear in the distance. As the car came closer, he saw the license tag and verified the identity of the driver. The Mercedes slowed down. A slight panic came over him. What did it mean? Was he going to sit on the bench next to him? He wanted to leave, but in the few seconds available he could only look at the blue car as if paralyzed. The man who was painting his stall across the street, also heard the car. He raised his hand as it passed. While Meyer hid behind the newspaper he heard a voice calling:

"Buenos dias, Señor Oliver!" and then an answer he did not understand. He heard the driver accelerate and when he looked around his newspaper, the Mercedes had passed. He could not suppress a sigh of relief, but at the same time he wondered why he had been so anxious. It was absurd to suspect that a single person in this village should know him. He saw that the owner of Bar Ramon had returned to his chores. A weak sun broke from behind some clouds and he felt the perspiration under his hat. He had never before worn a hat and he could not get used to it. A hat was too hot and in some way it irritated him. But he knew that a hat could change the face completely, especially in combination with the horn-rimmed glasses. Now that the sun started to shine, however, and nobody was in sight anyway, he took the thing off his head and placed it on the bench next to him. He had been dozing for about fifteen minutes like that, when he heard a door close. He opened his eyes and observed the owner of Bar Ramon in the process of putting away his things. After closing the door for the last time, he took a large padlock from a ledge under the awning and locked the door.

He took the key out of the padlock after closing it and replaced it on the ledge from where he had taken the padlock. He mounted his moped and disappeared in the distance.

Meyer closed his eyes again and enjoyed the sun of this early spring day.

16. Sitges, Friday Night, March 17, 1989

The previous day, before boarding the bus to Sitges, Meyer had bought the clothes he now wore in a department store in Barcelona. A pair of jeans, loafers, a jacket and a cap. Everything in earth tones that did not match too well. He carried an imitation Adidas bag in his hand. He felt uncomfortable in the clothes. First, because he found them tasteless and cheap and second, because they were new. That could be noticed. He carefully studied his fellow passengers on the bus, but nobody paid any particular attention to him. He walked in the direction of the Promenade and because he was still early, he decided to get something to eat first. He entered a small bar and ordered some *tapas* and a glass of beer. He sat down in a corner of the room and hid behind his newspaper. Around a quarter to seven he paid the bill, left the establishment and walked in a northerly direction along the Promenade. In the distance he saw the letters of the apartment complex against the twilight sky: "Apartamentos Las Coronas". The neon lights were not lit up. Just a single light on one of the balconies was visible. He passed the building on the opposite side of the street and a little later he crossed the street and walked back. After making sure that he could not be seen and checking again that nobody was there, he turned into the alley between two of the buildings. The alley curved slightly and after a while he arrived at the small parking lot, surrounded by cypresses. The blue Mercedes and a few smaller cars were parked to the left of the service entrance. Behind the cypresses to the right was a building with a view of the gorgeously maintained garden, the swimming pool and a number of extended terraces. He wriggled himself in between the cypresses, squatted down with his back against the wall and waited.

He placed the bag next to him, opened the zipper, took out a heavy whip and put on some black leather gloves. He heard voices and through the branches he saw a man approach one of the cars, get in and drive away. By the lighted dial of his watch he was able to ascertain the time as 7:20PM. Not much longer to wait. There had been no deviation from the pattern for the last three days. He was just surprised that there were two additional cars, in addition to the Mercedes. The previous evenings the work crews had left promptly at seven. It was now twenty minutes past and there were still two cars that did not belong. From inside the building he heard the voices of a number of men, engaged in an extended conversation. He heard the hollow sound of their footsteps and, every once in a while, the sound of an elevator. Obviously some sort of conference regarding the work was in progress. He felt his legs falling asleep and carefully he rose to a standing position. For minutes nothing happened. A half hour went by. The hands of his watch moved forward with agonizing slowness. Meanwhile it was five minutes to eight and nothing had changed. What if he could not complete his mission tonight? He would have to wait until Monday. Nobody worked on Saturday and Sunday. Three people appeared in the lobby at half past eight. Two carried papers and the third was making hasty notes. Probably contractors, or architects. Despite the fact that he did not speak the language, he noticed from the intonation that the discussion was winding down. They stood near the elevator and one of the men opened the elevator and entered. They shook hands with Señor Oliver and closed the elevator doors. Matias stood for a moment undecided, looked around and then walked toward the side corridor. From his hiding place he had been able to follow the events in the hall. Two men remained in the building. It had been empty the previous nights. Quickly he reviewed the new situation, took the whip firmly in his right hand, with lead-filled monkey's fist forward, and carefully crossed the parking lot. He squatted down behind the car next to the Mercedes and waited.

A few minutes later Matias Oliver appeared, walked toward his car, took out his keys and was standing next to the left-front door of the car, as Meyer quickly and silently rose from his hiding place. He lifted his weapon high above his head and before the victim had time to react the end of the whip hit him on the head. The body collapsed with glazed eyes and Meyer caught it. He opened the rear door of the car, and struggled the unconscious body onto the back seat. Quickly he crossed the parking lot and returned with his bag. He fished some handcuffs out of the bag, pulled the victim's arms on his back and put the cuffs around the wrists. He took a piece of rope and tied the ankles together. The remaining end was fastened to the steel cuffs. He pulled the mouth open and inserted a ball-gag. He picked up the car keys that had dropped on the ground during the assault, sat down behind the wheel of the Mercedes and drove off. After about a mile he turned into a dark street, parked on a small square, switched off and thought. What now? The first part had gone perfectly well, but he could not use the apartment building. He could kill the man now and leave the Mercedes to be found, but that would be too easy. The man on the back seat was an accomplice in the fiery death of hundreds of people, including his Aunt Marie and Uncle Jan. No, he had to be punished, there was no other way. He wanted to see animal fear in the eyes of his victim. The same fear known by the people trapped in the confined space, while flames encircled their defenseless bodies. Like sardines in a can, a red hot, glowing sardine can. Trampling each other to reach an exit that was unattainable. No, it would be too easy, the guilty was not going to get off that lightly. During the hate filled years behind him, while the hate had grown to immeasurable proportions, he had imagined the execution too many times to be thwarted at this juncture. It had to happen that way. Now especially. It had become a holy quest as far as he was concerned. He glanced at his watch and saw it was almost a quarter past nine. Now what? There was one possibility and perhaps it would serve even better.

He started the engine and drove back in the direction of the Promenade. Everything was deserted and a cold wind blew in from the sea. He stopped the Mercedes in front of Bar Ramon, got out and opened the rear door. He dragged the unconscious body toward the low wall that separated the sidewalk from the beach and threw the body over the wall. With a soft thud it fell on the sand of the beach. He put the car in a parking lot, took out his bag and calmly walked back. On the ledge below the awning he found the key for the padlock, opened it and dragged the body inside. His flashlight revealed a lamp, mounted on a gas bottle. He struck a match and the lamp lit with the usual puff. The space was filled with crates of empty lemonade and beer bottles, refrigerators, a large stove and a sink with two basins. Everything looked dirty and neglected. He opened his bag, took out a pair of black coveralls and put them on. He took a chair and placed it under one of the beams supporting the golf plated roof. From his bag he took a hand drill and used it to make two holes in the beam. In each hole he mounted a hook, normally used for the hanging of a child's swing.

17. Sitges, Friday Night, March 17, 1989

Meyer replaced the padlock on the door of the beach place and replaced the key on the ledge. It was half past eleven and it had been raining for the last few hours. He had heard the drumming of the rain on the golf plated roof. The last bus for Barcelona had left and it would be too dangerous to take a cab. Before jumping over the retaining wall to get on the sidewalk from the beach, he carefully looked around, but there was nobody in sight. He crossed the Promenade, disappeared into a street until he reached the road that encircled Sitges. It was a road that serpentined its way through a destroyed landscape. On both sides of the road was a never ending string of campgrounds, bungalow parks, nightclubs and discos with such names as "El Paradiso," "the Talk of the Town" and "Las Vegas." Poverty breathed through the cracks of the plywood buildings and billboards. The exotic and foreign names could not hide the tackiness. The area was the ultimate tourist trap. Fortunes were paid for illusions and imagined pleasures. The little man and his wife and two children were placed in a Japanese trailer with a canvas roof and for two weeks they were bamboozled into believing that they were world travellers, explorers, and adventurers.

At this time of the year everything was empty, however, and no lights showed anywhere. He found himself opposite a deserted campground, surrounded by a fence, but unguarded. He had decided that it would be unwise to take a cab to Barcelona and to wait in the street until daylight was just as risky. He could not afford to be seen. He approached the fence around the campground and spotted a number of camper trailers. He followed the fence and looked for an easy way in. Near the back he found a hole in the chain link and he crawled through. He felt the slippery mud of red clay ooze along his body. Drenched, he rose to his feet on the inside of the fence. He was cold and he felt dirty. A trailer, green with mold, was nearby and he walked toward it. Flowery curtains covered the windows and a Spanish license plate was barely visible. The door was locked. He picked up a stone and smashed a window. He removed the remaining shards from the bottom of the window, threw his bag inside and hoisted himself through the opening. The inside smelled damp and musty. In the light of his flashlight he discovered a small kerosene lantern above the table and he lit it. He opened the tap above the wash basin and was surprised to see the water come out. Perhaps a permanent connection, or a tank on the roof. He stripped off all his clothes and threw them in a corner. From his bag he took the plastic garbage bag in which the blood spattered coveralls had been wrapped. He washed himself and put on the clean clothes from the bottom of his bag. He then unfolded the bed and laid down. An excited feeling overcame him. Despite the horrible surroundings he felt elated. He no longer belonged to the common herd of mankind. He had done a great service for the world and he was the supreme judge.

Laying on his back he had a weightless feeling, as if he were floating in space ...

18. Sitges, Saturday Morning, March 18, 1989

Ramon tossed off his cognac, placed a 100 peseta bill on the counter top and left Bar Esquina. He started his moped, drove across to the other side of the Promenade, placed the moped against the low wall and walked toward his establishment. He felt on the part of the ledge where he usually placed the key, but could not find it. He tried again, but again without success. He was convinced that the key had to be there. With his hand he felt along the entire length of the ledge and found it almost at the end. Somebody had been inside, he was sure. He unlocked the padlock and opened the door. Even the dim light that came through the sky lights was enough to show him the revolting scene. His mouth fell open as he stared at the naked body, swaying slightly from the hooks.

"Dios mio," he said.

He felt the urge to vomit, turned and ran toward the low wall. Climbing on top of the wall, waving both arms, he yelled:

"Policia, policia, socorro, socorro!!"

The few passers-by across the Promenade stood still, looked at the wildly gesticulating man, shrugged their shoulders and walked on. Nobody reacted. Ramon jumped on his moped and without paying any attention to traffic regulations, he drove across the road and disappeared into one of the side streets. Within minutes he had reached the police station and panting he ran inside. The officer tried to calm the distressed man.

"Calma, calma, Ramon, quiet down, take it easy, what's the matter?"

Stammering and faltering, trying to keep control, Ramon told his story. It was not a clear report but the little that was understood by the cops, was enough to make them scramble for the car in order to investigate on the spot. In the back of the patrol car Ramon carried on. Once started, he could not stop talking. Sirens blasting, the patrol car arrived at the beach within two minutes. They jumped onto the beach and Ramon led the way. The door was still open. The younger of the two policemen entered and came out almost immediately, gagging and trying hard to swallow. The second cop, obviously in charge, steeled himself and entered. A little later he reappeared, looking white as a sheet. He stopped in the door opening and said:

"En seguida! Call the Inspector and assistance, urgente!" He went back into the bar. Ramon, knowing he was no longer alone and gaining courage from that, wanted to follow, but the cop stopped him and ordered:

"No! Prohibido! I don't want you to come in."

Attracted by the police car, rubberneckers were gathering near the scene. The young police man, while reporting via the radio, ordered the curious to maintain a respectful distance. Inside, the older cop immediately recognized the victim.

"Madre mia, Señor Oliver! Que passa!?"

There was no doubt that the man was dead. He had seen enough corpses to be absolutely sure about that, but the way in which the corpse hung in the chains was something he had never encountered before. Revolted and disgusted he looked at the scene. The man was nude and had been tortured. A madman must have been at work. What sort of idiot would do this? He noticed two empty beer crates stacked in front of the corpse. A white envelope had been placed on the topmost crate. Without touching anything he looked around. Coagulated blood covered the floor underneath the corpse and blood had spattered all around. One of the sinks had been used to rinse something, traces of blood were still visible. He decided to wait outside for his boss and the forensic team, because this looked to be a complicated business. In the distance he noticed the blue flashing light of the police van which parked on the sidewalk a little later. The three cops that emerged immediately started to rope off the area and urged the crowds behind the barriers. The crowd was becoming a mob, cars had stopped and were double parked. The inspector stepped onto the beach and the cop met him halfway. They exchanged a few words while they walked toward the bar and entered. Disconcerted, the Inspector looked around and uttered hoarsely:

"I have never seen anything like it! My God! Who found him?"

"Ramon, about half an hour ago."

"Touched anything?"

"Nothing, he was so upset that he didn't even dare to enter."

"I can imagine. Matias Oliver, how is it possible, in heaven's name? One of the nicest people I know in all of Sitges."

"You can say that again."

"Family been notified?"

"No, there hasn't been time."

"Pardona me, stupid question."

"Did you reach the Captain?"

"He was at home, but is being fetched. This is no case for us. We'll need the specialists from Barcelona."

Without touching a thing, the Inspector looked at every detail, the heap of clothes in the corner, the leather cuffs around the wrists of the victim, the hooks so carefully placed in the beam and he saw the envelope on top of the beer crate. Undecided he returned to the door and said:

"We'd better wait for the Captain."

Captain Adrover was still in the shower when the phone rang. He took the receiver with wet hands and received a preliminary report on the crime. He dressed while the car was on the way to him.

Five minutes later he got into the car, dressed in a spotless uniform with wet, uncombed hair hidden under his cap. The driver filled him in on the way.

"Do we know the name of the victim?" he asked.

"Si, Señor Capitan, it is Señor Oliver."

"Oliver? Which Oliver?"

"Señor Oliver of the Hotel Cristina, un amigo suyo, no?"

"Si," he said and crushed, he sank back in the cushions of the back seat. Indeed, Matias was a friend of his. But that was impossible. Matias? Was it really Matias? But the driver had specified the Oliver of the Hotel Cristina. He needed a little time to absorb it.

The Inspector saw the car approach and walked toward the curb. The sidewalk was being kept clear of the curious by a number of cops, assisted by the temporary police barriers. As soon as the car stopped, the Captain opened the door and, without greetings, he asked:

"Is it true ...? It is Matias?"

The Inspector, well aware of the long friendship between the two men, answered timidly:

"Si, Señor Capitan, I am afraid so. It's terrible for you."

Tears filled his eyes, after he had gone in and looked at the soulless body of one of his best friends, oblivious to the fact that this was not the expected behavior of a police officer. The helpless body was that of Matias. They had gone to school together. Together they had quarreled, made up, chased women and, many times they had gotten drunk together. His wife had been a girl friend of Matias and they had been best man at each other's wedding. They both had four children each and they had grown old together. And now this. At a loss he turned to the Inspector, rubbed his eyes and, without realizing how ridiculous it sounded, he said:

"I played tennis with him only yesterday."

"I know, señor, and you won," said the Inspector sadly. He put his arm on the shoulder of the Captain, pushed him gently in the direction of the door and said:

"For the time being, let me do the dirty work, sir."

An hour and a half later the specialists from Barcelona were on the scene. Meanwhile Captain Adrover took upon himself the difficult task of informing the family. He was the only one able to do so. They were all people he loved, with whom he had lived a lifetime. Despondent and confused he got into the car, mumbled directions at the driver and sank back in the cushions. He felt old ... ancient.

The driver pressed the intercom at the gate, a voice answered and the gate opened. Slowly the car approached the villa. Magdalena was waiting for them on the front porch. Her usually so cheerful face looked tired. Last night she had waited dinner for Matias. By midnight, when he had still not arrived, she had called the contractor and the architect. She knew that he was going to have a meeting with them. She had been unable to sleep and had gone to the apartment complex as recently as four in the morning, but everything was closed. She had stopped by the police station to ask if an accident could have happened. She could see from Juan Adrover's attitude, as he stepped out of the car with ashen face and lowered eyes, that something dreadful had happened.

When the Captain returned to Bar Ramon it was easy to see that he was troubled. His orders, usually given in such a precise and commanding tone, where now uttered in a soft voice and had lost their power. The Promenade, decorated with the red and white ribbons of the police barricade, managed to look the opposite of cheerful. He observed the carnival of photographers, fingerprint experts, laboratory technicians, Inspectors and other police officers with sad eyes. About a dozen patrol cars and an ambulance were parked behind the improvised barricade. Inside a priest kneeled next to the body, already laid out on a gurney. The police officers restricted themselves to a modest and suppressed murmur. One of the Inspectors approached the Captain and showed him a plastic folder with a white envelope and a postcard inside.

"This was found in front of the body," he said subdued.

He read the text. It said:

"ESPANA-HUNGRIA: 1-1."

He recognized the text and said:

"There's a madman on the loose in Spain."

19. Sitges, Saturday Morning, March 18, 1989

"As far as can be determined, he was first hit on the head, that rendered him unconscious but did not kill him."

The medical examiner was speaking and the Captain asked:

"How long ago did he die?"

"I would say about twelve to fourteen hours ago. That is to say, between ten and midnight."

"What was the cause of death?"

"The killer made a mess of it. The victim has been tortured, as you can see, massive loss of blood, but that can be survived. Two cuts, one through the artery in the neck and the other through the windpipe. This was the coup de grace." He lifted a tip of the blanket that covered the corpse and pointed to a spot, just at the base the skull. "That was fatal," he said and covered the body again.

"What was used?"

"Difficult to say, you'll have to give me a little time for that. At first glance it could have been a hammer, a pickaxe maybe. Has anything been found that looked like the murder weapon?"

"Not a thing."

"That might mean that the tools used by the killer, had some value for him."

"What was used for the torture?"

"Iron pins, as you can see." He pointed to a number of evenly spaced, deep lacerations in the skin. "And a whip, but not a normal whip, or even a bull whip. Something much more deadly, a scourge maybe. In any case, a whip with metal at the tip, or tips. Perhaps lead."

"What sort of person are we looking for, in your opinion?"

"An insane person, a fanatic. Somebody with orders, a mission. It is obvious that we are not dealing with an ordinary murder. It is a punishment. Perhaps a vendetta."

"The victim would be the last man in the world I would imagine as being involved with shady dealings."

"Exactly. That's what makes it so mysterious. I promise, I'll sacrifice my Sunday to get you a report as soon as possible."

"I would be obliged, doctor."

The captain was slowly regaining his decisive manner as he turned to Inspector Ubillo and said:

"How much personnel is available?"

"If you mean our own people, about twenty two."

"Cancel all leaves, I want everybody at the station, with the exception of those needed for guard duty here."

"I'll give the orders, señor."

"I want you there as well, because I intend for you to lead the investigation."

"But of course, señor, I'll be there all right. There is little I can do here. They'll be busy for a while."

The Captain left Bar Ramon and went to his car. His driver opened the rear door, but he said:

"You stay here, I'll drive myself."

When he arrived at the station he called the desk sergeant and said:

"About three weeks ago we received a message regarding the murder of an airport employee in Madrid. Find it and bring it to me, please." He went to his office. He placed his cap on the peg, took off his coat and pulled the knot of his tie down. There was a knock on the door. The desk sergeant entered and placed the requested message on the desk. Adrover opened a drawer, stirred around in it, did not find what he was looking for and opened a second drawer. Then he felt in his jacket pocket, cursed and found it in front of him, on the desk. His half glasses. He put them on and read: "File number ... February 24, 1989 ... Victim: Jose Antonio Maria Rodriguez-Vidal, employee of National Airport at Madrid ... No police record ... found dead in Hotel Pinar in the Calle ... hung from the wrists ... tortured ... presumed perpetrator registered under name of Van Kleef ... Dutch passport ... Espana-Hungria: 1-1 ..."

Before reading further, he grabbed the phone and said:

"Call Madrid, urgent, Captain Cortez. I don't care where he is, but I want to talk to him within the hour. The sooner the better."

He read on, while he murmured to himself:

"Damn, that's him, it's the same!"

The telephone rang and Cortez was on the line.

"Buenos dias, Capitan. This is Cortez in Madrid. Returning your call."

"Buenos dias, Capitan, this is Capitan Adrover in Sitges. I don't believe we know each other personally, am I right?"

"You are right."

"Capitan, I was just reading a report from your office about a murder, last February 24. The victim was Jose Antonio Rodriguez."

"Yes, a terrible business."

"We have a second case, just like it."

"Why are you so sure?"

"Exactly identical. Strung up, tortured, even including the postcard with Espana-Hungria: 1-1."

"Who is the victim?"

"Matias Oliver, a hotel owner here in Sitges. A personal friend of mine."

The line remained silent, as if the news needed time to penetrate at the other end. Then Cortez said:

"I'll take the next flight to Barcelona. Please have a car waiting for me at the airport around two o'clock. Of course, your case is outside of my jurisdiction, but we can worry about the red tape later."

"I agree. I'll make sure you're met." Adrover broke the connection.

Despite it being Saturday, a number of files needed his attention. He read them carefully, made a notation here and there, or initialed, as needed. After an half hour there was a knock on the door and Inspector Ubillo entered. The Captain asked, without looking up:

"Everybody here?"

"Two missing, but we are locating them."

"Bien, then we'll start." He got up and both men left the room. When they entered the room where everybody was gathered, the conversations stopped immediately. He stepped on a low dais and spoke:

"Buenos dias, señores, señora," with a slight bow in the direction of the only female police officer.

"As you all know, we have an animal among us. I will not go into all the gory details about the butchery we found, you can all read that in the official report when the time comes. But I want to emphasize that this is not the first instance. A similar murder was committed in Madrid on February 24 of this year and we are certain that it is the same killer. We are looking for a foreigner, a Dutchmen who operated in Madrid under the name of Van Kleef."

He took a piece of chalk and wrote the name on the blackboard behind him. As he wrote each letter down, he compared them to his notes.

"He entered the country under an assumed name, we know that as well. The passport was stolen in Amsterdam. It is unlikely that he would have used the same name twice in a row, but one never knows. According to the desk clerk at the Hotel Monte Carlo, in Madrid, we are dealing with man of about fifty years. Well dressed, grey at the temples. Here is a composite picture provided by Madrid.

"First: Check all hotels, campgrounds, hostels, in short all lodgings, that were open during the last three months and check the registers. Not just in Sitges, but in all surrounding towns.

"Second: Find the car of Matias Oliver. You know the number, the blue Mercedes 230SE.

"Third: Don't forget restaurants, bars or other establishments. He had to eat and drink somewhere.

"Fourth: Check car rental agencies and don't forget cab drivers and bus drivers. Check what cars have been stolen lately, he had to have some sort of transport. The man is insane, but also extremely cunning and precise in all his actions. He hardly leaves any traces. Nowhere, not even in the hotel in Madrid, did he leave any finger prints. The clerk noted that he wore gloves, even when signing the register.

"Inspector Ubillo will be in charge of the investigations. He will assign specific tasks and assign the reports. Keep reports short and to the point. Don't waste time with a lot of paperwork. As much as possible, stay on the streets until we find this lunatic. Any questions?"

One constable raised his hand: "Señor Capitan, is it possible that we are dealing with a group of terrorists, perhaps the ETA?"*

"No, there is no reason to believe that. If that were the case, they would long since have claimed responsibility. But we do believe that this is some sort of revenge. Neither one of the victims had any connection with political organizations, past or present."

"Thank you, señor."

Another hand was raised.

"Señor Capitan, you speak of one man. Could there be more than one?"

"In my opinion, no! I just reread the report from Madrid. The man is very cunning, but he works alone."

"Señor, you mentioned revenge. You were talking about torture. The victims have been disfigured. Does that not indicate some sort of drug connection?"

"Of course, that's a good assumption. At first Madrid thought along the same lines. But no connection, of any kind, could be established. As far as the second victim is concerned: I have known him personally since grade school. Everybody understand? ... Fine ... I expect the first reports at 5 PM."

While Inspector Ubillo assigned the various tasks, Captain Adrover went to his office, adjusted his tie, put his jacket on and walked calmly in the direction of Bar Ramon. That was his way of working. Walking and thinking. Something he could not do in the office. There was always something to interrupt him. And he could do without the endless paper mill and all the red tape. He needed hands-on involvement. He was a man of action, not a paper shuffler.

He noticed the remote truck of Television Espanola when he reached the Bar Ramon. They were quick! He saw a man with a camera on the shoulder and a reporter, microphone in the hand, was talking into the lens. When they recognized him, they swarmed toward him like greedy bees after a fresh pot of honey. A number of print journalists followed in the wake of the camera. Before he realized what was happening, the camera was aimed at him and his vision was being obstructed by a microphone and a number of hand-held tape recorders. Every word was going to be recorded.

It would have been pointless not to respond to the questioning. However, he only told those parts of the case that he wanted them to know.

---

* A Spanish terrorist organization.

20. Sitges, Saturday Afternoon, March 18, 1989

Captain Cortez arrived in Sitges at three o'clock. Adrover was waiting for him in his office. They shook hands and after the usual polite phrases, Adrover said:

"I take it you missed lunch?"

"That's right, there was no time."

"Then let's have lunch together. There is not as much choice in Sitges as in Madrid, especially at this time of the year, but I think we can find something."

"Very good."

They rose, walked outside and stepped into the car which was still parked in front. Adrover told the driver:

"Restaurant El Picadore, please."

The owner found a secluded place for his two visitors where they could talk without curious ears and without unnecessary interruptions. The story about the death of Matias Oliver had done the rounds through the village, so when the Captain entered he was stared at with more than casual curiosity. After they had made their choice, said "salud" to each other with a glass of Marques de Risçal, Cortez came to order.

"I will first tell you how we found Rodriguez and how far we have come with our investigations. I left all the reports in your office and we can go over the details there, in private."

"Please begin, my dear colleague."

"Rodriguez was an employee of the Airport and had an unblemished record. No police record, good family, no hanky-panky, nothing to criticize. We went over his past with a fine tooth comb: bank accounts, family, relations with other women, you know, the usual routine and were unable to find anything out of order. I want to emphasize this because the manner of his death looks like some sort of punishment. A gangland revenge."

"The doctor used almost the same words this morning: vendetta!"

"Exactly! Of course, we considered it. But there is no doubt. The man is as innocent as the driven snow. We do know for sure that the perpetrator originates in Holland. He identified himself in the hotel where he registered as 'Van Kleef', a typical Dutch name, according to a good friend, a commissaris in Amsterdam. All forensic research, finger prints, post-mortem, you name it, all came up negative as far as the perpetrator is concerned. The man has disappeared without a trace. The investigations in Holland are also at a dead-end. I know that they spared no efforts, but all without results. It is obvious that the man—if it is a man, although that's almost certain—is extremely intelligent and cunning. He stayed at the Hotel Monte Carlo, but just for a single night. He must have been in Madrid for at least four or five days, but he did not rent a car, at least not under the name of Van Kleef. As a matter of fact, there is not a single Dutchman registered with any of the car agencies during that period. The receptionist of the hotel gave a very vague description. The hotel has more than 450 rooms and is virtually always booked. Add to this the number of conventions being held in the hotel and it is easy to imagine that a lone person can easily be overlooked in the crowds. The owner of the flophouse, where the body was found, is an untrustworthy character with a record and we have been keeping an eye on him for some time. He is almost never there and when he is, he's usually asleep, or recovering from a binge. The perpetrator rented a room for three days and paid cash in advance. There were few guests, which you would find understandable, if you had seen the dump. All guests have a key to the front door, because there is no doorman. But we may assume that he never slept there, at least, according to the owner. I don't know how far we can believe him, but it makes little difference to the case. That drunk would not be able to recognize the suspect if he had been living there for the last two years."

The owner of the restaurant interrupted Cortez by placing the appetizers on the table. Two large portions of snails in a sauce of mayonnaise and garlic. While they extracted the first snails with care, Cortez continued.

"We are completely at a loss and have made no progress. Bakkenist, that's the commissaris in Amsterdam, checked the address the perpetrator gave when he paid in advance, but found that the address does not even exist. The passport which he used in the better hotel, turned out to be stolen. It disappeared in Amsterdam, just a few days before the killing. The real Van Kleef is a man in his fifties, so we can assume that our killer is roughly the same age. The bastard is so shrewd that he plans exactly what passport to steal, before he leaves on his killing expeditions. He most certainly picked somebody who more or less looks like himself. Again, this is a rough outline, details can be discussed later."

He removed another snail from its shell, dipped it in the sauce and ate it with relish.

"Espana-Hungria: 1-1, what is known about that?" asked Adrover.

"It was a soccer match played on March 27, 1977 in the Rico Perez Stadium in Alicante," answered the other.

"And?"

"Nothing unusual. Just a game. No fights, no mobs, no vandals, no pay-offs, no scandals of any kind. Just a soccer match, nothing else to say."

Captain Adrover looked thoughtfully into the distance and murmured:

"March seventy seven, that's twelve damn years ago. What does it mean?"

"It's been driving me crazy, but I have no idea. The killer obviously is trying to tell us something, but what?"

Both reflected on their own thoughts when Cortez broke the silence:

"And now the next case. Please tell me, Captain."

"The victim was found at eight o'clock this morning by the owner of the Bar Ramon. As I told you, it concerns one of the best friends I ever had."

There was a moment's silence and the emotion was tangible.

"I am so sorry for you. It must be difficult."

"You are right. But nevertheless we carry on. Matias was suspended from a beam wherein two large hooks were mounted by the killer. Wide leather cuffs were around his wrists and chains connected the cuffs to the hooks in the overhead beam. The body was disfigured in a most awful manner. Pins, whips, knives and other instruments had been used. The medical examiner was able to ascertain a few preliminary facts. The neck artery and the windpipe were severed. The fatal blow was administered to the base of the skull. It is not certain what instrument was used. It is of interest that not a single instrument, or tool was found. It is certain that the sink on the premises was used for cleaning purposes. Perhaps for his tools. That could mean that the instruments have some sort of value for the owner. Matias probably expired between ten and midnight last night. That's all we know at this time."

"All the known details are identical to what we found in Madrid. Everything had been cleaned and, except for the corpse, left in the state in which it was found."

The restaurant owner approached the table again and said discreetly:

"Pardone me, Señor Adrover, telephone for you."

The captain put his napkin down and followed the man. He returned a few minutes later.

"They found Oliver's car. It was parked on a small square, with the keys in the ignition."

"Any clues?"

"Nothing yet. He did not stay in a local hotel. There are just a few hotels open at this time of the year and they were easily checked. He also did not rent a car here."

"That bastard doesn't rent cars. He works with a stolen passport. If he wants to rent a car, he has to show a Driver's License and he cannot afford that. He uses only cabs, buses, public transportation."

"There are just seven cabs operating in Sitges at the moment. We checked, but no results."

"We are dealing with a madman, Captain!"

"Yes, but a very intelligent madman."

"Let's hope we get some clues from the current investigation."

"I wonder why the idiot selects Spain for his executions. Why doesn't he do that in Holland?"

"There is something we don't know, something we're missing."

21. Barcelona, Saturday Afternoon, March 18, 1989

While Adrover and Cortez were having lunch in Sitges, Meyer approached the concierge of the Trans Mediterranean Shipping Company to pick up the small suitcase he had stored there. From the harbor he proceeded, passing the statue of Columbus, to the Ramblas. The shops along the way were already closed and shuttered. In the center of the road thousands of people strolled past the flower sellers, street sellers and other hawkers and peddlers. After looking around for a bit, he turned a corner to find himself in the labyrinth of narrow streets and alleys which is almost a hallmark of Barcelona. He spotted a small bed-and-breakfast in one of the streets and went inside. A plump lady sat behind a counter decorated with a vase full of plastic roses. Behind and above her was an enormous picture of Jesus Crucified, enhanced with a halo constructed from flashing Christmas lights.

"Bueneas tardes," was the friendly greeting which indicated that she had finished her noon meal.

He spoke little Spanish, but enough to indicate his wishes for a room. The lady placed a registration card in front of him, but before filling it out, he asked:

"Pasaporte?"

The lady waved nonchalantly, which is what he had hoped for. If she had insisted on a passport, he would have told her that it had been stolen, that he had just come from the police and that it had even caused him to miss his plane. Instinctively he knew that he could not afford to register, not even under the name Kranedonk. Once arrived in the room he first took a long shower and then he put on the clean clothes from the small suitcase. He upended the Adidas bag on the bed. The shiny whip with the handwoven handle and the lead re-enforced monkey's fist at the end rolled onto the bed. Also the handcuffs, two old-fashioned razors, a number of black leather straps studded with sharp iron pins and a number of marlin spikes with extremely sharp points. From the suitcase he produced a bottle of neat's foot oil and a number of soft cloths and lovingly he rubbed the oil into the leather accoutrements. With a yellow flannel cloth he rubbed it out until the items shined like new. He inspected each item minutely and when he detected the smallest blemish, he took a small toothbrush and brushed until it was clean. Satisfied, he displayed all the items on the table in front of the window. Fondly he looked at the display which showed up as a sort of sadistic pop-art against the white formica of the table. Next he took out a rectangular black flannel cloth with pouches at regular intervals. All his stuff fitted snugly in their own places in the pouches. Only the whip did not fit. It annoyed him a little. When he originally made the carry-all for his instruments, he still had his previous whip. The nice one from England. This one had a slightly longer handle and did not fit. It irritated him. Four pouches remained empty. They had been used for the swing hooks, the chains and cuffs that had remained with the corpse. He rolled the cloth up tightly, secured it with a short black leather strap and placed it in the suitcase. Dressed, he laid down on the bed and thought about what he had done. A satisfied smile lit up his face as he fell asleep.

It was eight o'clock when he woke. Because meals had been a hit-and-miss proposition for the last few days, he decided to spoil himself this time. He walked outside and drifted through the neighborhood until he saw a restaurant to his liking. Expansively he ordered a large meal and ate at leisure. He deserved it, he felt. He had just completed the second part of his self-imposed task and nobody around him had any inkling. He had to complete his task away from the limelight of publicity. Around ten o'clock he asked condescendingly for the check, almost arrogant. He had never before dared to be this self-assured. But now, for the first time he felt superior. A new sensation. He left the restaurant and walked along the Ramblas toward the harbor. The crowds around him were relegated to a hardly noticed background. He felt elated and relaxed and able to tackle the world. On the left, the fronts of the buildings formed a semi-circular widening of the main thorough-fare. It gave the illusion of a square. The square was filled with door-to door bars, dives and sex theaters. Whores of all sizes, ages and colors patrolled the sidewalks. He stood still and saw a prostitute dressed in high leather boots, a short leather skirt and a minuscule leather halter. He crossed the road and walked over to her. She smiled at him, glad of the business, and dropped one eyelid in a knowing wink.

"You want nice fuck?" she asked with a Spanish accent, grabbing him by the arm.

"How much?" he asked.

After they settled on the price she took him to a small hotel. An unwashed and unshaven man behind the counter silently took his money, after which he followed the whore, up the stairs to the next floor. The room was furnished with an old double bed. She took off her skirt and halter. She was now dressed in a G-string and a half-bra that presented her breasts as if on a tray, the dark-brown nipples peeked over the top. She came closer, opened his zipper and took his flaccid penis in her hand. He took her wrist, twisted her arm behind her. She groaned. With his other hand he took a handkerchief out of his pocket and stuffed it in her mouth. A quick blow to the left temple and she collapsed, unconscious. He put her on the floor, tore the sheet from the bed and quickly ripped it into four strips. He put her on the bed and tied her wrists and ankles to the corners of the bed. He undressed and a moment later he stood naked under the bare bulb in the ceiling. He took a towel, held it under the tap and hit her in the face with it. Slowly she came to, realized the situation in which she found herself and became icy calm. In her profession she had encountered sexually frustrated clients before. She knew there was just one way to survive: she would cooperate. She moved her pelvis sensually, as if overcome by desire. He tore the G-string away and saw the shaved genitals. Her Mound of Venus looked innocent and soft as that of a baby. How did that whore dare! A stinking Spanish whore who hid the darling spot of a nine-year old girl in her pants and who degraded it to no more than a hole! Who for payment would imitate a rape for her clients. With his belt he administered the first blows. She groaned with pain and that's what he wanted. The belt descended on her belly and on her thighs, where the welts became obvious and visible. He felt his erection, took his penis in the hand and masturbated while he hit her. It was an added sensation for him to know she was a whore. Whores had to be punished.

Frau Vollmer was also a whore to him. But *this* whore was here in front of him, powerless, abandoned to his will. The frequency of the blows increased with the movement of his masturbation. Finally he was ready to ejaculate. He sat down next to her head and spurted the seed over her face.

He washed himself at the sink, dressed and left the room.

A little later he was back in his pension and thought about Monique. What a noble creature she was. Tonight reinforced that feeling. When he compared her to the mobs in the street and that whore! Just good enough to receive his sperm all over her face. People were filthy, untrustworthy and for sale. He loved Monique. He had proved that tonight. He had not laid a finger on that whore.

22. Sitges, Sunday Morning, March 19, 1989

At eight o'clock Juan closed the trunk and sat down behind the wheel. His wife was next to him on the front seat and the three children frolicked on the back seat. The trunk contained a plastic bag with four pounds of chuletas de cordero (lamb chops), a head of a lettuce, tomatoes, bread, a bag of charcoal and some fire starters. Mama had taken care of the cleaning stuff and Juan had borrowed a portable sandblaster from a friend. They left Barcelona and reached the main road to the south. During the drive they discussed the murder which had apparently happened in the village where they were wont to spent their summers. Last night they had followed a detailed report on the television and they had recognized a lot of places. About an hour later they entered Sitges via the road with the disco's, nightclubs and campings. The gate to Camping Vera Cruz was open and they drove inside. The man, who had for years been the regular guard of the place, stood near the entrance and greeted them like long lost friends. During the chilly and mostly rainy winters which are so typical for the north of Spain, the camping too, had been closed for the season. Now that Easter was just around the corner, this was the first Sunday that he was back on regular duty. Juan drove in the direction of his camper and quickly saw, from a distance, that not everything was as it should be. The door was open and that was impossible. He was certain he locked it the last time he visited. He stopped the car and the family looked with surprise at the camper. They not only noticed the open door, but also that the big window on the side had been smashed. Juan cursed softly and went inside. He looked around and quickly ascertained that nothing had been stolen. A bundle of unrecognized clothes was thrown in a corner. He picked them up and angrily tossed them through the window. The rest of the family, still outside, looked at the pieces of clothing and when the daughter looked closely at the pair of jeans in her hand she noticed with consternation the large bloodstains on the garment. Prompted by that discovery, Juan took a closer look at the remaining clothes and found bloodstains on the coveralls as well. He scratched his nail over one of the spots an noticed the redness under his fingernail. Coagulated blood and relatively fresh. Frightened, he dropped the garment and said:

"Eso es sangre, this is blood!"

Juan got into his car and left his family alone with the ghastly find. While driving away he called from the window:

"Leave everything alone, don't touch anything!"

A superfluous warning for the family stared at the camper with horror and fear, as if it were possessed by a ghost. Ten minutes after calling the police, two patrol cars, sirens blaring, drove onto the terrain. Inspector Ubillo came out of the first car and looked at the clothing. Undoubtedly it was blood. He took a quick look inside the camper and noticed vague traces of blood in the wash basin. An official limousine drove up a few minutes later. Captain Adrover stepped out, followed by Captain Cortez. After a brief conversation with the Inspector and a longer inspection of the interior of the camper, Cortez said:

"I'll bet you anything that we have found the blood of the victim."

"Then we now know where the killer spent the night."

Additional police was called in and the police barricades went up. Every square foot of the terrain was searched and bloodhounds led the men to the hole in the fence, which the perpetrator had used to gain access. The prints near the fence matched the soles of the shoes found in the camper. The clothing was scrutinized further and it was remarked that they were all apparently new. Perhaps just worn once. Tags and labels indicated that all had been bought in Spain. Adrover, lost in thought, began to realize what that meant. Tomorrow they would try to locate the store that had sold the clothing. The manufacturers would be able to provide a list of stores and hundreds of police would be needed to visit every one of them. The jeans and the shoes would generate the longest list, but the coveralls might be easier to track down. After all, coveralls were generally sold in stores specializing in work clothes and that list had to be shorter. Nevertheless a long and painstaking job. He wondered where he could find all the necessary personnel. The first place to ask for assistance would be in Barcelona. Inspector Ubillo was a good man, he had a lot of experience in large cities and would remain in charge. Not for the first time, he wondered if he was suited for his profession. It had all become so technical. Layers of red tape and legions of specialists in disciplines he did not understand any more. Hardly any regular street cops left to do the real legwork that was going to be so necessary.

Added to this was his emotional involvement in the case. Although he had apparently overcome that and, at least outward and toward his colleagues, was able to behave as if this was just another case, he knew that his strength and flexibility were being diminished. The man who had been almost a constant companion for the last fifty years, with whom he had walked through the orchards of their youth, dreaming and planning for the future, had become past history. He was dead.

*23. *Barcelona, Sunday Afternoon, March 19, 1989*

While the investigations in Sitges continued at a feverish pace, Meyer walked past passport control at the airport in Barcelona as if he did not have a worry in the world. The customs clerk hardly glanced at the black booklet, something that had become a habit in a Spain which was preparing to join the European Community in 1992. Meyer reflected that it might be ridiculous to have a second passport with a different name. Obtaining the extra passport did carry a certain element of risk, after all. He most certainly would not be able to use the Kranedonk passport much longer, because in less that two, or maybe three weeks, the number would be known at all border posts as belonging to a stolen passport. Perhaps via Interpol, or some other organization. He was not altogether too clear about such things. But as long as he made sure to transfer in another country on his way to Spain, they would have a hard time finding him. Almost impossible, as a matter of fact. Lodging remained the main obstacle. Good hotels asked for passports and had alert and professional front-desk staffs. He had to find another way to take care of lodging. Maybe a tent? Although he abhorred the idea of having to travel with a rucksack, it might be the best solution. He would have to buy a lot of those revolting sports clothes and a pair of the preposterous sport shoes, mainly worn by middle aged men, jogging through the suburbs. He refused to think about it! He was just a little too chic for something like that. He could afford to buy the best clothes in the best stores and that's what he was going to do. He hated cheap stuff. That was contrary to his image: he was not part of the common herd. Especially not now, after all his accomplishments.

A metallic voice sounded through the departure hall and announced, in incomprehensible English and too fast Spanish, the imminent departure of the Lufthansa flight to Frankfurt. One hundred and fifty people rose en-bloc in order to press themselves through the single exit from the gate area.

People are really disgusting, he thought. They're no more than rats. And this is just the departure of an airplane, where everybody has an assigned seat. What happens in an emergency? If they had to push and shove for their life? Carnival in Rio, a soccer stadium in Belgium, the Subway in New York, cattle cars to the concentration camps. If you were unlucky enough to stumble, you'd be trampled to death. He knew, he had been there. Just like rats. Rats also feed on each other.

He remained quietly in his seat until everybody was crammed in the bus. The people at the podium were counting tickets and he waited for them to finish. Then he rose, slowly walked over to the gate attendant and disdainfully handed her his Boarding Pass. With a look full of contempt he looked at the crowded bus, crossed the few steps from the gate to the bus, and entered.

When the bus stopped in front of the plane he alighted first and left the mob behind. That felt good. The stewardess handed him a Spanish newspaper and he looked with interest at a photograph of the Bar Ramon in Sitges. A screaming headline, across the full width of the page, announced: SEGUNDO ATENTADO HORRIBLE EN SITGES! He could not read the text completely, but he saw the name Matias Jesus Oliver-Amador. He was seated next to an English speaking Spaniard and he asked for a translation. The man provided a synopsis of the article and tried so hard to do a good job that he did not notice the fleeting smile that played over Meyer's face from time to time. When he reached the last paragraph, he translated:

"There is a suspicion that the killer is Dutch."

A reckless feeling overcame him and in a casual tone of voice he said:

"I'm from Holland. I live in Polderkerk."

*24. *Barcelona, Monday Morning, March 20, 1989*

At eight o'clock the official limousine stopped in front of Captain Adrover's house to take both him and Cortez to Barcelona. Despite his protests about too much trouble and unwanted interference in family life, Cortez had been persuaded to stay at Adrover's house over the week-end. Of course, he had been much more comfortable than in a hotel. Originally he had planned to depart for Madrid, from Barcelona, the previous Sunday afternoon, but the discoveries at the camping grounds had decided him to stay an extra night. Today his plane would leave at 2PM. Therefore he and Adrover had agreed to use the morning for a visit to the pathologist and the more fully equipped forensic departments in Barcelona. Sitges simply did not have the various technical facilities available. Although some reports had already been forwarded and more would be delivered as the case progressed, both men knew that it could be invaluable to speak face-to-face with the various specialists.

Shortly after nine they were seated at a spotless table in the laboratory, opposite a man in a white coat. Concerned, he looked at his two visitors over the gold-rimmed frame of his glasses.

"I am afraid," he began, "that I have little to report at this time. We have not completed all our investigations. It was Sunday, after all, and not all personnel can be easily located on short notice. In any case, as far as I can tell, we don't foresee any spectacular discoveries."

"How do you know?" asked Adrover.

"Did you read the report?"

SLEUTH OF BAKER STREET
Now TWICE as good!
1600 Bayview Ave. (416-483-3111)
604 Markham St. (416-537-9099)
1-800-361-2701; Fax 416-483-3141
MYSTERIES, THRILLERS & SPIES.
Like nobody else!

Wed Jun29-94 12:08pm #0112 S

Title/ISBN	Qty	Price	Disc	Total	Tax
TENERIFE					
1881164519	1	10.99		10.99	1
		Subtotal		10.99	
		GST (Tx1)		0.77	
Items	1	Total		11.76	
		Cash		11.76	

THANK YOU.
No cash refunds, sorry. Exchange
only, AND only with the receipt.

*9PROMO sales final.

GST# R 106 322 092

"Just before coming to see you, briefly."

"Well, to begin, the blood is simple. It belonged to the victim. The blood group and RH factors match. Finger prints have not been found. The Mercedes and the camper were both clean. The killer must have been born with gloves. In our opinion the perpetrator changed clothes in the camper. He did not sleep there. We concluded that from the mud on the shoes. The mud matches the consistency as of Saturday night, after the rain. The prints near the hole in the fence confirmed that the facility had only been used once. We did find remnants of gravel that corresponds with the gravel found in the parking lot of the apartment complex. We also found earth, garden dirt. We discovered that the killer must have waited for his victim between the cypresses on the right side of the parking lot and then sneaked up on him to administer the first blow. We also found remnants of the same gravel on the clothes of the victim and in the threads of the Mercedes. The victim was almost certainly attacked in the parking lot and transported to the beach bar in the Mercedes. The car was then abandoned while the killer returned to his victim. No leads have been found in the beach bar. The killer was extremely careful. The chains, the cuffs, the hooks in the beam, none are traceable as far as we have been able to determine. The chains and hooks can be bought in any hardware store, all over Europe. The leather work has obviously been done by an amateur. As you observed, all clothes found in the camper were new. Although we will not neglect it, it is a wasted effort to look for dust in the seams, or pockets. The conclusion so far, gentlemen: you are dealing with a shrewd and intelligent criminal who, for the time being, is always one step ahead."

"What about the postcard left with the corpse?"

"Little. A common postcard and a common envelope, not sealed, no traces of saliva. The lettering has been applied with a modern Olivetti typewriter. There is a slight deviation in the right bottom leg of the "H" of "Hungria." He picked up an enlargement of the typewriter letter H and pointed to the slight irregularity with a pencil.

"I am afraid that is all for now ..."

Captain Adrover stood up, Cortez followed his example, they shook hands with the laboratory technician and said good bye. Silently they walked through the long, impersonal corridors of the building, so typical of the architecture of Franco's time. They took the elevator down to the morgue to visit the pathologist. They felt the clammy coolness of the area and Cortez remarked, looking with loathing at the surroundings:

"Why in the world would anybody want to be a pathologist?"

"Perhaps he feels the same way about our profession."

The doctor received them with a hearty gesture and preceded them to his office. The room looked like such an office would be depicted in a horror film. Bare, stark, old and unkempt. The few pieces of furniture were decrepit in the extreme and a chaos of files, folders, books and papers was stacked against all four walls. The doctor, noticing their bemused stares, said:

"Yes, well, administration isn't my strong point, as you can see. But I do know where everything is. Upstairs they're all involved with computerizing everything but, thank God, they haven't found the basement yet. That's the advantage of working in the morgue."

He laughed and took the top folder of a stack, in no way discernable from any other, opened it and commented:

"Terrible case. Just once before encountered. In Burgos, 1956, a Guarda Civil felt compelled to interrogate a suspected communist. Oh, well, happily that is past history. What can I say. A lot of blood, but you already knew that." Absent mindedly he leafed through the papers, then continued: "I won't bore you with all the medical terms. To begin: death occurred around ten thirty as the direct result of a blow to the base of the skull, about where the spinal cord meets the skull. It must have been applied with considerable force and the perpetrator knew exactly what he was doing."

"You mean, he has done this more often?"

"Not necessarily, he could have been lucky. But he *knew* that death would be instantaneous as the result of such a blow. And that is what he achieved. If he had been experimenting, we would have noticed it. There would have been more damage in that spot. The severing of the artery and the windpipe happened before the victim died. Indications are, forgive me Captain but it must be said, that the victim was fully conscious when that happened. As preliminary investigations concluded, it has been confirmed that the torture instruments consisted of a whip with a weighted handle and metal tip, tapered iron pins ranging in size from pencil-thin to perhaps 3 inches in diameter and some sort of brass knuckles. The abrasion to the head, which rendered the victim unconscious, was administered approximately 45 minutes before the fatal blow to the head. The victim was in good physical condition. We investigated the possibility of a heart attack during the torture, but that has been ruled out."

"Can you add anything regarding the murder weapon?"

"A blow with a hammer, or pick axe, is easily recognizable. The angle under which the blow is administered can be accurately measured from the nature of the wound. In this case, however, we are dealing with a round object. Perhaps I can describe it best as a sort of sling, or a ball attached to a rope, or chain. That's the limit of my speculation. In any case it is not an everyday object. We did find something in the wound which just increases the mystery. We detected slight traces of a kind of oil. Roughly the same chemical consistency as shoe polish, but colorless. That could mean that we are looking for a leather object. And that's what makes it so strange. A leather object is not designed to break the skull. The skull is the hardest bone in the body. One needs something a lot harder and heavier to get the desired result."

"You mean a leather preserving oil?"

"That is possible."

Cortez rose, shook hand with the astonished doctor and said: "Thank you very much for this last remark, doctor. I am very grateful." Then, turning to Adrover he said: "Come on, we have to make a phone call. I've got an idea."

*25. *Amsterdam, Tuesday Morning, March 21, 1989*

Detective Arie De Berg had barely sat down behind his desk in the Headquarters Building of the Amsterdam Municipal Police, when a colleague warned him:

"You're supposed to report to the boss at once, Arie, he seems in a hurry."

He stood up immediately and walked the few steps down the corridor to the office of Commissaris Bakkenist. He knocked and after the impatient "yes, yes, come on in," opened the door.

"Oh, glad to see you, Arie, I have a fax from our friend in Madrid."

He picked up the paper on his desk and handed it to De Berg, who read it carefully. After a few minutes he dropped the hand with the fax in his lap and said, with barely controlled excitement:

"It's him, sir. It's the same guy."

"I had come to the same conclusion."

"That son-of-a-bitch is good, though, the Spanish have almost nothing to go on."

"Yes, but it looks like we have to get involved again, don't you think?"

"Absolutely, but as you know, sir, we checked everything that could be checked, but found nothing, niente, nada, nix."

"Yes, but think, what did you tell me about the robbery of Van Kleef, the one who lost his passport?"

"I'll be damned if I can remember, sir."

"Oil! Arie, oil used for leather!"

"Sorry, yes, you're right, sir, when I called the quack, he told me ..."

"That traces of some sort of oil, used to preserve leather, had been found," completed Bakkenist.

De Berg looked again at the Madrid report an found the paragraph that mentioned "leather-oil". Followed by a chemical formula.

"I'll check this out, at once," he stood up and on the way to the door added a belated "sir." Just before closing the door he grinned at his boss and said: "Don't call us, we'll call you," and disappeared.

He went back to his desk and called Records for all the information concerning the robbery of Van Kleef. Within five minutes the print-out was on his desk and he read: "... blow with ball-shaped weapon ... faint traces of high grade oil, identified as similar to neat's foot oil ..."

But the chemical formula was missing. Again he grabbed the telephone and called the doctor who had initially treated the wound. He was told that the doctor was out.

"It's ever so," he murmured, oblivious that the same thing was said about the police, "they're never there when you need them."

"What did you say, sir?" asked the friendly girl at the other end of the line.

"Ach, nothing, I didn't mean it, miss, but I do need him rather urgently for a case in progress."

"I can try to reach him, he's in a meeting."

Why the hell didn't you say that right-a-way, he thought angrily, but said, in a syrupy voice: "If that's not too much trouble, miss, I would be very obliged." He gave the number of his direct line.

Meeting! He should have known. Everybody was always in a meeting these days. There was so much bullshit generated at these meetings, it was a wonder the dikes didn't break. A meeting, or a training course. Another thing he hated was a "special" training course. And if there was no meeting, no "course", they would take a "compensation" day. A "compensation" day! He grinned, somewhat ruefully, at himself. If he ever took all the "compensation" days he was entitled to, he could go with early retirement.

The telephone rang and the doctor was on the line.

"I'm sorry, Mr. De Berg, but I just learned that you wanted to speak to me urgently. I was in a meeting, you see."

"They're also necessary, doctor," he lied.

"How can I help you, Mr. De Berg?"

"Doctor, a few weeks ago we discussed a case regarding a certain Van Kleef."

"Van Kleef ... Van Kleef ... I don't remember."

"Somebody had bashed him on the head."

One of this doctor's peculiarities was that he could never remember names, just injuries.

"Ah, yes, now I remember, I know exactly what you are talking about, Mr. De Berg." He dropped a string of medical terms that were so much Greek to De Berg. He interrupted:

"In your report you mentioned a type of oil, oil used for leather."

"Yes, yes, I remember that very well. Rather strange, that. A sort of shoe polish in a wound. Don't see that every day."

"Doctor, if I give you a chemical formula, or analysis, or whatever you call that, from another doctor, can you then tell me if it's the same stuff?"

"But, of course, my dear man."

"But we're rather in a hurry, doctor."

"Well, come right over."

"All right, but what about your meeting?"

"They'll never even miss me. It's always the same thing, anyway."

"I have to make a few more calls, doctor, and then I'll be right there."

"I'll wait for you, Mr. De ... eh ...Berg."

Arie disconnected and rang another number at once.

"Station Warmoes Street, desk sergeant speaking."

"De Berg, Headquarters, detective Gelder, please."

Click.

"Gelder speaking."

"Hey, Jan, it's Arie."

"Well, well, a call from the upper reaches. Stuck again, eh, boyo?"

"Listen Jan, no kidding, I'm in a hurry."

"You're always in a hurry. Well, tell me."

"Do you remember a Van Kleef who was robbed of his passport?"

"Yes, I wasn't on that case, but I know what you mean, because a few weeks later almost the same thing happened."

"What!? How?"

"Well, a robbery, almost the same spot. Same area, anyway. A man arrived from Paris by train, bashed on the head. Except he didn't realize at first that he had lost his passport."

"How's that?"

"Well, they had stolen his briefcase and that was recovered the same night."

"Really? How?"

"Two of our boys happened to patrol the pedestrian tunnel under the Central Station when they spotted two miscreants with a brand new briefcase. One of them was an old acquaintance, so our men checked it out and it turned out the briefcase had been stolen. A little later the owner, a lawyer from the provinces, Arnhem I think, came in to report a robbery and it turned out to be his briefcase. He checked it, but found nothing missing. Frankly, he seemed mostly concerned about some papers. In any case, he called a few days later to tell us that, after all, his passport was missing. It had been in the briefcase. I can get the report for you, if you want."

"Not necessary, I can find it, if I need it."

"We checked on the culprits, but they professed to know nothing about a passport, but you know how it is, probably sold right-a-way. For drugs, or something."

"Nothing further?"

"No, why?"

"Well, anything peculiar? Different? Out of line?"

"No, oh yeah, now that you mention it, one of those guys had a whip."

"A whip? What kind of whip?"

"Well, a formidable thing, you know, bigger than a riding whip. Martinet, somebody called it."

"Leather?"

"Yes, beautiful workmanship. Seemed new."

"Could it have been polished?"

"Of course that's possible."

"Solid handle?"

"Yes, certainly, hand-plaited, with a sort of reinforced monkey's fist at the end. You know, as they use on ships, for decoration. A sort of knob made of metal, or wood, all covered in plaited leather. Very intricate."

"Where is that whip?"

"Where else? In the depot, of course. Evidence!"

"Would you please, as fast as possible, get that thing from the depot and then meet me, with the whip, at the lab. I'll be there in about ten minutes."

He broke the connection without waiting for an answer. He ran outside, hailed a passing patrol car and gave the address. Sirens blaring, he arrived at the lab in less than ten minutes. The doctor had just arrived.

"I found my original notes," said the doctor.

He compared the illegible scribbles with the notations on the Madrid fax, took off his glasses, cleaned them elaborately with the slip of his laboratory coat and said:

"No doubt about it, Mr. De Berg, it is the same substance. As I said: a sort of oil, transparent, colorless. Can be used for polishing shoes, or waterproofing boots."

"The shape of the wound, any additional observations?"

"Not much, no. Most of it was in my report. A round object, a lot different than, for instance, a blow with a baseball bat."

"What would have been the estimated size of the object?"

"Maybe one and a half to two inches in diameter."

"A colleague of mine, from the Warmoes Street, is bringing an object for you to look at. He'll be here any minute. Will you wait?"

"But of course, perhaps a cup of coffee while we wait?"

"Yes, thank you, doctor."

They talked while sipping their coffee and then Gelder entered with the whip, wrapped in a plastic bag. The identifying label was still attached. The three of them closely examined the probable murder weapon and hefted it in turn. De Berg felt the ball at the end of the handle and remarked:

"There's some sort of metal inside, it doesn't give and just feel the weight."

"I think it's lead," said Gelder and then, turning to the doctor, asked: "Doctor, could this have been the object that was used to bash Van Kleef on the head?"

"That could be entirely possible. It's leather and it's certainly dangerous enough. Especially the way the perpetrator handled it." He took the whip, reversed it and made swinging gestures with it.

"This thing is more dangerous than a cosh, or a nightstick."

"Could the leather have been treated with the same oil?"

"We can examine that."

"How long will that take?"

"If you can spare fifteen minutes, you can wait for it. It's not that difficult."

De Berg and Gelder spent the next fifteen minutes in front of the coffee machine in the corridor and talked while drinking a plastic tasting cup of coffee. The doctor came out of the lab, spotted them and said:

"Gentlemen, there's no doubt. It's the same oil."

After a hasty greeting, a thank you and a "please send the report", the two detectives left the building.

When De Berg heard the "come on in" from Bakkenist, he entered and shouted:

"We've got him!"

In a more sedate tone he made his report.

"Where are the two suspects?"

"Gelder of Warmoes Station is already picking them up."

*26. *Amsterdam, Tuesday Afternoon, March 21, 1989*

Gelder came in with the two suspects at quarter past one. They were Abdul Mohammed Wahab, born in Amsterdam on November 23, 1967 and Jan Ockhuyzen, born in Rotterdam on August 12, 1962. They were led to a bare room, somewhere in the sprawling Headquarters building. A plain table and some chairs stood under a harsh light. The door seemed more substantial than usual. A tape recorder was placed on the table and the suspects were told to sit down. Detectives De Berg and Freriks sat down opposite them and placed a file on the table, while Gelder walked up and down behind the suspects.

"Well, gentlemen, we would like to go a little further into the incident of last Monday night, the thirteenth."

"We told you everything we know," hissed Abdul.

"Come on, listen now, we want to be friends."

"Oh yes, is that why we're here?"

"We just want to talk about it, nothing else. You've been treated fairly, isn't that so? We didn't cuff you, or beat you, or anything, did we? We didn't even use a paddy wagon, now, isn't that so? Just an unmarked car, right? We just want to be friendly. Come on, you can at least try."

"Friendly, he says," Ockhuyzen looked resentfully at Gelder.

"We just want to know a little more about that business behind the Station. Tell us again, what happened exactly."

Both men started to talk at the same time and De Berg raised a hand in protest.

"One at a time, please," he said. "You start, Ockhuyzen."

"All right, you know, nothing special. We seen the car behind the Central Station with this geyser in it, you know. Abdul here, he opens the door, on the left, you know, and he hits him, like that, you know. Real quick. I opens the other door, you know, and there's that briefcase and the whip, you know, and I grabs it and that's all, man."

"And then you were arrested at once, in the pedestrian tunnel?"

"Yeah, thasso, mebbe five minutes later, you know. Thassall. You gots to believe me, mister. Look, I knows we ain't no good guys, you know, but tha' wassall. I dunno whadda ye want, but whaddever it is, ain't no part of us, you know."

"Where were you on the 22nd of February and during the night from seventeen to eighteen March, That's last Friday and Saturday?"

"I'd have to think of February some, you know, but last week I was here, in Amsterdam, no sweat, man."

"And you?" De Berg pointed at Abdul.

"When in February, did you say?"

"Twenty second."

"Ah, yes, the twenty first, that was the birthday of my little sister, charming child, I was home, of course. But I am sorry, I cannot tell you how I spent the next day."

"And last week?"

"We were out, together, Jan and I."

"Where did you go?"

"Well, first we visited Jan's girl-friend, for the purpose of asking her to accompany us. But she was otherwise engaged and therefore we proceeded together, just the two of us."

"Anybody see you?"

"But of course, half of Amsterdam."

"Tell me again about the night you stole the briefcase and the whip. Did you see the man?"

"Yes, very briefly. I hit him very precisely, not too hard, such is not my wont, but it was dark so I am at a loss as to his exact features."

"You're sure it was a white car.?"

"Yes," they answered in unison.

"What color was the interior?"

"Did you see it?" one asked the other.

"I really cannot help you, it was most certainly not leather, fabric, not plastic."

"Last time you said that it was a Citroen BX, are you sure?"

"Absolutely, I am certain, my brother-in-law has the identical vehicle."

"You too?"

"Yeah, a BX, you know, for sure, man."

"Did you notice a license tag?"

"No, I did not remark upon it." Abdul turned to his partner and asked: "Jan?" Jan indicated ignorance.

Addresses, telephone numbers and names were being noted and both detectives left, only to return almost two hours later with the knowledge that both alibis were irreproachable. While the two rascals were courteously driven home by two constables, De Berg phoned the Department of Motor Vehicles.

An hour later he had a complete print-out on his desk of all the owners of a white Citroen BX, registered in the Netherlands. Dejectedly he looked at the stack of paper, there were more than twenty five thousand names and addresses. That was looking for a needle in a haystack. He took the whip from his desk and carried it to the elevator and to the next floor up. From a passing constable he learned where to find Goren. He knocked on the door and entered without waiting for an answer.

"Hello, Jan, I need your help."

Goren was the chief of the mounted police. A horseman since the day he was born.

De Berg placed the whip on his desk and asked:

"Is this kind of whip used around horses?"

Goren took the whip in his hand, looked at it closely and then said, thoughtfully:

"Good God, no! Certainly not in this form. For one thing, there are *four* tails, each with a lead tip. That's got nothing to do with horses. Look, the handle is of the same size as that used on long whips, used for dressage, you know, as in a circus. But with four tails and lead tips. I don't know about that. Beautiful craftsmanship, by the way. Must have been expensive. Between five hundred and a thousand dollars, easily."

He slid the leather lovingly through his hands, appreciating the quality.

"What sport uses a whip like this?"

"I cannot say. As far I would guess, this whip has been specially made for somebody. This is not just a whip, it is a murder weapon. Feel the ball at the end. That's lead."

"Who could make such a thing?"

"Not in Holland, in any case. This type of handwork is no longer available. You can still find the necessary craftsmen in England, though."

"What is your feeling about this? Which direction would you look?"

"Arie, I am a horseman, not a detective. You know that. But this is a whip meant to be used. To provoke. This is a macho thing. The Hell's Angels at the time. Sadists, Masochists."

"The S&M scene?"

"That could very well be possible, they get a kick out of this sort of thing."

On the way back to his office, he warned Freriks:

"We'll be going out together, later."

He picked up the phone and made a number of calls. After some time he wrote down a name and an address. He grabbed the information from his desk and called Freriks. Together they commandeered a car. On the way he informed his colleague about the conversation with Goren and his suggestion about the S&M world. The suggestion did fit extremely well with the way in which the killer treated his victims. The car stopped in front of a house on the edge of the Red Light District. They rang the bell and a beautiful Thai boy opened the door. De Berg told him that Mr. Roy Garner expected them and they were allowed to enter. The boy led them to Roy's office. After a few moments, Roy, supported by his inseparable walking cane, came in and shook hands with the two detectives. In his suggestive and mocking voice he said:

"Well, well, the police. How nice. Are you going to put cuffs on me? I'd like that, you know. So deliciously helpless." He laughed at his own joke.

De Berg placed the whip on the glass top of the desk behind which Roy had seated himself and said, businesslike:

"Mr. Garner, we would just like some information, or rather, some technical advice."

Roy looked at the whip, caressed the leather and said: "What a cute item, how did you get it?"

"Mr. Garner, we are investigating two murders and we have indications that, in the execution of least one of them, this whip was used as a weapon."

"And now you have come to arrest me?" Again the shrill, effeminate laugh. Without showing any of the irritation he felt, De Berg continued:

"We would like to know if you sold this whip to anyone."

"No, much too expensive. There's no market for that, here."

"Where could it have been bought?"

"I wouldn't know."

"Mr. Garner you own and operate a boutique specializing in accoutrements for the sado-masochist. That's the right expression, is it not?"

"Yes, yes, but we don't just sell, we also have a studio."

"Do you sell wholesale, or retail?"

"Both, but our largest volume is, of course, retail."

"So you sell to individuals?"

"But of course."

"They come to the house?"

"Yes, although they usually call in advance."

"Do you have a list of your retail clients?"

"But no! I understand that you are not familiar with the scene. Look, Mr. De Berg, sado-masochism is still a taboo. People who are not familiar with the scene, find it bizarre, strange, dirty, unnatural, disgusting, you name it. People in the S&M scene cannot afford to let their sexual preferences be known because of a family who would not understand, colleagues on the job, a good job, and so on. The majority of the people interested in S&M know each other, but only on a first name basis and that is usually fictitious. If an individual shops here, it is always cash on the barrel head. Not because of me, you understand, but that's what the customer wants. I don't know where they live and I don't know their names."

"But you do know your regular clients by sight?"

"But of course, do you have a photo?"

"No, unfortunately. Last question, Mr. Garner, where are the meeting places, clubs, etcetera, apart from the classified ads one sees in the paper?"

"I'll give you some addresses."

He picked up a plastic ball point, shaped like an erect penis, and wrote down the addresses. He underlined one and said:

"This is the most popular club at the moment. The "in" place to be, pun not intended. You should go on a Wednesday night. They put on something special on that night and it always draws a crowd."

Outside again, ready to step in the car, Frcriks turned to look back at the house and remarked, idly:

"I better not tell my wife where I've been today."

*27. *Amsterdam, Wednesday, March 22, 1989*

An old storefront, in a quiet street at the edge of the inner city of Old Amsterdam. Windows boarded up with black painted plywood. A spy hole is installed, roughly at eye height, in the solid door. Visitors can be closely scrutinized before being admitted. An innocuous sign, no larger than a three-by-five card, announces that "Club NOW" is located on the premises. De Berg pressed the buzzer. He could hear a cover being pushed aside on the inside of the spy-hole and he knew somebody was carefully looking at him. Shortly thereafter the door opened to reveal a lady, dressed in a close-fitting top which left her arms bare and stopped just below her breasts, a very short, low slung and tight pair of leather pants and a pair of incredibly high-heeled boots that covered her legs to mid-thigh.

"You must be new," she said.

"Yes, this is my first time, I heard about your Club from Roy Garner, he suggested a visit. My friend is coming a little later."

He had agreed with Freriks that they would arrive with about fifteen minutes interval in order to avoid as much attention as possible.

"Oh, Roy, our own, dear Auntie Roy. But you know that this Club is heterosexual, don't you?"

"Yes, I know, I am a healthy boy."

"Well, come in then, we can always use another healthy boy. My name is Giselle, what's yours?"

He mentioned a name while he took his coat off and hung it on a hook. Mistress Giselle led the way and showed him around. There was a bar, some seating arrangements in a number of booths, separated from each other, but open in front, and a small dance floor. There was also an open fire with imitation logs sparkling underneath a gas flame, surrounded by an imitation marble fireplace. A clock and the statue of a dancer were placed on the mantelpiece. The main area was full. There were a number of couples, dressed in black leather, or imitation black leather, made from a shiny plastic material. Female slaves, dressed in black leather, or less, took orders and served drinks. In front of the bar a naked man was tied to a chair, ignored by everyone. Behind the bar was a man, dressed in a complicated harness decorated with chrome studs. His genitals were encased in a piece of leather clothing, shaped in the form of his penis and scrotum, with pubic hair sticking out on all sides. Freriks arrived fifteen minutes later and sat down next to his colleague at the bar. De Berg nodded almost imperceptibly in the direction of the barkeeper and murmured with a straight face:

"We should invite him for the police ball."

"We'd have to increase the dues."

Shortly after Freriks, a nude couple entered. She was dressed in high heels and carried a small purse elegantly under one arm. He wore a small piece of cloth, the size of a washcloth which only partially covered his genitals, suspended from a narrow chain around the waist in addition to a small bag, suspended from one wrist.

"I think we should search those two."

"Not enough time, can take hours."

Everybody seemed to know each other and hearty greetings were bandied about. At ten o'clock the music stopped and Mistress Giselle appeared on the small dance floor. A few weak, colored spotlights came on and Giselle welcomed everybody to the club. She then announced two performances to be followed by a cold buffet around midnight.

A man, dressed in leather pants, boots and a simple harness around his torso strode onto the dance floor and announced, in a vulgar Amsterdam accent, that he would now discipline slave Caroline. He sat down on a stool and ordered a young girl of around twenty, to remove her skirt and to put on the handcuffs he handed her. A heavy cable, ending in a loop, came down and by means of a mountain climber's carabiner he connected the cuffs to the cable. The cable tightened until she was standing on her toes. He then requested one of the guests to strip her. The naked man came forward and pulled her tube top down below her buttocks, simultaneously loosening the G-string. Next he took off her brassiere and caressed the naked breasts under loud approval from the audience. He then slid all remaining garments down to the floor, again with loud encouragements and approval from the audience. He was rewarded with applause when he went back to his seat. The slow and soft beginning of Ravel's *Bolero* came over the loudspeakers. The man in the leather pants picked up a whip and circled the naked, suspended girl like a animal trainer in a circus. Then he began to hit her, each blow a little harder and stronger than the previous one. At intervals he would stroke her neck and caress her breasts and shaved genitals. Next he wrapped her in ropes, also between her legs, and pulled it tight. Suspended in a forward position she now had to endure another ten blows with the whip. He then picked up a paddle, covered with leather and hit her on the buttocks until they were red as tomatoes. He rubbed a lotion on her buttocks and then placed her on the horse, a leather covered instrument, shaped like a barrel with legs. He positioned her on her back with widespread legs toward the audience. Additional cables came down and he attached her ankles. He then pulled her legs in the air. Utilizing a whip made of rope and leather, he attacked her clitoris. She groaned with pleasure and pain. Slowly he brought her to a fever-pitch of excitement, the audience participating audibly. Many hands looked for, found, felt and pinched or stroked their own, or other body parts. The girl struggled in the ropes and the man in the leather pants took a vibrator and slipped it into her vagina. He kept her down until the inevitable orgasm happened. Silence reigned. Mistress Giselle stepped in front of the couple and said:

"Thank you very much, Peter and Caroline."

A long applause rolled through the room.

A man next to De Berg remarked: "Technically, extremely well done."

"Yes, I agree, but I felt the text lacked substance," he answered.

The man looked at him strangely for a moment and then turned abruptly away. De Berg turned to his colleague and said:

"I do think that's enough for tonight, what do you say?"

"Whatever you say. I just want to register as a member, if you don't mind."

They asked the barkeeper for the check and paid the bill. They walked toward the exit, followed by the hostess in the leather outfit and the high-heeled boots. De Berg turned toward her and said in a regretful tone of voice:

"Unfortunately, we have to leave, but we'll be back."

She opened the door and just as they wanted to leave a well dressed, middle aged man entered. They passed each other in the entrance and just before the door closed behind them, they heard the woman say:

"Hello, Jacques, how nice to see you again."

*28. Amsterdam, Thursday Morning, March 23, 1989

The next morning at nine De Berg sat down at his desk with a spiritual hangover, to write his report. He could not forget the suspended girl in the tackles. Such an elfin face. No more than twenty. He couldn't understand it. He saw much, almost too much and one had to be constantly on guard against losing all faith in mankind in this job. That was possible. He knew colleagues who had been so embittered and changed by all the misery and sadness they saw on a daily basis that they had lost the ability to think and act objectively and professionally. Marriages went to hell and more often than not a solution was sought in the bottle. If you became bitter, if you could no longer differentiate between the good and evil in people, then everything you did as a police officer had lost its value. Again he saw the pale, lovely face before him and the cruel marks, caused by the cuffs, when she had finally been released. He recalled her poor buttocks, the same behind that had once been lovingly powdered and caressed before she had been sung to sleep in her cradle. And that filthy man, who, with such obvious pleasure, had wielded the whip on her defenseless body. He had two daughters, almost the same age as the girl in the tackles. He shivered at the thought that briefly flashed before him. He gave up smoking more than a year ago, but now he suddenly needed a cigarette. He bummed one from one of his colleagues and lit up. He typed the report with two fingers and finished in about half an hour.

He knocked on the door and entered.

"Sir, we're at a dead end. No clues at all."

"Tell me about it," said Bakkenist.

"Those two gutter snipes have alibis that cannot be touched. Incontrovertible. It is certain that they did not steal the stuff from the Arnhem lawyer, but from some guy in a white Citroen who was parked behind the Central Station. Here is the list from the DMV, there are more than twenty five thousand likely suspects." Disgusted, he tossed the stack of paper on the desk.

"What else do we have?"

"The oil in the wound of the first victim coincides with that found by the Spaniards and also with that found on the whip. To recapitulate: we know that the suspect is a middle aged man, he has been in Madrid with the passport of Van Kleef, he drives a white Citroen BX, he uses the back end of a whip to hit his victims with and ... he likes soccer," he added ironically.

"A check of Citroen owners?"

"I thought about it, but where to start?"

"You're right, that's not going to solve anything."

"The only clue we have is the whip. Freriks and I have been following that up."

He gave a concise report of their investigations and when he stopped talking he placed the written report on the desk.

"Would it be productive to pursue the S&M world?" asked Bakkenist.

"Where to look? We haven't a clue. They all cover for each other, they hardly know each other, they have no membership lists in the clubs, nothing!"

"So you're stuck, you think?"

"As I said, nobody has ever been more stuck."

"Then there is only one thing to do. We wait!"

"I was afraid of that."

"Until he catches the next one."

"It looks like it."

"I'll send a fax to Madrid."

"I'm sure they'll be very happy."

De Berg stood up and left the room.

29. Polderkerk, Friday Evening, March 24, 1989

While he made the last arrangements in preparation for Monique's visit, he thought about the performance he had seen, last Wednesday, at the Club NOW. He looked around and compared his own playroom with what he had seen at the club. Satisfied he concluded that the comparison did not put him to shame. Fourteen days ago he had seen her for the last time and again he had been unable to persuade her to use the new playroom. Perhaps he would succeed tonight. Perhaps he would have to force her. Is that what she wanted? Was that perhaps her silent, unspoken wish? He felt himself able to do so, that wasn't the problem. He had closely watched the performance in the Club and made careful note of the number of variations. He was sure she would enjoy them. He loved her and he did not want to give up their little games. But sometimes the games became a bit repetitious, almost boring. He needed some variation.

He heard her park the car in front of the house and he went downstairs to greet her. He kissed her on the doorstep and they went inside.

"How are you, tell me, what have you done for the last two weeks?"

She kicked off her shoes and with pulled up knees nestled in a corner of the couch. Yes, he thought, what have I done in the last two weeks. I cannot tell you what I have done and what's left is hardly worth the trouble.

"Puttered around a little," was all he could think to say. He poured two glasses of red wine. They drank the wine and there were long silences. Long silences, pregnant with erotic thoughts and unfulfilled desires. Suddenly she stood up, left the room and returned about ten minutes later. She had dressed herself in high, black boots, a short, black plastic skirt and an a harness that supported her breasts, but left them completely bare.

"Is my master pleased?" she asked coyly.

Disdainfull, as if not interested, he stood up, left the room and went upstairs. He undressed in the playroom and made a careful selection from among the new purchases he had bought from Roy. He put wide leather cuffs, decorated with chrome studs, around his lower arms. He put on black cowboy boots with sharpened points and spurs. A wide leather belt, also decorated with chrome studs, went around his waist and a thin piece of black cloth, attached to the front of the belt, was pulled back between his legs, just covering the genitals. A short narrow strap ran between his buttocks and was attached to the back of the belt. Finally he donned a leather hood which covered his head like a balaclava. Only his eyes and mouth were visible. He picked up a whip and went downstairs. The moment she saw him, she threw herself on the floor and groveled at his feet. He pushed the handle of the whip under her chin and ordered her to stand up. He administered a number of firm blows on her behind and chased her up the stairs. She ran into the bedroom and he ordered her to take the skirt off.

She opened the zipper on the side and it fell away. With bulging eyes he looked at her genital area, which had been shaved bald.

Suddenly he saw the despised Barcelona whore in front of him, and also the face of the tormenter with the female face of 1945. A sexual excitement mixed with uncontrollable rage overcame him. With tears in his eyes he approached her and hit her in the face with his open palm.

"God damn, you shaved yourself, you dirty, filthy, horny bitch," he yelled.

He hit her on the back with his whip. Suddenly scared, she crouched down on the floor and raised her hands over her head to try and protect herself.

"Whores shave their cunts, you hear, whores do that, so they won't get crabs, when every hour they take a new prick into themselves for a couple of bucks. That's why they shave, you bitch! Get UP!"

Afraid, she rose, this was going wrong, she felt. For weeks she had this feeling that there was something wrong with him. She would suffer it all stoically, there was no other way, after all, she had started the games herself. But this went too far. He hit her on the bare behind and said, threateningly:

"You come along with me, you little whore. Master Jacques is going to give you a lesson in his own little, secret hideaway." He gripped her upper arm with such strength that she almost screamed. He pulled her with him to the playroom, kicked the door open and placed her in front of the cross. In no time at all he attached her wrists to the tops of the X. A belt went around her waist and the center of the X and was tightened until it almost took her breath away. Around her ankles he fastened leather cuffs, attached to ropes, which led across pulleys to the opposite walls. He picked up his whip again and looked with blazing eyes at her scared face.

"Yes, now you're really scared, aren't you? You should have thought about that *before* you shaved yourself, you bitch."

He hit her with the whip and ordered her to count. Meanwhile he raged on.

"Do you know where they used to shave people? Eh? ... Well? No, you don't know that, do you?" He continued the punishment.

Oh, my dear God, she thought, what has come over him? The pain racked her body. What have I done wrong? I just shaved myself! Never, in her wildest dreams, could she have expected this violent reaction. Something was wrong, something was bothering him. What could it be? Mixed feeling of fear and pity dominated her thoughts. And he kept on hitting her. It had all started with this horrible room, this blasphemous cross ...

"And do you know what's so funny, you delicious little whore of mine? Well, do you? Again the whip descended across her breasts. "Well, I tell you, you filthy whore! A shaved cunt reminds me of a shaved head. Do you hear? Number 89219!! You're bald, number 89219 and a bitch without hair on her head is no woman. Not anymore, do you know that, 89219!? That's no longer human, that's a number 89219!!"

He walked to the wall and pulled on the ropes which were attached to her legs and used them to spread her legs wide. He fastened the ropes in that position and pinched and squeezed her labia till she screamed with pain.

Sweat ran down his body, foam showed in the corners of his mouth and he raged on. Always the same number, yelling, cursing, hitting. There seemed no end in sight. She begged for mercy, she called his name, all to no avail. Then the whip descended on her face and she felt the skin break as the leather lacerated her cheekbone. She could taste the blood in the corner of her mouth. Then suddenly, he collapsed. Exhausted and completely desolated he sank to the floor. Softly he began to cry. His hands were clenched behind his back and his entire body shook in uncontrollable spasms. Just one word, repeated over and over and strung together came from his lips, between the heartrending sobs:

"mamamamamamamama mamamamamamama mamamama-mama mamama ..."

She looked at the crouching, crying and devastated human being at her feet and felt her own tears blurring her vision. She let herself go and uncontrollably she cried. She had not done that for years.

"Jacques, darling, help me down, come on, my dearest, come on now, I love you."

Slowly he lifted his head and regarded her, helpless in her bonds.

"What I have I done, what I have I done to you!?"

"Never mind, darling, it's all right, I understand. Help me, then I can hold you. Please, darling ..."

Crushed, he approached the cross and loosened her bonds. When she was free they embraced each other and tasted each other's mingled tears.

*30. Amsterdam, Saturday Morning, March 25, 1989

She woke at ten o'clock and rubbed her wrists. They were still sore from the leather cuffs that had chafed her while she was hanging on the cross. She looked in the mirror and noticed that her face was blue where he hit her. She could not go to work this way, that was certain. Tears filled her eyes when she thought again about the previous night. What had she gotten herself into? Was it a lost cause? It looked that way. He had been crying almost non-stop and tossed and turned like an overwrought child. He had begged her forgiveness, over and over again for everything he had done to her. She had put him to bed, she had consoled him and suddenly, without warning, he had fallen asleep and started to snore hard and insistent. Almost like an epileptic after an attack. She had left a note for him and had gone home. How could such a tender, dear person have changed so much, so quickly? Would she be able to help him? She doubted it. The doorbell rang, which surprised her, at that hour of the day. She engaged the intercom and heard his voice.

"May I come upstairs, please, I need to talk."

She walked to the elevator and waited for him to come up. When he saw her, his hands began to tremble and his eyes became moist.

"I didn't want to use your key, I might have scared you."

"Come," she said simply.

He remained hesitantly on the doorstep when they reached her apartment and said:

"I won't stay long."

"Just sit down for a moment. Do you want some tea? Have you had breakfast?"

"I don't feel like eating."

"Just eat something, a snack, it will make you feel better."

"No, never mind."

"Don't be that way. Won't you take your coat off?"

She prepared a cheese sandwich and poured him a cup of tea. She placed it in front of him and he silently ate what she put down. After a long silence, he stammered:

"I have spoiled everything."

She did not answer, at a loss for something to say. Then she said:

"Not necessarily."

"Sometimes I think I'm going mad."

"Why? How?"

"I don't know. It's so difficult to talk about."

"If it is that difficult, you don't have to."

"We had such great plans, but I don't know if I can go on. If I'm the right man for you."

"What are you afraid of, Jacques?"

"Of everything, of myself, of loosing you."

"I am still here. I am sitting right next to you."

"I know."

"I want to help you. I don't know what's the matter, but I'm sure you cannot face it alone."

"It's wonderful of you to say so, but I have to face this alone. I cannot understand how I could have let myself go like that, last night. I went completely round the bend. I was convinced you'd like the playroom."

"Would you be very disappointed if I told you that it went too far. It's so loveless, so technical, so sterile, so ... so ... distant, you know what I mean?"

"Yes, I know that now. Now I understand what you mean, but, you know, it was going to be so different between us. We had a deal. I'd never imagine that this could happen. The new room was actually still part of the previous period. I was just blind to the facts."

"I understand, but ..., what ... eh ... was the matter last night? What happened?"

"I don't know. I'm not sure. When you stood in front of me like that, so dear, so childlike, I loved you with all my heart, you must believe that. But I just don't know what happened, what made me so angry. I really wasn't angry with you, I hardly saw you after a while. I mean, I saw you, but I didn't see it was you anymore. As if you were two different persons at once. It was the association with something that made me so very, very angry."

"Something from the past?"

"Yes."

She stood up and took him in her arms. She rocked him slowly, like a baby. The she sobbed:

"Oh, my dear, dear, dear darling, what is the matter, what have they done to you. You'll never have to be afraid again. I'm here and I love you. Do you hear me, Jacques Meyer? Listen to me. I want you to feel safe with me. Life has beaten you, hurt you, but we will overcome together. I *know* that. I don't want you to think small about yourself any longer. I don't want you to feel like a failure. And I want to tell you something. In your eyes I may be a successful businesswoman, with an expensive apartment and a high income and everything, but do you know how lonely I've been all these years? Me, the decisive woman, able to solve the most difficult problems, involving millions of dollars, with efficiency and with admiration from all. Yes, me, who is in charge of hundreds of people, all dependent on me for an income and for guidance. Yes, me, have you any idea how rotten I feel when I come home at night, alone, to a goddamn empty apartment of half a million? There's never anybody to talk to in the morning. I breakfast alone, always. Nobody here to talk to. Always, always surrounded by yes-men, or people who are after my job, or are looking out for the main chance. But now I've got you! You have given meaning to my life. Yes, you, and I don't care who you are, or what you were, or what you did. I love you because you are who you are and nothing else. Do you hear me!?"

31. Amsterdam, Monday Morning, March 27, 1989

Monique parked her car along the curb on the north side of the Sarphaty Park. The park was a long, rectangular widening of the Sarphaty Street. The center space, about two hundred feet wide, was filled with trees, grass, bushes and a well-kept playground. Sarphaty Street traffic split up into two one-way streams on either side of the park. She had cancelled all appointments for the day. She was very conscientious about her work and never failed to have her business well organized. She was always where and when she had to be. She had, after all, reached her present exalted position on sheer ability. This also allowed her, if necessary, to quickly and efficiently rearrange her schedule to take care of personal matters. And this day was going to be devoted to her quest of finding out more about Jacques. The revelations of the previous Friday and the following Saturday, made that imperative. Apart from that they had enjoyed a wonderful, bittersweet week-end together. She thought about it with gladness and sadness. More than ever she was determined to help him and keep him.

For weeks now, she had postponed a serious search into Jacques' past, after her initial conversation with the barman. She knew more or less where he had lived in his youth, but that was all. There was something in his past that had to be discovered, if she was ever going to help him. He did not want to discuss it himself. Something had damaged him and he was still not able to overcome that. Perhaps she could help him with love and patience. After the conversations on Saturday, she was firmly convinced that nothing could be more important. For the moment everything else had to take second place. He was the man she loved. No matter how crazy, or incomprehensible, it was a fact.

If anybody had told her, as recently as six months ago, that there would come a time for her to love again, she would have dismissed the thought with scorn and ridicule. No, never again! A friend, perhaps a number of friends, just for the physical aspects, that fitted in with her ideas of the possible, especially in consideration of her career. That would be all right. To be completely without a man, would be even more impossible. Once in a while she had to feel a man in her. A man who would hurt her, physically, who would play her games and would allow her to be his slave. A man, any man, who appreciated her dressed in black stockings and provocative corsets, who would treat her roughly, with his hands and with a whip. That should have been enough. But now, how ironic, one had come by who was able to arouse her love. Of all things, via a classified advertisement. How banal!

She walked along the houses. Every once in a while a small storefront interrupted the endless string of row houses, but they were few and far between. People lived here. Children of all skin colors and nationalities played in the street. Moroccan and Turkish women, covered from head to toe in voluminous robes, walked shyly and furtively in and out of stores and in the direction of the shopping center at the end of the long street,

In marked contrast to the beautiful, colorfully dressed black women who, proud and bold, strode down the center of the sidewalks, exuding eroticism, health and a calm sense of self esteem. A hodgepodge of exotic faces, dress and customs, which compared favorable with the pale, nondescript Amsterdam natives.

She looked carefully at every house, but had no idea which would be the right one. She was looking for the house where the Kellenbachs had lived. Next to a dairy store, according to Harry, the barkeeper. She spotted an old lady with bucket and sponge in a hallway. She approached.

"Madam, may I ask you a question?" she asked with a sunny smile.

The woman placed the bucket on the floor, turned around and looked at her with curiosity in her eyes.

"Have you lived her long?"

"Are you from the City?" she asked suspiciously.

"No, no, not at all. I am looking for somebody who might have known the Kellenbach family, who used to live here, but I don't know where."

"What was the name, you said?"

"Kellenbach."

She thought carefully, for a long time and then shook her head.

"They are supposed to have lived here? How long ago?"

"I think, about fifteen years ago, or something."

"Kellenbach ... Kellenbach ... No, means nothing to me. It could have been on the other side of the park, you know, we didn't mingle with them. Those were people you met, you know what I mean, they weren't neighbors. Yes, on this side I knew everybody. Not anymore, though, there are so many new faces, now. The ones that lived here before are all dead, or they are in a rest home, or live in the provinces, somewhere. I am just about the last one of the old guard, me and my neighbor upstairs, but, well, what do you want, she's also been bedridden for some time already. That won't last long, anymore. But Kellenbach, it doesn't ring a bell."

"They lived close to a dairy store, does that mean anything to you?"

"A dairy store? Yes, of course! You mean the dairy store of Jan Van Strumpel, but he's been gone for some time, too, you know. All the supermarkets, you understand. But Jan Van Strumpel, yes, he had a dairy store. He also delivered at the door. Just in this neighborhood, you know."

While the woman was talking, Monique realized how terrible it could be to grow old. To slowly see the environment disappear in which you had grown up, had lived and loved, to see it fade away and disappear until you were left, all alone, with just your memories, in a neighborhood where nobody recognized you any more.

"Where exactly was that dairy store, ma'am?"

"On the other side, I don't know the number, you'd have to ask over there. Jan Van Strumpel was the owner, I remember that very well."

"Thank you very much, ma'am."

"No bother," she answered with the typical Amsterdam intonation that left you doubting whether it was meant, or not.

Monique crossed the park to the other side and started with the first house. If there had been a dairy store around here, it was possible that the facade might still be visible, even if it had been remodelled to living space. Or perhaps there was now a different store on the premises. This neighborhood was riddled with hundreds of small stores, catering to the special diets of its polyglot inhabitants. Suddenly she saw a facade which was different from the others. A large window with a door next to it. Curtains flanked the window and flower pots were displayed both inside and outside the glass. That could be it. This had obviously been a store at one time. She decide to ring the bell and ask. She heard the bell ring in the distance and waited. The house remained silent.

She tried again, but again no result. Upstairs a window opened, the head of a woman appeared, who yelled:

"They're not at 'o-o-ome!"

Monique looked up and said:

"Perhaps you can help me, ma'am. I am looking for anybody who might have known the Kellenbach family, who used to live here."

"Then you're in the wrong place. That used to be the dairy store of Jan Van Strumpel."

"So, that *was* here?"

"Yes, that used to be a dairy store. Before my time, you know, because I've lived 'ere only five years."

"So you haven't lived here that long?"

"No, if you want to talk to somebody who's been 'ere forever, you want to talk to Uncle Gert. 'E's been 'ere since before the war."

"Where can I find that gentleman?"

"Just wait up a mo! I'll come downstairs and go with you. 'E knows me. If 'e sees a stranger all of a sudden 'e might get a shock. 'E already 'as a weak 'eart."

A moment later the door opened and she came out.

"Come on," she pushed a bell knob on the door next to hers, while using the string, which hung from the letter slot, to unlock the door. She opened the door and stepped inside.

"Uncle Gert! It's me, Alice!"

An old man appeared at the top of the stairs and looked curiously at his visitors. When they came upstairs, the woman, still panting from her climb up the stairs, said:

"This lady wants to ask you some questions."

Monique shook hands with the old man and introduced herself.

"It's about the Kellenbachs, if you knew them," said the woman.

"Of course I knew them. They lived next door, one floor higher. What is this all about?"

"Perhaps you will find it strange that I want to know something about the family, after so many years, but I have a reason that is difficult to explain."

Suddenly she realized that she had not prepared herself for this part of her investigations. How was she to explain the "why" of her visit to a man who didn't even know her? She should have thought of a good reason before she set out on her expedition. A reason that would sound plausible.

"Well, come on in, then." said the man.

"Shall I make you a nice cup of coffee, then?" asked Alice. "You will stay and 'ave some too, won't you, madam?"

The man was at least eighty, but his eyes still retained a boyish twinkle, full of life.

"Doesn't happen too often anymore, that a young lady comes to visit me, up the stairs and all," he said and laughed.

"Just control yourself a bit, won't you, you old rogue," came from the kitchen.

"May I ask you, sir, ..."

"Just call me Uncle Gert, darling, you could have been my niece."

"Uncle Gert, you knew the Kellenbach family?"

"Yes, most certainly, nice people they were too. It was a shock for the entire neighborhood when they were suddenly taken from us. I even went to the memorial service, although I never go to church, otherwise."

"What happened to them?"

"You don't know? They were killed in an airplane crash, in Spain. They had never flown before and for the first time they were going to go on vacation, for three weeks, by plane. I remember it well, the newspapers were full of it, at the time."

"Where did the accident happen?"

"In Tenerife, ach, it was terrible. They were such good people. His name was Jan and hers was Marie."

"Did they have any children?"

"No, they couldn't have children themselves. She told my late wife once. You know, one of those typical female talks. But they did have an adopted son. Jacques. I can still see him arrive, just after liberation, it was. Goddamn Nazis killed his whole family, he was the only survivor. God, oh, God, the way that child looked! I remember telling my wife: he won't survive. So thin. And they were so happy with him. Proud as peacocks they were. They used to take him for walks on Sunday. I have children myself and I'd do, and did, anything for them, but the way those two were with that boy! No, you don't see that too often, anywhere. The sacrifices. Nothing was too good for him. Poor chap, but you could measure the improvements by the day. He used to come here a lot. My son, Kees, was of the same age. But the kid always remained a quiet child, sort of withdrawn. Never really let himself go, you could tell that he had experienced a lot. None of it good. You could just tell. Dirty , goddamn Nazi's! Even today, when I meet some of them in the street, I'll walk across to the other side, because I'll never forget!"

"Did you ever hear anything about the family of Jacques?"

"Yes, Jan told me one time. His parents had a furniture store, somewhere near the center of town. On the Langedijk. I remember were that was. A well-known store at the time. "Meyer's Furniture Palace." They were Jews. He also had a sister, older than Jacques, she didn't come back either. All of them gone ... but what can you do. It happened."

Then they were both silent, immersed in their own thoughts, until Alice came in with a tray.

"Would you like sugar and milk, ma'am?" she asked.

32. Polderkerk, Monday Morning, March 27, 1989

While Monique talked to the old man at the Sarphaty Park, Meyer awoke. Last night he had needed a sleeping pill. He had been so depressed that there was no other way to get much needed rest. It was the only thing that would allow him to sleep. Today was the 27th of March and it was exactly twelve years since it happened.

He just knew the day was going to be bad. This day his memories were even more vivid than other days. He could so well visualize it all. He had taken them to Schiphol Airport, twelve years ago. He in his best suit and she in a new summer dress, despite the winter weather. Because *there* it would be almost eighty degrees. For the first time they would be flying and they had never been abroad, except once to Antwerp and once to Brussels. He had been so proud of being able to give them this present for their thirty fifth wedding anniversary. The night before he had taken them out to a restaurant. How he would have liked to give them grandchildren. How proud they would have been. They would have accepted them as their own grandchildren, despite the fact that the children would have had his own name. Uncle Jan had never wanted him to change his name from Meyer to Kellenbach. They had discussed it often, but Uncle Jan had always told him that he was the son of Jewish parents, that he was the last of the line and he should keep his name with pride.

The memories about his parents didn't really start until the day of the man-hunt. One of the infamous razzias, or pogroms, designed to round up the entire Jewish population. The only thing he remembered from before that time was the day they went to the beach. He remembered the blue streetcar that started on Admiral Way. He remembered just one day, but there must have been others, because they often went to the beach. Perhaps that's why he remembered all the days before the capture as sunny days. It was always summer, then. From that day his recollections started, the faces of his parents and his sister. Everyday he still saw his sister. The way she walked, the way she talked. How she consoled him and how she took him by the hand. In his memory she was always old and wise, much older than the three years that separated them. But a sister of nine, when you were only six yourself, was, of course, a *big* sister. He could still hear her voice. Such a darling voice. And also that day in the camp: "I'll come back to you," she had said. Uncle Jan had been right, he should keep his own name, he owed it to the people that were no longer here, that had gone forever. And it made no difference, anyway. Just changing his name would not have stopped the dreams. He had loved Uncle Jan and Aunt Marie more than anybody else in the world.

And now it was again the 27th of March, Why were calendars ever invented? To be confronted, again, with your birthday, every year? But also with Memorial Day and the 27th of March. Normally his memories were almost unbearable, but during such days they were terrible. Every year again he felt guilty. He paid for the trip and he had persuaded them to go. At first they didn't want to go. They were a little afraid. Not the flying, they both looked forward to the experience. No, a holiday abroad, there was something scary about that. People spoke a foreign language and ate different foods. Why had he not given them another present? New carpets, maybe, or new curtains? He knew Aunt Marie had been saving for that. He should have done it. Nothing would have happened, then. He could have just picked them up in the car for a little sight-seeing trip. Uncle Jan, who had never owned a car, was so proud of his son's car. As he used to tell everybody who asked: "No, on Sunday we're not available. My son will pick us up. He's got his own car." When nobody was looking, he would lovingly caress the hood, or the dashboard. Then he would sit next to him, his inseparable fisherman's cap on the head, and Aunt Marie in the back, with a bag full of snacks and sweets. Then, after they died, he had to go to their small apartment and clear things up. He had found the Will. Then he discovered that they had lived so frugally, all these years, in order to save enough to leave him a small inheritance. That was their pride and their joy. He had offered them the trip from which they had never returned and he had outlived his parents and his sister during the war. That was his fate. He was left with a feeling of guilt that ate away at his very being. Everybody was gone and he, alone, always remained.

But this time he was not going to carry all the guilt by himself. Frau Vollmer and the rest of the German population could no longer be held accountable. Not even the man who had burned the number in his mother's arm. On the inside, just above the wrist.

He could still see and smell it. He had seen the number just once, but would never forget it. The face of the man still haunted his dreams. How he would have liked to meet Frau Vollmer just one more time. The beast that had whipped his mother until she had collapsed and died. All of them had escaped their just punishment. They probably all still strutted arrogantly around, somewhere, with as big a mouth as ever. But what happened twelve years ago did not have to remain unpunished. He had been able to look straight in the eyes of two of the guilty. He had watched as they pissed in their pants from fear, after they regained consciousness and discovered themselves hanging from the hooks. Those were the first two, the others would follow. And the day would come that everybody would know that he had made it possible for justice to triumph.

He would spend the day in planning. And to take appropriate measures in preparation.

He took the phone off the hook and called a Travel Agency ...

33. Tenerife, Sunday Afternoon, March 27, 1977

There was still a thick fog over Tenerife. Two Boeing 747s had landed just hours ago: KLM with 229 passengers and 15 crew and PanAm with 373 passengers and 14 crew. Both planes were destined for Las Palmas, KLM from Amsterdam and the American plane from Los Angeles. The airport at Las Palmas, however, was closed because of a bomb threat. At one in the afternoon, shortly after the take-off of the last domestic flight, there was an explosion on the first floor of a flower shop. The owner, Doña Marcelina Sanchez Amador, was seriously injured and among the six lightly injured was the Chief of the airport, Don Pedro Gonzales. The airport was closed immediately and planes were diverted to Los Rodeos at Tenerife. After a thorough search of the airport and all arrival- and departure halls, the airport was re-opened at four o'clock in the afternoon.

Fog was still heavy at Tenerife. Both 747s taxied in the direction of the runway at approximately 5PM. The KLM flight reached the beginning of the runway, and after completing its checklist, received permission to depart. The PanAm plane had taken a turn and found itself in the middle of the runway, near the center. The KLM plane revved up, released the brakes and started its take-off roll. Suddenly the crew of the PanAm plane saw the Dutch Jumbo bear down on them. Distance was already minimal. The PanAm plane tried to get away and avoid a collision. The KLM plane collided with the tail section of the American plane and both airplanes immediately caught fire.

Local time was 18:14 hours.

*34. Amsterdam, Monday Afternoon, March 27, 1989

At one o'clock she was back in her office, ignoring the stack of mail on her desk, she stared silently into the distance. She thought about what the old man had told her and more and more she began to understand Jacques. All the scraps of conversations, the odd remarks, started to fit together. The story about his parents, who had died at an early age and his sister who died at the age of nine. It fit, except for the way they had died. He had not talked about that. Also the inheritance fit into the puzzle. The furniture store on the Langedijk. The inheritance must have been the property. Then the sad, accidental death of his foster parents, it was terrible. She picked up the phone and called one of her assistants.

"Fons, Mrs. Vanderlaan here, I'd like you to do something for me."

"Of course, ma'am, what can I do for you?"

"Look up and see if we have anything in the records about a plane crash in Tenerife."

"I don't think we were involved in that, as far as I can remember."

"No, no, I am not interested in the insurance questions, I just want some general information."

"I'll see what I can find, ma'am."

She broke the connection, pushed the intercom and said:

"Irene, will you please get me the State Institute for War Documentation?"

"Should I ask for anybody in particular?"

"I don't know, just connect me and I'll take it from there."

She made a few notes and then picked up the receiver at the first sound.

"State Institute for War Documentation."

"Good afternoon, ma'am, my name is Mrs. Vanderlaan. I wanted to know how I go about getting information from your organization. It concerns a family that died in a concentration camp."

"Just a moment, I'll connect you to Mr. Nagel."

"Nagel here, good afternoon, how can I help you?" asked a friendly voice and she repeated her question.

"What exactly do you want to know, ma'am?"

"Mr. Nagel, we do not know each other, but I want to be as frank as possible. I have a friend for whom I care very much. He is now fifty years old and as a child he was interned in a concentration camp, where he lost his family. He never wants to discuss it, but I found out on my own. Mostly because of a number of changes in his behavior patterns over the last few months. Depression, sadness, all in all not nice changes. I want to help him, but it would be a lot of help to me if I knew a little more about his background."

"CC Syndrome?" *

"I considered it."

"Yes, that can become more marked with ageing, that's well known."

"May I ask you some questions?"

"But of course."

"If I give you the name of the family and their address, here in Amsterdam, can you find the missing details?"

"It depends, I assume they're Jewish?"

"Yes."

"Do you want to give me the name now, or would you like an opportunity to reflect?"

"No, no, that's not necessary. It concerns a family Meyer from the Langedijk, at the time they owned a well-know furniture store."

"Do you know the Christian names, or dates of birth?"

"Only of the son, the man in question. He is Jacques Izaak Meyer, born on August 20, 1939 in Amsterdam. It was his family, consisting of the father and mother and a daughter of about nine, and the son, of course."

"I will see what I can find. Will you ring me back, later this afternoon?"

"Gladly, Mr. Nagel, and thank you very much for your trouble."

"No trouble at all, ma'am."

Finally, she turned her attention to the stack of mail and started to work her way through it. She accepted phone calls, solved a number of problems for her assistants and gave advice when asked by colleagues. Quickly, routinely and efficiently she followed the normal pattern of her office. Fons called back after about an hour and a half:

"What did you find?"

"Just the general information, number of victims, dispositions and a synopsis of the judicial consequences."

"No names of the victims?"

"No."

"What was the date?"

"Twelve year ago, today."

"What? Did you say today?"

"Yes, March 27, 1977, a Sunday."

"Thank you very much, Fons, I have enough." She hung up.

Today! And he was home alone! On this day!? She could not let him be by himself. Not today, of all days. She thought a while longer and then picked up the phone again. She dialled his number.

"Meyer here," she heard on the other end of the line and without mentioning her name, she asked:

"Do you have any nice suits?"

"You call to ask me that?"

"I am just asking if you have any nice suits and then you're supposed to answer yes, or no."

"Nice suits is all I have."

"Put one on and make sure to be at my place at seven o'clock."

"Why?"

"Escort service. I need a companion tonight."

"Who's paying for that?"

"Payment will be strictly in kind." She broke the connection.

It so happened that she had obligations for an informal dinner with some clients and their partners. Business was not to be discussed at this particular meeting. Jacques would fit perfectly in that company and it would do him good, she knew that. No matter what, she wanted to start introducing him to her colleagues, acquaintances and business relations. This was a perfect first opportunity. During the remainder of the afternoon she completed her agenda and she called Mr. Nagel again at the end of the day. When she got him on the phone, he told her the whole, harrowing story. The date of the capture, the names of the SS-officers who had been in charge at the camp, the date of transport, the name of the camp, the ages, the birth dates, the names of the family ... Rachel, Eva, Simon ... everything was on file and available in the old mansion on the Gentleman's Canal. Unbelievable. Mass murder in alphabetical order. Including the numbers that were burned into, or tattooed on, the wrists.

Eva Meyer-Salomons ... born April 14, 1914 at Amsterdam. Camp number 89219 ...

---

* CC Syndrome = Concentration Camp Syndrome—trans.

35. Amsterdam, Monday Evening, April 3, 1989

When she opened the door of her flat at a quarter past eleven that night, she immediately smelled the scent of his after-shave. She recognized it and she saw the light in the living room. A happy feeling came over her. Jacques was here! The first time that he had come without asking her in advance if it was convenient. She opened the door of the living room and saw him waiting with two glasses of red wine.

"Oh, Jacques, what a wonderful surprise! I am so happy you're here! You're staying, aren't you?"

"I brought my toothbrush."

"Oh, darling, how nice. And a glass of wine, delicious!"

"Do you want to eat something? I bought some cheese on the way."

"And a candle? It takes me back to my student days when I lived in rooms: red wine, cheese and a candle."

"And ham and eggs."

"Yes, most hot meals were just ham and eggs, in those days. I always loved it. Tonight I dined with a couple of expensive gentlemen in Excelsior, but that's nothing compared to ham and eggs. Did you wait long?"

"Since about ten. I watched television for a while."

"How absolutely wonderful to see you." Again she embraced him and placed her cheek next to his.

"And it was such a bastard of a day in the office."

"How's that?"

"Ach, you know, I like my job, after fifteen years the job has started to adapt itself to me. But there are always people who feel stepped upon, or passed over. Especially my chief-assistant, he just cannot get used to the idea that I'm his boss and he shows it, from time to time."

"He wanted your job?"

"You bet, he would have done anything to get it, and he did. Lobbied within and without the company, kissing behinds, flattery, favors for the Directors, you know the sort of thing. But it's been settled for some time. He's been passed over and I got the job. Now he tries to trip me up every chance he gets."

"Can he do that?"

"Of course, he can do that, if I let my guard down. He can suppress, or delay, vital information, work against me in a thousand subtle ways, you name it. And always in a way that is just almost undetectable, and if it is discovered, in such a way that somebody else gets blamed while he remains blameless. He's a coward too. Furthermore, the fact that I'm a woman really works on him like a red flag on a bull. We're in the middle of a gigantic project. The insurance of the Singapore Airport. We're talking hundreds of mil lions of dollars. I'll even have to go out there, one of these days. And I have to be doubly careful that I watch everything, because he would love to see me fail."

"Well, forget it a for while, now."

"Yes, how fine! Are you really staying the night? I don't have any appointments until ten tomorrow, so I won't have to rush in the morning. Cozy, isn't it, my own dear little Jacques?" She nestled herself firmly in his arms.

That night he could not fall asleep. He heard her calm breathing and felt guilty. What had he done? What had he started? On the one hand he had finally found what he had been looking for, all these years, and on the other hand, it kept him from the plans he had made. He had started on that path and it was unthinkable that he should turn back. He felt no regret for the two he had been able to reach so far. They were criminals who shared the guilt of hundreds of deaths. But life had turned around so quickly for him. What now? What would happen if he made a mistake and the whole business would come to light prematurely? She, too, would be implicated and it would all be his fault. What would happen to her then? Would it be better to stop now? Stop what? Stop the relationship with her, or stop the executions?

36. Amsterdam, Tuesday Morning, April 4, 1989

She got up at eight o'clock and found that he had fixed breakfast and set the table. The silver service, precise to the millimeter, next to the two plates and the napkins folded into a perfect fan. The food displayed on serving trays and freshly pressed orange juice in bedewed glasses. The smell of coffee wafted through the house. Twenty minutes later, washed and made up, but still in her robe, she sat down at the table.

"How fantastic, what a service, what luxury!"

While they were eating she suddenly looked up and said, in a businesslike tone:

"I must confess something."

"Oh, yes?" he asked.

"I should have discussed it with you much sooner, but I never knew how to start."

"Sounds serious."

"First I must have your promise that you won't be angry and you must tell me when you want me stop with the story. Promise?"

"All right, I promise."

"Well then, I'm sure you know that I have worried about you a great deal?"

"Yes, I know."

"I hope you know that you can trust me?"

"What do you want to tell me?"

"I know everything about you, Jacques."

A shock went through him, but he controlled himself almost immediately.

"What do you mean?"

"Your past, about your parents, the Kellenbachs, Sarphaty Park, everything."

"How did you discover all that?"

"I talked with Uncle Gert who, by the way, sends you his heartiest greetings."

"Is he still alive?"

"Most assuredly, and still quite spry. He asked if you would visit him."

"Uncle Gert was a wonderful man. He used to keep pigeons and I was always allowed to help him."

"So, he was a real uncle for you?"

"Yes, he was."

"Go and visit him, once in a while."

"What else have you found out?"

"All about your father, your mother and your sister. I know the names, their birthdays. The store on the Langedijk: 'Meyer's Furniture Palace'."

"Yes, I still have a picture of that store. Father stands in the door opening."

"Do you have pictures of your mother, and your sister?"

"Yes."

"Where do you keep them? I didn't see them in the house."

"Somewhere in a drawer."

"Why? You think that will help you forget?"

"No, of course not."

"May I see them?"

"But of course."

"May I give them a place in my house, as well as in yours?"

"Why would you want that?"

"We're happy together and I would like to think that they be-long, that they're part of that happiness."

"Well ... I don't know."

"Do you mind that I know?"

"No, not at all, that's all right."

"I only want to discuss it when you want to, or when you think it'll do you good."

"I want to talk to you about it, but don't ask too much."

"I'll never do that, but you will show me the pictures soon?"

"I promise."

"Please understand, I won't ask for them, you'll have to give them to me on your own accord."

"Agreed."

She felt she had gone far enough, for the moment, and changed the subject. At the last moment she got up, dressed quick-ly, took her coat and briefcase from the hall closet, kissed him and said:

"Perhaps you'll still be here, tonight. In any case, I'll be home around seven. Decide for yourself."

"OK."

"You have a lot to do, today?"

"Nothing special."

"Well, then why don't you visit Uncle Gert, it'll do you good."

"I might do that, yes."

After she had gone he walked to the front of the flat, opened the French doors and stood on the balcony. From the seventh floor he could see the main entrance and he waited for her to appear. He whistled on his fingers when he saw her. Surprised she looked up and waved. He waited until she had stepped in the car and the car had disappeared. After he had gone back inside, he promised himself that he would get the pictures out and that he would visit Uncle Gert.

37. Poldercerk, Sunday, April 16, 1989

This Sunday, for the first time in weeks, he was again home alone. Yesterday he had taken her to the Airport for her business trip to Singapore. She would be gone at least ten days, which seemed like an eternity to him. The emptiness he felt, after she waved and passed passport control, was mingled with bittersweet and painful memories. He had stood on almost the same spot, twelve years ago. That time he had waved goodbye to the two dearest people in the world. The vision was still with him as a concrete reality and it scared him. It wasn't the fear of flying, but the coincidence of finding himself again in almost the same spot, worried and disturbed him.

Everything in his life had been a string of coincidences. It was a coincidence that they had been discovered at their hideaway in 1945 and it was a coincidence that there was a bomb threat in Las Palmas and an airplane had been diverted and it was a coincidence there happened to be a heavy fog in Tenerife. Everything was coincidence and happenstance. He stared without seeing anything. It was already one o'clock and he not yet eaten. The house was a mess. The dirty dishes from the previous day were still stacked on the counter. He had not taken a shower, he wasn't shaved yet and was still sitting around in a robe.

Dejectedly he thought about the mess his life had become. He had nobody to blame but himself. He should never have let it get this far. When would there be an end, and also, how would the end be? A dragnet had been set out for him, it but waited for the final command to let it descend and trap him like an animal. But he could not turn back. The horror of his deeds did not affect him, nor regrets, just the fear of discovery and the panic at the possibility of losing everything he had found.

He looked at the nicely framed pictures on the sideboard. His father, his mother and his sister. Monique had them enlarged and retouched and they looked as if they had been taken yesterday. The same photos were displayed in her house. He looked at these people from so long ago. The dear face of his mother, the sweet face of his sister with long, black curls and his father, proud underneath the sign of "Meyer's Furniture Palace". A feeling of sorrow and hate overcame him. He ground his teeth and balled his fists in a powerless gesture of frustration and fury. He couldn't stop, it had to happen, he would finish and he would not be discovered. Nothing was to be left to chance. Nobody would catch him. Nothing and nobody was going to stop him!

Slowly the familiar, exalted feeling returned, that feeling of power and being chosen. He stood up and left the room. As he passed the portraits he said:

"I'll get the bastards, Papa!"

38. Palma de Mallorca, Wednesday, April 19, 1989

The Martinair Airbus touched down at ten thirty in the morning at the Palma de Mallorca airport and as soon as the plane came to a complete stand-still at the gate, two hundred and fifty tourists rose en-masse. The usual confusion of crowded, twisting bodies who all needed their luggage from the overhead compartments at the same time and were all determined to be the first to leave the aircraft. At the bottom of the ramp, as usual, a photographer was making pictures of every passenger as they left the plane. Two, or three, weeks later, or whenever the charter was scheduled to depart, the pictures would be ready for sale. After most of the passengers had left the plane, Meyer stood up, took a small rucksack from the luggage compartment and strolled toward the exit. The stewardess in her pretty red and white uniform, wished him a nice holiday and as he smiled to acknowledge the wish, he spotted the photographer. Continuing as if nothing had happened he completed his turn, told the stewardess he had forgotten something and disappeared back in the plane. He walked back to his seat and pretended to look for something. Meanwhile he waited for the last passengers to depart, while keeping an eye on the photographer. The man, satisfied he had accounted for all the passengers, finally packed up and disappeared in his car. Again he walked to the exit, for the second time received wishes for a nice holiday and stepped in the waiting bus.

Everybody simply raised the black booklet in their hands as they walked through passport control and were waved on. While waiting for his remaining luggage, he could not suppress a slight attack of panic. Everything had been planned to perfection, and then suddenly, that damn photographer. Perish the thought that such an innocent slip would cause him to be traced. He calmed himself with the thought that nobody could know who he was. He had booked on a camping charter under a different name. That was easy. He had made the reservations himself, by phone, had gone to the Travel Agency and paid in cash. He spotted the bright blue overnight bag among the luggage on the carousel and picked it up, waited until a large family, with a lot of luggage, was ready to go trough customs and then attached himself to the crowd. He avoided the hostess from the tour charterer who was trying to round up as many people as possible for the first bus trip into town. He took a cab. A little later he had himself dropped off in the center of town. He drifted through the labyrinth of narrow streets, dead-ends and alleys that bend back on themselves. Then he noticed a neglected hostel in the Calle Bon Aire, one of those typical European institutions, a cross between a hotel and a boarding house. He entered and asked the man, apparently the owner, for a room for one night. He planned to do this all week. Every night a different place and just one night at a time. For a single night it was unlikely that he would be asked for his passport and he would not be long enough in any place to be easily recognized later.

He had bought sports clothes, a rucksack and an overnight bag, just for this trip. All of them the kind of items he hated. He felt cheap and ordinary. He was used to travel with a real leather suitcase, lined in silk, with specially made compartments for his shaving gear and other items. Also, of course, he was accustomed to travel first class. He was repulsed by his own appearance, the rucksack, the cheap bag and the fact that he looked just like hundreds of others. But the others liked it! They bought the cheap trash because it satisfied their taste. He was firmly convinced that the majority of the world's population was uncouth and without any taste for the finer things in life.

After arranging his things to his satisfaction, he went out and walked around town. He knew the town from previous visits, as a regular tourist. From Borne, with the large fountain, he strolled down the Jaime III, the expensive shopping street with arcades on both side, equivalent to Rodeo Drive. He walked past the exclusive boutiques and shoe stores and the marble facade of Cartier until he reached the Travel Agency he was looking for. Months before he had memorized the phone number. "Viajes Palma" was written on the sign. This was it. The man he was looking for was inside!

He resisted the urge to go in. He looked at the window display of posters and model airplanes, each painted in the colors of a different major airline. He saw a number of young people behind terminals and a few customers, either talking to the agents, wandering around, or reading brochures. In the back of the space was a man, obviously in a management position. His desk was larger and his corner was semi-private. A glass partition separated him from the main floor. This could be the man he was looking for. He had known his name for years, but had never seen him. Tonight he would be certain, after he followed him to his home address and the last piece of the puzzle would fit into place. Then he would have to locate an isolated place where the punishment could be meted out, undisturbed by anyone. That was still a problem. He had been lucky, the last two times. In Sitges he didn't even have to rent a car. The victim had conveniently provided that. In Madrid it had been different. He had been forced to show the British Driver's License that he had stolen, more than a year earlier, from a coat in the lobby of a London hotel. It was relatively simple to replace the picture on the license with one of his own.

Leisurely he strolled in the direction of the sea and the fishing harbor, opposite the gorgeous examples of renaissance architecture. To the left was a break in the buildings, filled with old palms and orange trees. Behind the buildings around the square was the entrance to the Yacht Harbor, closed off by a rusty fence, a hanging gate, a thin chain and an enormous, old fashioned padlock. To the right of the gate was a Ship's Chandler and to the left was a small chapel. The massive, oak door of the chapel was closed and from the notice pinned to the wood, he learned that the chapel was only open on Sunday. A shiver ran up and down his spine. A holy place, consecrated ground, could it be a sign?

Upon closer scrutiny he was able to ascertain that the square only contained commercial establishments. More than likely it would be deserted in the evenings. He walked away and made a left turn in the direction of the Yacht Harbor. The paved ground behind the chapel was filled with pleasure craft. All were being worked on. Small, nondescript sail boats, but also a few multi million dollar power boats of more than sixty feet in length. He noticed that the chapel did not have a back entrance. He had noticed no fence, when he approached the Harbor from this side and wondered if it was guarded at all, even at night. The gate separating the Harbor from the square had obviously not been used in a long time. He walked back to the Ship's Chandler and went in. A big man with a reddish beard greeted him in English. He was the only customer and he asked permission to look around. After having looked at a number of items, asked a price here and there, he told the owner of the store that he had just arrived in Palma with his sailboat. It was his first visit to the island and because he needed some maintenance done anyway, he would like some information. The man had time, so he assured Meyer, and patiently answered all his questions. Toward the end of the conversation he mentioned the security of the Yacht Harbor area.

A little later he took a closer look at the structure that had been pointed out to him. A small shed, built on poles, gave a bird's eye view of the entire Yacht Harbor. He looked at the distance between the shed and the chapel and estimated it to be at least one hundred and fifty yards. It could safely be assumed that the walls of the chapel would be at least two feet thick and the nearest surveillance was more than one hundred and fifty yards away. The guard could not possibly hear anything that happened in the chapel. He had firmly decided. This was the spot were it would happen, this was the spot to which, as if by an unseen hand, he had been sent. Even more than before, he felt as if a holy task had been assigned to him. After all, he had been drifting around, wandered without any specific goal in mind, just taking in the sights, without any ulterior motive. And suddenly he had been confronted with the perfect spot, in front of the heavy oak door and he had *known*: This was the place! Again he felt a cold shiver go up and down his spine, despite the sun and despite a temperature in the eighties.

**39. Palma de Mallorca, Monday, April 24, 1989*

It was eight o'clock in the evening when Meyer strolled into the parking garage behind the "Galerias Preciados" department store in the center of Palma. It was a stifling building without sufficient ventilation and permeated with the clammy clouds of carbon-monoxide created by the more than four hundred cars that were parked here on a regular basis. Near the entrance, under a weak light, an unhealthy looking man breathed this atmosphere for more than fourteen hours per day. Perhaps in an attempt to get some fresh air, or at least poison of a different kind, he chain smoked cigarettes made of a black, heavy tobacco. The walls were black from the exhaust gasses and the narrow ramp went up five floors along the individual parking stalls that could all be closed off with a roll door. Less than half of the lights in the building seemed to function. It was a somber, dirty and somewhat menacing place. He took the elevator and a few minutes later he stood in front of the closed door of stall number 237.

Knowing the door to be unlocked, he opened it, entered and closed it behind him. He unscrewed the only lamp capable of lighting the place and put it carefully in a corner. A small passage remained on either side of the parked car. He opened the left rear door, removed the cover of the dome light and took out the tiny bulb. He wrapped the business end of his whip around his right hand and gripped the handle with the monkey's fist projecting forward. Then he crouched behind the driver's seat and waited.

He heard cars start up and drive away. He heard the footsteps of the owners pass the door behind which he was hiding. It was busy in the building at this time. During the previous nights, while exploring the situation, he discovered that nobody was likely to pay any particular attention to slot 237, or any other slot, for that matter. First of all it was too dark and secondly, people were concentrating on getting home and paid attention only to the specific spot where *their* particular vehicle was parked. They wanted to go home, all of them, and as soon as possible. He felt for the big key to the chapel, safely tucked away in his pants pocket. There had been two on the wall, next to the door on the inside, when he visited the chapel last Sunday. Two! One for the priest and one for him! Perhaps they had been hanging there for years, in the same place. Undisturbed.

Last night he had visited the chapel again. He had placed new candles in front of the altar and mounted two large hooks, normally used to suspend a child's swing, into an age-old beam. Then he had lit the candles and stared in rapture at the murals of the various Saints. He had always avoided religion and made a special effort to stay away from Catholicism. Although he was Jewish, from a generation of Jews, circumcised* and all, he had never visited a Synagogue. Vaguely he remembered the Sabbath of his youth, but that was all. The key was in his pocket, proof of his special quest, it had to be enough. He couldn't remember how long he had stood in the damp chapel, lost in the sight of the ancient paintings. He only remembered that it was already daylight when he finally arrived in his hostel and went to sleep. Suddenly he heard a noise. Somebody opened the roll door and came into the garage.

The light switch clicked, but the light did not come on. From his hiding place he heard something that must have been a curse. Then a shuffling sound along the side of the car. He tensed and took a firmer grip on the handle of the whip. The timing and the accuracy of the first blow had to be perfect. It had to be quick. There was a risk that somebody might pass at the critical moment and be alerted to something suspicious. The driver's door opened and the car, also, remained in the dark. This time he clearly heard the irritated curse from the voice he had heard earlier. A fist impatiently tapped against the dome light, but the light remained off. Finally, with a sigh, the man let it be and started to get ready to drive off. As he closed the door, Meyer rose and hit him precisely with the lead-reinforced whip. With a soft rattle, the head slid aside and then against the backrest. Meyer emerged from his hiding place, stepped out of the car and closed the garage door. He took the bulb from the corner, fitted it and turned the switch. There was light. Quickly he secured his victim at wrists and ankles. He moved the passengers seat as far back as possible and then reclined the backrest. He placed the victim on the reclined seat and then shoved as much of his body under the dashboard as would fit. To the casual passer-by, here slept a man while being driven home. He opened the garage door, seated himself behind the wheel and backed out. In passing he waved at the man with the unhealthy pallor, who gave a dry cough as answer.

It was just eight thirty, too early to go to the chapel. That too, had been taken into account. He drove over the Jaime III in the direction of the Paseo Maritimo and turned left, toward the cathedral. He took the exit to the beltway and another ten minutes later the exit to Valdemossa. He turned into the first street on the right and arrived at the ruins of what once had been the Municipal Sports Center. He drove to within the walls, the only parts that were still standing. Protected by darkness and the lonesomeness of the place, he waited for midnight. Then he drove slowly to the chapel, parked the car on one of the parking lots and looked carefully around. He opened the door of the chapel with the purloined key. A small light burned brightly in front of the Maria statue.

He walked back to the car and drove to in front of the entrance. He opened the passenger door and again looked carefully around, he dragged the body from the car and then quickly into the chapel. Just as he stepped into the car in order to return it to the parking lot, a police car drove by, sweeping its headlights over the half-open door. He saw what happened from his place behind the wheel, but calm as ice, he started the engine and drove off. He drove past the fishing harbor and parked the car. After making sure that he was not being followed, he walked back to the chapel. From the opposite curb he noticed that the police had disappeared. He crossed the street and entered the chapel. The body was near the entrance and groaned.

That was right. The victim was supposed to be fully conscious when punishment was being meted out. They had to feel it. Just like his mother, his sister and his Aunt Marie and his Uncle Jan. The guilty would feel the same pain. He placed two benches on top of each other and hung a pulley with pre-rove rope from each of the hooks. Quickly he lowered the ropes and attached them to the leather cuffs around the wrists of the victim. Then he pulled the body up, facing the altar. Slowly he lit the candles until the scene was brightly lit. The light reflected in the gold leaf of the altar and the murals. The victim, now fully conscious and in pain, evacuated his intestines. A wet spot appeared near the crotch of the beige trousers. Meyer knelt in front of the altar, placed his forehead on the floor and prayed. A half hour later, with a dazed look in his eyes, he stood up and cut the victim's clothes away with a knife. Then he took the whip with the weighted tips and administered the first blow ...

---

* Circumcision is not generally practiced in Europe and is strictly a religious rite - trans.

*40. Amsterdam, Thursday, April 27, 1989

At four o'clock he was in the arrival hall at Schiphol Airport and saw that the KLM flight from Singapore had just landed. At least three hours delay! At least, thanks to a computer program and the proper modem, he had avoided an unnecessary wait. With happy anticipation he looked from behind the tall windows at the arriving passengers who, after having cleared passport control, where gathering their luggage. He kept his eye on Carousel #7. That was *her* flight. The first passengers started to approach the designated carousel and he knew it could not be much longer. She didn't know he was picking her up. That was a surprise. She had just left a message on his answering machine, announcing her arrival today, via KLM. There was just the one KLM flight from Singapore, so she had to be there. A few moments later he spotted her, accompanied by a number of gentlemen in grey, or blue business suits. She had left alone, ten days ago, but he knew that a number of specialists were to follow her. The carousel started up and the first pieces of luggage started to appear. They were soon picked out and the first passengers were moving to the exit. One of the gentleman picked a suitcase off the carousel and handed it to her. Hands were shaken and goodbyes were being said. Monique walked toward the "NOTHING TO DECLARE" exit and walked past customs and through the automatic doors. Almost at once she saw him, her travel-weary face lit up and she approached him enthusiastically. She dropped he suitcase and embraced him.

"Oh, Jacques, what a wonderful surprise to see you. How are you? Did you miss me?"

She swamped him with questions. He just managed the occasional "yes", "no", or "you bet". He took her suitcase and she pressed his free arm tightly to her body. Talking, they crossed the parking lot to his car.

"Are you tired?" he asked.

"Dog tired."

"Was it difficult?"

"Doing business with orientals is always difficult, for us. Patience, patience and again patience. You just have to have patience."

"How was the weather?"

"Hot and humid, but I loved it. Now that I've had a taste of the atmosphere, I've decided that one of these days, soon, I'll take a vacation in Indonesia. I still have family there, you know. My father's oldest brother, my uncle, lived there and married a native. They've both been dead for some time, but I still have a lot of cousins there. Come on, how are you? What have you been doing with yourself?"

As she asked the question, he could visualize the chapel in Palma.

"Nothing much."

"Nothing to talk about?"

"Well, no, I wouldn't know what to talk about. I lead a rather dull life, as you know."

"Were you bored?"

"Yes, a little," he lied.

"You should get a hobby, darling, that would do you good."

"What kind of hobby?"

"I don't know, maybe we can think of something."

"Well, let it be for now. You're home again and that's a full-time hobby, too. What do you want to do tonight? You want to go out to eat, or shall I order something in?"

"I don't even want to think about food. I just want to sleep."

"You want me to stay, or would you rather be by yourself?"

"Jacques Izaak Meyer, what are you thinking of? Of course, you're staying! You're on duty!"

"Oh yes, I meant to tell you, the last time I went to see Uncle Gert he wasn't home, although I'd told him I was coming."

"Is something the matter with him?"

"He's in the hospital."

"Serious?"

"I don't think so."

"Still, the poor old man."

"You want to come with me, when I visit?"

"But of course, he's your uncle! Tomorrow morning I have a Board Meeting, but I had already reserved the afternoon, because of jet-lag. It always takes me a couple of days to get over it. We'll go see Uncle Gert tomorrow afternoon."

On the way to her apartment she told him about her trip. The city, the people, how clean everything was, the reception in the Dutch Club in Singapore, but he only listened with half an ear. Today she had arrived from Singapore and only yesterday he had returned from Palma. She could tell him about her trip, but he couldn't say a word about his. They had both completed a task and perhaps that was the only thing they had in common. The tasks themselves couldn't be more different. Now he was with her again, in the other world, that had just barely opened up for him. The world that was so far removed from the holy task to which he had been appointed. The two worlds just did not mix. To, try and combine them was almost too much for an ordinary mortal. But he had to be able to switch from one to the other. Not just his actions, but above all, his thoughts. He must be able to hate intensely but at the same time he must be able to love, perhaps even more intensely. Simultaneously he felt as one of the chosen ones and as one of the common herd. A dual personality that had to be controlled to the last detail. He had never suspected that this could be so. That he would be able to do it, to make it work. Him, the grey, nondescript little man from the municipality, the kid that in 1945, alone and orphaned, faced a hostile world. What was it that Monique had told him once? He had to be more aggressive. He shouldn't feel small. That was it! He had something to be proud of. Himself! He just couldn't let it be known ...

*41. Palma de Mallorca, Sunday, April 30, 1989

Shortly after seven in the morning the priest of Establiments mounted his motor scooter and drove off in the direction of Palma. A transparent blanket of morning fog shrouded the landscape and gave it a mysterious appearance while accentuating the complete tranquility of the Sunday morning. This was the most beautiful time of day. Dew had imparted a varnish to all plants and flowers, bringing out the colors and aromas that were so much a part of making the day friendly and happy. He loved this time of day and especially on this day of the week. The busy week-day traffic was absent and most people were still sleeping, recovering from a raucous Saturday night. Now the island was in its prime. Leisurely he drove on, along the narrow paths, marked on both sides with low stone walls, which had separated the fields since time immemorial. Wild geraniums grew in a profusion of enormous, red clouds of cotton wool along the road and under the gnarled trunks of the age-old olive trees grew a carpet of yellow flowers that stretched out as far as the eye could see. In the distance he could hear the bleating of sheep mingled with the sound of the bells around their necks. The herd was being driven in his direction. When they were close, he dismounted from his scooter and let them pass. He talked for a while to the shepherd and then continued on his way.

Arriving at Palma he rode past dirty industrial terrains and modern suburbs. Streets full of unimaginative apartment buildings, one after the other. Impersonal storage bins for people, with not enough light and not enough space. He crossed the Avenidas and reached the old part of town, toward the sea. Through the lifting haze he saw the dozens of fishing boats, already returned from their early trips. It was beautiful. He stopped a moment in order to savor the view. Five minutes later he turned left and parked his scooter against the front of the chapel. He took the key from his pocket and opened the heavy, oak door. Before entering he looked at his watch and noted the time as eight thirty.

In Polderkerk, about twelve hundred miles further north, Meyer's alarm clock rang ...

42. Amsterdam, Monday Morning, May 1, 1989

As usual, De Berg entered at the stroke of nine and immediately saw the fax, waiting on his desk. He picked it up and read. A little later he put the paper down and said dejectedly:

"Goddamn, another one!"

He picked up the fax and went to see Commissaris Bakkenist. He knocked on the door and entered as a result of the usual "yes, yes, come on in".

"Good morning, sir."

"Morning, De Berg, I take it you saw?"

"Yes, another one."

"Yes, they keep sending the details because they're convinced it's a Dutchman."

"After all, it's all they have."

"Yes, that's for sure. I haven't yet spoken to Cortez, because he isn't in yet. I'll call back in about an hour and maybe we'll know more, then."

"Look, the only thing we know for sure, is that the weapon used was a whip. But that particular whip isn't the only one. There must be a number of crazies in Spain as well. I'm really starting to wonder if we should be looking here."

"You forget that he used a Dutch name and passport, Van Kleef, in Madrid."

"No, I'm not forgetting that, but it is possible that he bought the passport from somebody. What other proof is there? The desk clerk at the hotel states that our bird bought a Dutch newspaper, everyday. That too, doesn't mean too much. Perhaps it was a German paper, or a Swedish. For a Spaniard the difference is hard to determine. Maybe he just assumed it to be a Dutch paper, because of the Dutch passport. It's certain that no Spaniard can detect the difference between a German and a Dutch accent."

"Of course, I've thought about that, but what do you want? We cannot ignore the case."

"What can we do?"

"Travel Agencies. You read in the fax that the victim must have been dead for at least five days. Therefore he must have returned around that date. Start with the charter flights. Passenger lists. A middle aged man, traveling singly. There shouldn't be too many."

"Want me to start right-a way?"

"If you need help, take Freriks."

"OK, I'm on my way." He stood up and left the office.

Back at his desk he first called the three charter companies and within the hour he had received a stack of faxes, containing the passenger lists of the last three weeks. Carefully and patiently he went through them. At the end he had the names of two gentlemen who had travelled by themselves and the names of the travel agencies that had booked them. Again he picked up the phone and called the charter company. The first passenger turned out to be the twenty two year old boyfriend of the Mallorca hostess of the company. The second one was more interesting. A certain Mr. Spit from Amsterdam. The tour operator could provide little information. The customer had booked through a small agency in the center of town. He called and a friendly voice told him that the agency was closed until one o'clock on Monday. The voice belonged to a machine. Temporarily stuck, he and Freriks used the time to go over everything again. After discussing the cases for almost two hours, making arguments and rejecting conclusions, they were as far as they had been in the beginning.

"There must be something we're missing. It must be possible to locate the guy!"

"We have nothing. Our bird doesn't make mistakes."

"He must have made them, they all do, we just don't know yet what mistakes he made."

"You think the boss already talked to the big cheese in Spain?"

"I'll find out." De Berg called Bakkenist on the inside line.

"Have you heard anything more from Madrid, sir?"

Freriks, listening on an extension, also heard the voice of the commissaris.

"The usual pattern. Without a doubt, the same killer and no clues, whatsoever."

"Fingerprints?"

"Nothing! Hotels are still being checked, so far without result."

"Yes, but there are quiet a few on that island. This afternoon we'll be checking the travel agency."

"Do so, let me know." The connection was broken.

"Short and sweet," said Freriks.

De Berg completed some left-over administrative items and left shortly before one o'clock, rode the elevator down and took a car from the pool. He identified himself at the travel agency and asked to speak to the manager. He was shown to a small office and after the usual handshakes and introductions, he said:

"You took care of the booking for a certain Mr. Spit, a trip to Mallorca from the 19th to the 26th. I want to ask your people if they remember anything about the man. To be frank, I don't hope for much, but every little bit helps."

"You said Mr. Spit?"

"Yes, left on the nineteenth of April."

"One moment, let me check the file."

The man left and returned almost immediately with a thin folder.

"Here you are: Mr. Spit, residing at number 14, Peter Minuet Street, second floor. Reserved by telephone and came to pick up the ticket himself."

"How did he pay? A check? Credit card?"

"In cash. Here you are: four hundred and seventy five guilders. That's the price for a camping trip. No accommodations."

"Did you see the man?"

"No, this was handled at the counter by one of the clerks. Here you are: Annie. You want to talk to her?"

"Yes, please."

Although the agency was small enough to be able to have a conversation with anybody in either of the two room, even with the connecting door closed, he importantly pressed the button on an intercom and asked for Annie, who entered almost immediately.

"Annie, this is a gentleman from the police and he wants to ask you a few questions."

Apprehensive, the girl looked at De Berg and stammered:

"Y-yes, sir."

"I would like some information about one of the customers for whom you did the booking. Perhaps you'll remember some detail. Any detail, no matter how small, can be important."

"Yes, I understand, sir."

"We're concerned with a certain Mr. Spit. He picked up a ticket on the 17th and paid in cash for a camping trip to Palma. Look, here are the papers." He gave her the folder.

"Oh, yes, I remember, sir," the girl said, after looking through the file. "It was an old man."

"How old?"

"Well, at least fifty."

De Berg, forty eight himself, felt his age.

"What did he look like?"

"Distinguished, a real gentleman."

"How come you remember so exactly?"

"Well, you see, sir it doesn't happen too often that people pay in cash. In a way it's a bother, we're not really geared for it. We don't even have a cash register."

The manager supported her statement.

"The usual way is that we receive a down payment, via check, bank draft, or Money Order. We then send an invoice a few weeks before departure and that's paid in the same way. Of course, we accept credit cards, but that doesn't happen too often, in this neighborhood."

"I understand," said De Berg, and turned again to the girl:

"Tell me a little about the man. Anything peculiar, anything different you noticed?"

"No. I wouldn't know what."

"Hair?"

"Normal, nothing strange, it was grey."

"Along the temples, or all over?"

"Just the temples, maybe."

"How tall?"

"Average, just under six feet."

"Thick or thin?"

"No, he looked good, no stomach."

"He said his name was Spit. Did you feel it was his real name?"

"Yes, no, I mean, why not? How would you know?"

"I admit it's difficult. But sometimes, when somebody is used to write his own name for years, they'll hesitate before writing a fictitious name."

"But he doesn't have to write anything. I do that."

"Yes, exactly, but didn't he have to sign anything?"

"Yes, the form for the receipt, here it is." She handed it over.

He looked at the signature and asked the manager:

"May I take this with me? I will return it."

"But of course. Would you like me to make a copy for you?"

"No, I'd rather take the original, I want to have it examined by experts and the copy is less useful for that."

After thanking the manager and the girl for their cooperation, he returned to Headquarters. On the way he reflected that the vague description given by Annie, was more or less similar to the description provided by the desk clerk in Madrid. The suspicion that the perpetrator was indeed Dutch, seemed to become stronger.

*43. Amsterdam, Thursday, May 4, 1989

Today she wanted to be home early. He had not gone home since the day he picked her up at the airport. In fact, he had moved in, although they never discussed it. He had just stayed. He had gone to get some clothes from Polderkerk and she had emptied a closet to accommodate them. It was a sort of trial period, they were both still free, no obligations. If he wanted to go home, he could do so without breaking a promise. That was all right. He was on the front balcony when she came in. She went to him and saw the changes. A number of large flower boxes had been fastened to the railing, filled with bright red geraniums. The concrete deck had been covered with astro-turf and four adjustable lawn chairs and a table with a large umbrella had been grouped on the imitation grass. After recovering from her surprise, she covered her mouth in ecstasy.

"Oh, how nice, why did you do it?"

"I have a feeling it's going to be a wonderful summer."

"Jacques, how much did you spent on all this?"

"I never said it was a present. If I leave I'll take it with me. Like it?"

"Wonderful, but why didn't you tell me?"

"I am not allowed to surprise you?"

"Oh, how terrific."

"Tomorrow I'll put a light over the table, then we can eat outside in the evening."

"Will you stay forever?" she took him by the shoulders and placed her cheek next to his.

"You shouldn't *beschrieje*."

"That's my little Jewish boy, full of superstition!"

"You're nice and early."

"I have a surprise too. I reserved a table at the best Italian restaurant in Amsterdam and I have tickets for *A fish called Wanda*."

"This is not the week-end, it's just Thursday."

"Oh, darling, don't be so old-fashioned, what's the difference. I felt like it and thought you would too. Let me freshen up. Let me get rid of the dirt I picked up today."

"Still the same?"

"Don't talk about it," she disappeared in the direction of the bathroom.

Around seven they were at a table in the small Italian restaurant, owned and operated by a married couple. She was in the kitchen and he was the waiter. The six tables were filled every night. Nobody knew the names of the owners. Everybody called them Papa and Mama.

"Another hectic day, today," Monique sighed.

"Problems?" he asked.

"I don't know what's the matter. Ever since we started this business with Singapore, everybody seems to have gone crazy, especially my esteemed assistant, my so-called deputy."

"What's his name, anyway?"

"Smet. He has been behaving like a real bastard, the last few days, the underhanded son-of-a-bitch."

She had long since determined that she would share her life with him. The good and the bad, including her business triumphs and problems. In the first place it was wonderful to have somebody to talk to and secondly she wanted him to feel that she appreciated his opinion. And she did.

"He's against everything, tries to sabotage things and sometimes he's downright insulting. He's acting as if he owns the place and his condescending manner to everyone is enough to make me want to spit nails."

"He's planning something. He smells power. That seems obvious."

"But on what can he base that assumption? Does he think there's something connected to Singapore that can be used against me? I've watched everything like a hawk, it seems impossible that he'll be able to embarrass me with a wrong calculation, a mistake, or whatever. I've studied every detail to the last comma and crossed all tees and dotted all eyes. I've had everything double checked by the Comptroller's staff."

"Still, I've seen this type of behavior before. There's always more behind it than is apparent at first glance."

"You're telling me! I know that people who are being lured away by the competition will change their behavior overnight. They become careless, sloppy, or arrogant."

"You think he's had an offer?"

"It seems that way and he sold himself dearly."

"Singapore?"

"Of course Singapore. There have been long discussions, but no contracts yet. Nothing is yet definitive. And he knows everything, so he's a good catch for a competitor. They'll receive him with open arms. We're talking about the insurance of a $500 million property. The premiums could put a lot of companies in the black."

"Would Singapore be receptive to certain pressures?"

"I see what you mean, it depends how far you want to go with business gifts."

"Bribes?"

"No, they are very sensitive about that, believe me. Bribes wouldn't work. They worry about a calendar, or a desk set."

While talking they enjoyed the meal Mama had cooked for them and *A fish called Wanda* closed the relaxing evening.

She felt wonderful when they arrived home at midnight.

She had dragged him through the fourth of May* without him noticing.

---

* May 4 is Memorial Day in Holland and May 5 is Liberation Day. Both commemorate primarily World War II.—trans.

*44. Amsterdam, Friday Morning, May 5, 1989

When she entered the office of Galen, the president of the company, she saw a weekly on his desk. Without greeting, he said:

"Did you read this?"

"No, what are you talking about?"

"Well, here's a nice piece of prose for you," he handed her the opened periodical.

She read: "ASUCO, INC. PAYS BRIBES."

"My God, what a disaster!"

"That's one way of putting it, yes."

She read the entire article and met one surprise after another. The Singapore project was described in detail. A complete report of all the negotiations was included. Copies of letters were printed as proof. Names of company personnel were named, as well as some of the names from Singapore, among them the name of their most important contact, Mr. Chen. The investigations had gone as far afield as the Far East! After reading the article, she put it on the desk and looked pale as a sheet.

"They did a thorough job."

"I feel the same," said Galen.

"My God, what a sewer journalism."

"Yes, but how do we handle it?"

"How could they possibly get all the details?"

"I've been asking myself the same question."

"It has to be somebody from within the company!"

"That narrows it down to four: You, Smet, Hagenaar and myself."

"What can we do?"

"I really wouldn't know."

"There's a leak in the office."

"Or in Singapore."

"What could they possibly gain by that?"

"A better price from a spiteful competitor."

"You have anybody in mind?"

"There could be a number of them."

"What they said about me in this scurrilous article, is complete fantasy and fabrication."

"But it is damaging."

"It's certainly not minor. Who's behind it?"

"Do you have any enemies within the company?"

"I wouldn't know who. Of course, the usual jealousies, but that couldn't possibly be the motive for destroying somebody completely."

"You'll understand that I will have to take this up with the Board of Directors and there's no telling what the consequences will be?"

"With a little bit of additional bad luck, we can forget about Singapore."

"I think it's a lost cause already."

"That would be disastrous."

"Monique, it would be disastrous *and* damaging. Not just from the financial aspects, but above all as it concerns our prestige and credibility. As you know, we're subject to closer scrutiny in those areas than any other type of business. I think the money losses will amount to much more than the loss of Singapore."

"It's terrible!"

"Let's keep a cool head and think about containing the damage, a plan for restoring our image and possibly revenge."

"Would Chen know?"

"We have to assume that he's part of the plot."

"I'll call him. It's just ten o'clock here, it'll be just about five in Singapore."

As she left the office, she encountered Smet in the corridor. He laughed and asked:

"Problems, Mrs. Vanderlaan?" he walked on and knocked on the door with the brass nameplate.

*45. Palma de Mallorca, Monday, May 8, 1989

The team of eight detectives and the police Captains of Palma, Madrid and Sitges were seated in a space that most resembled a small classroom. Tables and chairs were aimed at the wall, where a big blackboard had been mounted. A lectern stood in a corner to the side of the blackboard. Cortez had originally flown in from Madrid for this meeting, just to keep informed of the progress of the case. But now the three cases had, after a lot of red tape and jurisdictional backbiting, finally been coordinated and Madrid had been placed in overall charge. Cortez walked to the lectern, placed a file in front of him, cleared his throat, wished a good morning to the assembled team and welcomed them. His decisive way of talking, fast and with rolling r's, forced one to listen. He spoke a perfect Spanish with a slight Madrid accent, it sounded proud and manly. He was not a man to use a lot of flowery, vague words, so beloved by the average Spaniard. His sentences were short and to the point. All superfluous embellishments were discarded.

"What do we know?" he began.

"Three murders, all committed in the same way. The victims were tortured and then killed with a sharp blow to the base of the skull, just above the top of the spine. The antecedents of the victims have been investigated and there's no reason to believe that they are in any way connected with crime, or the underworld. The method is identical. Therefore we know it must be the same perpetrator. A middle-aged man with graying hair at the temples. The description provided by the desk clerk at the Hotel Monte Carlo coincides with the description received in Palma about the man who rented a car under the name of Webber. It's not usual to photocopy a Driver's License, thus we have just the name. The fact that the description of Mr. Webber coincides with the description from Madrid means little. There are millions of middle-aged men with greying hair at the temples. However, every detail is important and we cannot afford to ignore any of them. We are dealing with an invisible man and we'll have to give him substance. We are certain to be dealing with a Hollander. A Dutchman. Amsterdam has checked all the passenger lists from the fifth through the thirtieth of April and found just one middle-aged man, travelling singly. The name is Spit."

He pronounced it "speet" but spelled it correctly to make sure. He then continued:

"Spit booked a camping trip in Amsterdam and paid in cash. The address and phone number provided to the booking agency turned out to be false. We therefore have a strong suspicion that this is our man. We checked all the pictures taken upon arrival, but without result. Amsterdam questioned the personnel of the charter company and one of the stewardesses mentioned that a passenger returned to his seat during disembarking, supposedly because he had forgotten something. He was the last person to leave the plane, in the end. Apparently the photographer had already left by that time. She described a middle-aged man with greying hair."

He took a sip of water and continued:

"The ground personnel at Palma has been questioned, including the hostess of the charter company assigned to meet new arrivals, but nobody has seen him. The name Spit did appear on their records. Arrival on nineteen April and departure on twenty six April. No description. The victim in Palma was not discovered until the thirtieth, by the priest who came to open the chapel. The pathologist concluded that the victim had been dead for at least six days. No pension or hotel has been found where the perpetrator could have stayed. Finger prints have not been found anywhere. The man has been extremely careful. Sitges launched an investigation into the origins of the clothing found in the camper, but without positive results. The manufacturers deliver to a lot of outlets and special lot numbers, or other identifying marks were not attached. Laboratory research only discovered one peculiarity: Traces of a sort of leather oil has been found in all the fatal wounds. This oil coincides with two discoveries. The wound of Van Kleef was examined by Amsterdam, after he had been robbed of his passport. The same traces were found. It is also certain that the Van

Kleef passport was used in Madrid. The receptionist of the Monte Carlo registered him under that name and so did the owner of the hostel where the first victim was found. By coincidence two criminals were arrested after they had robbed the driver of a white Citroen BX behind the Central Station in Amsterdam. A briefcase and a whip were stolen. The whip was examined at the forensic laboratory in Amsterdam and it has been concluded that this was the murder weapon used in Madrid. Again the traces of oil were identical with the other samples and the shape of the wound indicates that it was caused by the ball-like protrusion, the so-called monkey's fist, at the end of the handle. The latest victim, here in Palma, has also been killed with a comparable weapon. Again traces of the oil were found in the wound, caused by a round object."

A short pause, another sip of water.

"The whip has been carefully examined in Amsterdam and the conclusion was reached that this is not the type of whip used as a riding whip, or in any other kind of sport. It was concluded that we are dealing with a luxury item from the sado-masochistic world. Speculations have also been made about groups such as the Hell's Angels, the Skinheads, or neo-Nazi and neo-Fascist organizations. Personally I'm convinced that the man does not belong to any organization but that he works alone. And very shrewdly. I also believe him to be an amateur, not a professional killer. But a highly intelligent amateur. A professional killer would not steal a passport in order to get a different identity. Too much risk. There are other ways to obtain perfectly forged false papers, if one has the connections. Our invisible man did not have such connections, therefore he was forced to steal additional identification. We have no clues regarding the motive. It is certainly a revenge action. But why? A sensible answer eludes us. The card with the inscription 'Espana-Hungria: 1-1' does not seem connected in any way. Just a soccer match of twelve years ago. The question remains, what next?"

The room remained silent until the Captain from Palma rose and said:

"Because the clues, such as they are, are most recent here in Palma, I would propose that we concentrate our investigation here first. Small hostels, off the beaten track, perhaps we'll have a better chance there, than with the regular hotels and pensions. I also thought about the restaurants. If we cannot discover where the man slept, perhaps we can discover where he ate. A single person in a restaurant draws attention."

"It is possible that the man slept every night in a different hostel," answered Cortez. "One is rarely asked for a name in that sort of places, let alone a passport. The owners are usually not very cooperative when it comes to giving out information. But we have to try. We must certainly not neglect the restaurants."

46. Rotterdam, Monday Evening, May 8, 1989

When the maid served the main course, Smet didn't feel like eating. He felt sick and nauseated. His wife asked:

"Why don't you eat, darling?"

"I don't know, I just don't feel like it."

"I bet you had another extended business lunch. I've told you many times you have to watch that."

"I had no lunch at all, Magda."

"Well, then why don't you eat?"

"I just don't feel too well, that's all."

"You'll be able to come to the Honigs, won't you?"

"Do you mind if we make our excuses?"

"That would be very unwise. Honig is an important relation you cannot afford to loose."

"Honig is no relation of mine."

"You leave that to me. I have a good nose for spotting people who can be important, or not important, for us. I know that Honig can mean a lot to you and your career. Especially when you move to Belgium."

"All right, good, you win, we go. But please excuse me now, I have to be alone for a moment."

He stood up and left the room. In his study he picked up the phone and dialed an unlisted number in Belgium. A little later he heard the jovial voice of Breughel.

"Did you read it, Mr. Smet, we've got those Dutchmen by the hairs, yes, by the short hairs!"

"Mr. Breughel, I don't know if I can admire this method."

"Admire? Admire? Mr. Smet have you ever encountered one single move in business that could be admired? And what do you want now? I get Singapore and you get Mrs. Vanderlaan. Couldn't be better, right? Couldn't be better."

Breughel had the habit of repeating himself.

"So you informed the press?"

"Of course I informed the press! You Dutch always do it in your pants when you think about an extra bonus for an important person. That doesn't bother us in Belgium. No, that doesn't bother us in Belgium."

"Did you get in contact with Mr. Chen?"

"Of course, a very nice gentleman, Mr. Smet. The matter is just about closed. We raise our premium slightly and then we raise his commission slightly and everybody is happy. Yes, everybody is happy! No, I have to tell you, we're certainly grateful to you. Yes, we're certainly grateful to you."

"And our other arrangements?"

"Ah, yes, good of you to remind me. Yes, we'll have to discuss that again, soon, yes, we'll have to discuss that again."

The connection was broken from the other end.

Smet was as pale as a ghost when he replaced the receiver. He had been used. And his only salvation was to continue the game. To go along. To the bitter end.

✻47. *Amsterdam, Friday Evening, May 19, 1989*

They had now lived together for three weeks and both felt that it was the way things should be. The memories of the years they had lived apart became dimmer as time went by. It was difficult to imagine a different sort of life. He had never dared hope that fate could be this kind. Especially to him.

The business worries that troubled her and which, at least in this form, were something new to her experience, were almost unbearable. Without his support, his understanding and his patience, she would probably have succumbed. The case of the bribes had gotten completely out of hand. Of course, gifts had been distributed in Singapore. In the form of so-called commissions. There was no other way of doing business in some countries. Everybody knew it, but nobody mentioned it. It wasn't done. But now, since the facts had been publicized, everybody suddenly washed their hands of it and tried to pass the blame as quickly as possible to a convenient scapegoat. And she was the scapegoat. The Board of Directors consisted of a group of scared old men, who professed total innocence. She had been called on the carpet and the only person to support her, had been Galen, the president. Nobody thought it strange that Smet had resigned. She was convinced that he had been the one to leak the information to the press. But it was impossible to get any proof. Proof would not be found until he started his new job and the entire Singapore project followed him.

But she wasn't going to let it get that far. She'd show them, all of them, how much she was really worth. The Board of Directors did not pass a motion of no confidence in her, but she had won with just a single vote. Even the sudden departure of Smet did not change their collective minds. Smet had been with the firm so long, in a number of different capacities, that the very familiarity of the name seemed to place him above all suspicions. But she knew how his behavior had changed, the moment he had been passed over for her position. There was no rational explanation for that. There had been a lot of little things, little irritants, sarcastic remarks, veiled hints. Smet had known exactly how far to go, he'd been around a long time. Undetected sabotage could not be explained, not if it was done subtly and if anything said about it, was immediately dismissed as gossip.

She could hardly present that sort of evidence to a Board of Directors that was still getting used to the idea that women could be more than secretaries, or waitresses. Even so, they were never totally convinced. They had finally accepted her on the basis of her knowledge and loyalty, but she was very well aware that she always had to be at least twice as good as anybody else in the same position, because she was, after all, only a woman.

How could she save the project in Singapore? Only by offering the powers-that-be a higher commission. But that was exactly the problem that could not currently be mentioned. They were dealing with a competitor. A highly unethical competitor, that was certain.

She opened the door of the apartment and kissed Jacques as soon as she entered. He saw her worried face and said:

"You're not letting it get you down, are you?"

"I'll get over it."

"You have to call Galen, he's home now."

"He wants me to call him at home?"

"Yes, you had just left, he needed you urgently."

"Well, it must really be important."

She walked to the phone and dialed the number.

"Mrs. Galen," she heard from the other end of the line.

"Hello, Thea, Monique here. May I speak with Edward, please? It seemed urgent."

"I'll call him at once." She heard her voice calling: "Ed, phone for you!"

"Yes, Galen here."

"Edward, Monique. You asked me to call."

"Yes, a very unpleasant business. The reporter who wrote that filthy article, called me."

"And?"

"He says he's got proof that a part of the commissions, he calls them bribes, found their way into the pockets of somebody in our management."

"My God, did he mention a name?"

"Yes, yours."

"What!? My name? Where does he come off? You don't believe him, do you?"

"If I believed him, I wouldn't have called you."

"This is incredible. What sort of proof does he say he has?"

"He says that he has a copy of a Deposit Slip to a numbered account with a bank in Luxembourg."

"No name?"

"No, no name."

"How can we find out?"

"That's impossible."

"What filth. What can we do about it?"

"Remain calm, for the moment, perhaps we'll think of something."

"Smet resigned. Don't you find that suspicious?"

"Yes, of course, I've thought about it, but you know how it is, in our company the name Smet is still above suspicion."

"Please understand, Edward, I do not accuse anybody, not even Smet, but you do know that he felt insulted and passed over?"

"Let's assume that there is a certain amount of spite. But so what? He resigned, more than likely to accept a better position. Why would he want to hurt us gratuitously?"

"But it would make sense to his new boss. You said yourself that the consequences of this affair would cost more than the entire volume of the Singapore deal. His new employer would be in an excellent position to profit thereby."

"Let's just let it simmer a while, at least for the week-end, then we'll talk again on Monday. I hardly dare wish you a nice week-end."

"I'll try to salvage some of it, I promise."

"See you Monday."

"Goodbye, Edward."

He had listened to the conversation and asked:

"What's the matter?"

"Just a minor thing. I am being accused of fraud, that's all."

*48. *Amsterdam, Wednesday Morning, May 31, 1989*

"Gentlemen let's call them as we see them," Galen said to the Board of Directors. "Let's face facts. In that part of the world, as in most places, everything can be had for a price. It's up to us to set the limit on our 'commissions'." He gave the word a distinct double meaning. "I'm convinced that somebody within the company has been bought and that same somebody has supplied the information to the press and to the competition."

"Industrial espionage?"

"Yes, Mr. Hordike, just industrial espionage. Perhaps we're still, both of us, from a period that ethics and reputation were more important than just profits. But that time is gone forever. The project we're discussing is watched by our competition with a vulture's appetite and many are ready to pounce on the remains of the feast, if we let them."

"I understand, but what's our policy to be?"

"I believe we'll have to go to Singapore and by 'we' I mean Mrs. Vanderlaan. I've talked a number of times with Mr. Chen by telephone and I feel that there is a bond of mutual admiration and trust between him and Mrs. Vanderlaan. Our option expires on this coming June 6. We'll continue to work out the details and we'll have the complete program ready for presentation in less than five day. We'll go to Singapore and stick to our agreement."

"Apart from everything else, that does seem to be the best tactic."

"This affair is going to cost us money, no doubt about that. Our competition knows our plans and our bids. The final offerings are not known, but I don't have to tell you that they can figure just as well as we can. They will almost certainly underbid our final price in order to get the order."

"Is there any room for negotiating?"

"That all depends on the amount of money we want to give up."

"This is a matter of prestige. We must win, at all cost."

"I agree with you wholeheartedly, Mr. Hordike," said Galen.

"I do want to be absolutely clear on the position of Mrs. Vanderlaan," continued Hordike. "I remain of the opinion that the entire affair is part of her responsibility. With, or without, the so-called industrial espionage. She is responsible for preventing this kind of calamity. That's why we pay her salary and that's what we can reasonably expect. This kind of sloppiness means, to me, a certain degree of incompetence."

The murmur that started after this speech was interrupted by Galen.

"I know that there are a few among you who have difficulty with a woman in this position, but I want to point out, once again, that this opinion is not based on the facts. I don't want to go as far as mentioning prejudice, gentlemen, but we must most certainly take care that prejudice doesn't apply."

"Mr. Galen, the opinion of Mr. Hordike is not based on prejudice, but is a practical matter. A woman is generally not accepted as a worthy opponent."

"Mr. Cohen," asked Galen softly, "have you already forgotten Golda Meir?"

It was quite still for a moment and then there were some hastily suppressed grins. Galen continued.

"As far as Mrs. Vanderlaan is concerned, gentlemen, I just want to add this. As president of this company I reserve the right to investigate the accusations leveled against her. We are dealing with an extremely competent person who means a great deal to this company and has always contributed greatly to the overall efforts of the company. But apart from her many contributions and apart from her competence, as a human being I feel obligated to protect her to the fullest from false accusations of fraud based on hearsay, gossip and innuendo. That's part of my duty. My duty to her and to every other employee of this company. If you cannot agree with this I do not feel able to continue managing this company."

A few of the gentlemen applauded carefully, the rest did not react.

*49. Polderkerk, Monday Afternoon, June 5, 1989

Monique departed for Singapore that morning in an attempt to save the situation there. He had been unable to solve her business problems the last few weeks, but he had been able to support her. He was there when she came home depressed and he listened when she needed to talk. The accusations which were being aimed at her were so personal and so devoid of any human feeling that they became almost unbearable. The Board of Directors had dropped her like a hot potato and she had only the president, Galen, to thank for the chance to vindicate herself. Galen was the only one within the firm who stood by her, through thick and thin. Therefore she had asked herself, justifiably so, why she bothered, if the company was worth the effort. Even if she was able to save the situation in Singapore, she was determined to leave the company. Smet had turned his resignation in on the 6th of May and yesterday, in a private interview with the president, he had asked for the resignation to be rejected. He saw his chance! Galen had told her about it in confidence and had added that he had denied Smet's request. The vulture was hoisted by his own petard.

When he saw her pass through passport control, yesterday, he had the feeling that he would never see her again. It had happened so often in his life. But if it happened this time, he did not want to be left alone again. Not again live through it. That was too much. People within the company were bent on destroying her. He had also experienced that and it still made him angry. They had been happy together for five weeks and six days. He had been given five weeks and six days and it was already over. All over again. Every time again. He would never see her again, he was sure of that. He looked around the room and wondered how he could have ever lived here, without her. If she were to be taken from him, he would be right back here. Alone. That loneliness didn't bear thinking about. If he didn't see her again, all would be for nothing. He would again be staring at the walls, day after day, and talking to himself. He had carried on complete conversations in this living room. Long conversations with people who weren't there and would never be there. Friends who had been imagined and a family that did not exist. He was one of the survivors and this was his punishment. The few acquaintances he knew had been met during meetings and parties of the S&M world. In reality that was a hollow world, geared for orgasm. Like drug addicts they were always looking for a bigger experience, a greater kick, more egocentric pleasures. Their entire thought processes had been canalized in that direction.

Love, or even affection for each other, could not be found in that environment. Friendship was reduced to a slap on the shoulder and a first name that might even be fictitious. And always the surreptitious use of the "in"-words that were supposed to suggest an intimacy and trust that was permanently absent. If you wanted to be lonely, you could be very lonely in that environment. And he didn't want that anymore. Slowly he started to cry uncontrollably and the visions returned. It was going to end, that was certain. Five weeks and six days. It had been a wonderful spring and he thought about the evenings they had eaten on the balcony and then looked at the stars. He wasn't going to allow anybody to take that away. Not this time! Three times in his life he had been powerless to influence the outcome, but it was different now. He regained his composure and stood up. The things he needed were ready.

He would leave tonight.

*50. *France, Monday Night, June 5, 1989*

Calmly Meyer drove along the highway to Paris. A luggage carrier had been mounted on top of the car and he carried a surfboard on top of that. Not because he liked surfing. On the contrary. He detested such a "poor man's yacht", but it was an excellent camouflage. At the borders he would be looked at as just one more tourist. He passed Lille, glanced at the map and continued on to Paris. It was ten in the evening. He would drive through the night and then would take a train to Gerona from Narbonne. He didn't want to take his car, with Dutch license plates, into Spain. He had also ruled against flying. He had done that three times already. He wasn't too sure about police methods, but felt he had to avoid a pattern. Perhaps it was an exaggerated precaution, but better be safe than sorry. He was convinced that he had not forgotten anything. The newspaper reports had confirmed this opinion. "There is no trace of the perpetrator" had been written and he had felt powerful, almost omniscient. Two police forces in two different countries were unable to catch one ordinary man. Every time he was one step ahead. He had not left a trace, anywhere, he knew. Power was such a wonderful feeling!

He had never realized that before. He had always been the nondescript public servant, unnoticed and unnoticeable. Just another little man, like millions of others. How relieved he felt when, after years and years, he had finally found the courage to live off the modest income from the store on the Langedijk. How he had hated the nonentities behind their typewriters and file folders. With their pale skins and cheap suits, smelling of cabbage and

Brussels sprouts. He had been one of them. For years. He had to, it was expected. Every day again, the same faces, the same office, the same desks. The same conversations, about the camper, two weeks on the Riviera, soccer, salary. They had never read a good book; a theater, or a museum, was foreign territory. What they knew about "art" was delivered during the annual office party with performances by the rock-band-of-the-moment. Politics was nothing but blowing in the wind and foreigners were a bother. But he had stayed, driven by fate and grateful for every hand that was, however briefly, stretched out to him. Ever since the day that the Americans liberated him from the camp, from which only he out of his entire family had survived, he had been dependent on others. That had been the foundation of his self, formed him into an inoffensive little man that nobody bothered about, but was also not allowed to bother anybody. He looked for an outlet in his clothes. That was his way of separating himself from the rest. His clothes were always well-made, fitted flawlessly, with colors and styles matched to perfection. His socks always matched his ties and he never owned a pair of white socks. It had been so for years.

Thinking, he drove through the night. Every once in a while he would stop at a restaurant for a snack, or gas, and he arrived in Narbonne around 4 o'clock in the morning. He parked his car in a garage and took a dark week-end bag from the trunk. He did not want to use the brightly colored overnight bag a second time. He was dressed in faded jeans, a leather jacket and wore glasses with plain glass. The grey hair at the temples had been tinted and his hair was now all black. It made him appear a lot younger, he thought. He wondered what Monique would say, if she saw him like this. He walked outside, and in his best French asked a passer-by for directions to the railroad station. He followed the directions and reached the station within fifteen minutes. The train to Gerona was due to depart at six. He bought a one-way ticket. He arrived at ten o'clock in the evening and went to look for a cheap hotel ...

51. Madrid, Thursday Morning, June 8, 1989

Despite the fact that his desk was stacked with unfinished business, Cortez was not in his office, but in a quiet spot in the bar next to the building wherein the Policia Nacional was headquartered. The case of the madman, who had now killed three times, was very much on his mind. It was impossible to forget it. His immediate superiors, the Judge-Advocate, the District Attorney, all wanted results. But there simply was no light at the end of the tunnel. Every day the newspapers would rekindle the public interest with stories which were at best half-true, mostly phantasy, but always concluded that the police was totally incompetent. In order to justify that impression, the papers were absolutely silent on any cases he and his colleagues had been able to solve. At this time of the year, the so-called cucumber time, when there was little, or no real news, the case was exploited and sensationalized to the nth degree. Full-page heads in the style of "The Dutch Executioner Strikes Again!" and "The Butcher Among Us!" were only designed to increase the sale of newspapers. An out-and-out slander campaign had been started that irritated him no end. Of course, the various obstacles caused by a combination of a sluggish bureaucracy and an excess of red tape, sometimes delayed, or even hampered, an effective investigation. The mutual rivalry between the various police forces did not make it any easier. There were at least three forces who all wanted the honor of nabbing the culprit: his own Policia Nacional, the Policia Municipal and of course, the Guarda Civil. And, instead of cooperating, all worked against each other and at cross purposes. Even in his private life he was confronted with foul blows about the efficiency of the police. He ordered another coffee and opened the paper he had just bought. He skipped the front page in order not to be irritated all over again. The owner of the bar, an old acquaintance, brought his coffee and said in a worried tone of voice:

"You don't look well, Señor Cortez, you should take it easier."

"Thank you, Juan, I'll get over it."

"They're nothing but vultures, señor," he pointed at the front page and walked away.

Cortez leafed through the newspaper without really reading anything. His mind wasn't on it. Suddenly he noticed an article on page 3. It was just one column wide. "Soccer team among dead in plane crash," he read:

> "A plane, owned by Surinam Airways, crashed yesterday near the Zanderij Airport of Paramaribo. Among the victims were the members of a soccer team from Amsterdam that was scheduled to play a match ..."

After reading the first few sentences he put the paper down and stared bemused at nothing in particular. Then he cursed loudly and with emphasis. Resolutely he rose and left the bar. Now he knew! The date! Espana-Hungria: 1-1, played on March 27, 1977. The plane disaster on Tenerife was also on March 27, 1977! There was the connection!

He practically ran through the corridors, refusing to be delayed, or interrupted by anybody. He ran into his office, pressed a button and barked:

"Get me the headquarters of Aeropuertes Nacionales, now!"

He took a file from the stack on his desk and looked through it as one possessed. He took out the biographies of the three victims and read them over, again. He had a lead, he felt it instinctively. If it was worth anything, was left to be seen. Here it was: Rodriguez worked as traffic controller at the airport in Madrid, Oliver from Sitges had also worked at the airport and the last one, Planes from Palma, also! Surprised and bewildered he put the three sheets in front of him and looked away, deep in thought. The sudden ringing of the telephone startled him.

"Aeropuertes Nacionales for you, señor Cortez," said a voice.

"Please connect me with Personnel," he asked the operator. A little later a deep male voice answered. Cortez said:

"You're speaking with Captain Cortez of the Policia Nacional. I want to speak to whoever is in charge over there. This is in connection with a serious and urgent case."

"Naturalmente, señor, un momento, por favor," said the man, clearly impressed by the authoritarian behavior of Cortez. Within seconds he spoke to the Vice President of Personnel. Without greetings, he again mentioned his name and came immediately to the point.

"I want you to give me the entire employment history of three people. I'll give you the names. I want to know exactly where they worked and complete details regarding dates, and functions. Do you have a pen ready?"

"Si, señor, please begin."

"First, Jose Antonio Maria Rodriguez-Vidal, born on December 3, 1936 in Cadiz. Second, Matias Jesus Oliver-Amador, born on January 23, 1927 in Sitges and finally, Pedro Alfonso Maria Planes-Marti, born on August 30, 1935 at Lluchmayor on Mallorca. Do you have all that?"

"I have it written down, Captain."

"I am this minute dispatching an officer to you to pick up the information."

Before the man could protest, Cortez broke the connection.

Cortez paced his room. What was the connection? Was it really a lead, or just another dead-end? Everything had already been checked and double checked and then checked again. Amsterdam had sent him the latest information: the false name for the reservation of the ticket, the probable description that fitted so well with that from the desk clerk in Madrid. But it wasn't nearly enough. No help at all. Bakkenist told him that the killer had not stolen a passport before the third killing, at least no passport had been reported as stolen. That could mean that he had operated under his own name. But what kind of help was that, if you didn't know the name in the first place?

He must have rented a car, that was undeniable. Where did he sleep? Would it help to place an ad in the paper, or perhaps, use the television? Even the few clues they had might trigger somebody's memory. Somebody must have seen him. He picked up the phone and called the Judge-Advocate. He pleaded for some time, and then received permission to act accordingly. He composed the text, walked outside and gave it to one of his people. The man read the text and went to the telex-and-fax department. Within minutes the message was on its way.

As Cortez walked back to his office, he full well understood that he had left himself open to an avalanche of questions from reporters and other news hounds. He decided to forestall them and hold a press conference. Perhaps he would also get a chance to stop, or at least limit, the flood of incorrect stories and theories that were being circulated. He would have to discuss that with the Judge-Advocate. What could he tell the press? Nothing, really. What did he have to loose? Also nothing, really.

There was a knock on the door and a motorcycle cop strode in, helmet under the arm. First the man closed the door, then came to attention, saluted and said:

"Captain Cortez, herewith an envelope with contents which I picked up at headquarters of Aeropuertes Nacionales, as per your instructions."

He placed the envelope on the desk.

"Thank you, son."

"De nada, Capitan," the man answered formally. With much clicking of heels and stamping of boots, he turned and left the office.

Impatiently Cortez tore the envelope open, relieved it of its contents and started to read.

Jose Antonio Maria Rodriguez-Vidal, born on December 3, 1936 in Cadiz. Traffic controller. Hired: February 2, 1961. He read most of the information diagonally across until he reached the part that interested him in particular. And there it was: From November 1, 1975 to July 31, 1978, stationed at Tenerife.

He picked up the second stack of forms.

Matias Jesus Oliver-Amador, born on January 23, 1927 in Sitges. Chief Air Controller. Hired: September 1, 1957 ... from March 15, 1973 to May 31, 1977, stationed at Tenerife.

Pedro Alfonso Maria Planes-Marti, born on August 30, 1935 at Lluchmayor on Mallorca. Traffic controller ... from October 1, 1975 to December 31, 1978, stationed at Tenerife.

A cold shiver ran up and down his spine as he compared the dates. Could it be possible? Was that the motive?

But what, in heaven's name, was the connection with a soccer match between Spain and Hungary?

*52. *Alicante, Sunday Afternoon, March 27, 1977*

It was four thirty and long rows of people were lined up in front of the ticket windows at the Rico Perez Stadium in Alicante. Despite the fact that this was only supposed to be an exhibition game, it looked as if the stadium would be sold out. The police tried valiantly to prevent a traffic snarl. This Sunday again, they would be doomed to failure. Steadily the stadium filled while the camera people of Spanish television did a final check of their equipment. Singing and cheering could be heard from the stands and the red-yellow flag of Spain was very much in evidence. There were barely a hundred Hungary supporters among the fans. A bench for the officials was placed on the edge of the field and at five minutes to five, the trainers and reserves of both teams, preceded by their respective coaches, trotted onto the field and sat down, each group on their own sideline. Baroti, coach for Hungary and Kubala for Spain. At exactly five o'clock the large doors at the end of the field opened and the two teams, jogged on the field, followed by the Frenchman Vautrot, the referee for this match. The stands chanted the name of popular Juanito, who pirouetted before the public, clenching fists above his head. The result of this exhibition game would give an indication of the real match, to be played in fifteen days, in Bucharest against Rumania. That would be for the cup.

Kubala knew that, although technically the Rumanians rated far below the Hungarians, they were a lot more aggressive. After the toss, the referee blew the whistle and play began. The stands swayed with emotion and the reporters, far above the field, started their commentaries. Cameramen tried to keep focused on the ball. It developed into a boring game. Hungary was indeed technically far superior and the Spanish team reached a new nadir. Both teams showed less than their best efforts and there seemed to be no team spirit on either side of the field. Every player was doing his own individual thing, playing to the fans, grand-standing. Hungary dominated mid-field and Vilar defended his territory efficiently. Zombori, a large, blonde Hungarian was the only one of the field who seemed to genuinely enjoy himself. His game was masterful at times.

A reporter was already writing his story: "Disappointing, little depth, sometimes a brilliant move by Juanito, Hungary better prepared and trained."

After fifty eight minutes of play, the Hungarian Kovacs made the first goal. 1-0 for Hungary. In the sixty seventh minute Juanito answered for Spain in a brilliant solo dribble across the length of the field. The final score:

ESPANA-HUNGRIA: 1-1!

53. Gerona, Thursday Morning, June 8, 1989

While Cortez, in Madrid, thought he had finally isolated a motive, Meyer walked through the inner city of Gerona. He had most carefully studied a street map of the city, while still in Holland and now he was surprised at the feeling of deja-vu that overcame him. He had felt the same inkling in Madrid and Barcelona. Also in Palma, but that he knew from previous visits. He found that he recognized most of the names of streets and squares and their connections. The city looked much as he visualized it, but yet different. It was like a voice on the radio. The image the voice called up was seldom accurate. It was a comforting, and at the same time, a very disturbing feeling. It was warm and the heavy traffic raced through the narrow streets. But he knew where he was going and walked without haste, but with a purpose, toward his destination: The offices of Iberia at Number 8, Plaza Marques de Camps. A little later he reached it and saw the red-yellow logo of the Spanish airline on the front of the building. Here it was. Here was Jose Jimenez, the ex-controller and now chief of this Iberia booking office. For years he had known the names of his victims, their addresses and their employment, but never the faces. He had visualized those as well, over the years, like the streets. They also, never matched the reality. Like the voice on the radio. He decided to enter.

A large number of people were waiting their turn in front of the various windows. This gave him the opportunity to look around at leisure. He read the name plates on the counters: Maria Ferrer, Jaime Morillo, Antonia Gonzalez. The man he was looking for would probably have his own office, somewhere in the back. In the back of the room he noticed a dark-brown, panelled door with a brass door knob. He went closer and read the name, inscribed on the brass name plate: Jose Maria Jimenez-Escanellas, Director. That was the next one. He walked closely to the door and heard a male voice, telephoning, or in conversation with a second person. He took a folder from one of the tables and sat down in an easy chair next to the door. Nobody at the counters paid any attention to him. He was just one of the crowd. There was a veritable cacophony of sound, telephone calls, ringing telephones, buzzing of ticket printers, slamming of doors and drawers, the continual loud sound of Spanish conversations, discussions and arguments. But behind the door was he, the one he was looking for. Partly because of the actions of that man, he had received one hundred and sixteen thousand dollars in blood money. That was the price that had been put on the dead. Fifty eight thousand dollars each. Not per person. Per piece. Each! For one hundred and sixteen thousand dollars they had bought off those that remained.

That was the tariff established by the Warsaw Convention of 1929! Legal hush money, no more. The money was designed to lull everybody asleep. That way nobody would go after the really guilty, the bastards who were responsible. The victims couldn't protest any more. One hundred and sixteen thousand dollars. That was a little over three hundred thousand guilders in 1977. A greedy tax department immediately demanded more than fifty percent.

It was a plot. Just a conspiracy of powers that could no longer be controlled. One hand washed the other and an "I scratch your back if you scratch mine" mentality. Obviously they knew, and fully expected, that apathy and plain disinterest could be bought for a mere fifty eight thousand dollars a head. But not this time!

The pretentious door with the brass nameplate opened and a corpulent man, cigar in the corner of his mouth, emerged. He was no taller than five foot two, or three, dressed in a dark blue summer suit that stretched perilously around him. He went to one of the counters and discussed something with a clerk who interrupted from time to time to voice a respectful "Si, Señor Jimenez". So, this was the man. He had seen him now. He memorized the face and left the office. He strolled through the town for a while, stopped now and again to drink a *cafe con leche* and at exactly one thirty was back in front of the office. The first employees were just leaving and Jimenez was one of the last. He followed at a distance. The man walked to a garage and approached a grey Renault 25. He opened the door and drove off a little later.

Meyer noted the license number and left the parking garage. He took a cab and was taken to Estartit. Tourists with white, undulating thighs and pink shirts filled the streets and the sound system of every bar was too loud. He went to the office of a small car rental agency, showed his British Driver's License and after he had filled out the necessary papers and paid a deposit, he received the keys to a small Seat Uno. Walking along the souvenir shops, all, without exception, peddling the same sort of junk, he found, after a little searching, a bar where no music was forced upon the patrons. At leisure he ordered a large lunch and a bottle of ice-cold *rosado*. After that he walked to the beach, rented a chair with a large parasol and slept within minutes.

He woke, looked at his watch, saw it was past six thirty and stood up. He picked up the rented Seat and drove to Gerona. He parked the car in the same garage to which he had followed Jimenez. He left the car and stalked along the rows of cars, looking for the grey Renault 25. When he found it, he went back to his own car and parked it in a free slot, diagonally across from the Renault. After half an hour he discovered the silhouette of the short, corpulent man. He started his own car and waited for Jimenez to get in his car. Then he followed the large automobile as it left the garage.

The parking fees were ready in his hand and he was able to follow the other car, almost bumper to bumper. Jimenez was a thoughtful driver, who navigated calmly and decisively through the confusing traffic patterns. They left the city and finally arrived in an impersonal suburb of bare streets at right angles to the main roadway. The houses were large and expensive, but tract houses for all that. They formed a strange contrast to the unimaginative infrastructure of the main roadway, with pretensions of being a grand boulevard that failed miserably. The few pining palm trees alternated with street lights that were rusted, missed a top, or glass, or were just not working. What was supposed to be a bounteous median, luxuriant with plants and flowers, had deteriorated into a dirty strip of weeds and rubbish.

Jimenez entered a dead-end street and stopped in front of a villa. The gate opened automatically in response to an unseen command and he drove inside. Meyer turned his car at the end of the street, noted the address and returned to Gerona.

This was the first step. He would follow him for the next several days. Day after tomorrow he would return the car to the agency and then would rent another from a different agency. A different make and a different color. It seemed safer. The last time he had rented a car for just one day and depended on public transportation after that, but that wasn't possible this time. He also needed time to find an acceptable place of execution and he had to prepare for his departure.

Monday night it would be June 12, Aunt Marie's birthday. She would have been seventy two if they had just taken a little bus trip. Along the Rhine, maybe.

*54. *Madrid, Thursday Afternoon, June 8, 1989*

Tense and impatient Cortez waited for the promised phone call from Tenerife. He had called more than two hours ago and requested the duty roster and the names of the staff on duty in the control tower on that fatal March 27th of 1977. It was just a thought, but you never knew. The killer had wanted to make a statement with the date of the soccer match. He was hinting at something. The fact that all three of the victims had been working in the control tower of an airport and that all three had been stationed in Tenerife on the specific date, was more than coincidence. There had to be more to it. If the motive was as he suspected than they were dealing with a vengeful madman. But why after twelve year?

His thoughts were interrupted by the sound of the telephone. Before the first ring had stopped he took the receiver off the hook.

"Duran here, Señor Cortez please."

"This is Cortez."

"Señor Cortez, I have the requested information. Do you want me to send it to you, or will you take notes over the telephone?"

"Both. I'll take it down now and then you can fax me the complete information."

"I'll take care of it. Can I begin? First: Chief controller was Matias Jesus Oliver-Amador."

Cortez didn't need to write that down. He knew.

"Then the names of the other three. First: Jose Maria Jimenez-Escanellas."

"Just a moment, not so fast." He wrote.

"All right, please continue."

"Next Jose Antonio Maria Rodriguez-Vidal."

Cortez interrupted again and said:

"And the fourth is Pedro Alfonso Maria Planes-Marti!"

"Exactly, señor Cortez, how did you know?"

"It's my job, señor Duran. That was all?"

"Si, señor."

After thanking the man from Tenerife, he broke the connection and asked to be connected to headquarters of Aeropuertes Nacionales. He pushed a button and one of his inspectors entered almost immediately.

"We've got him, we just have to catch him."

The inspector looked surprised and said:

"I'm really curious, señor."

"On March 27, 1977 there was a soccer match between Spain and Hungary. Does the date mean anything to you?"

"No, señor, I wouldn't begin to guess."

"On that same day there was an airplane crash on Tenerife, hundreds of people lost their lives."

Cortez paused for effect and then continued.

"The three victims in Madrid, Sitges and Palma de Mallorca were aircraft controllers who were on duty in the tower at the time of the crash. Are you getting it?"

"Well, goddamn, that looks like vengeance. What we suspected all along!"

"But ..."

The phone rang. Cortez answered it, listened, picked up a pen and wrote something down. With a "muchas gracias" he replaced the receiver.

"But ... there was a fourth, namely Jose Maria Jimenez-Escanellas, at this moment in charge of the Iberia offices in Gerona, living ...," he read from the paper on which he had just made some notes, "at Number 15, Calle Puerto Rico."

"We have to warn him, that's the next one," was the immediate reaction of the inspector.

*55. *Gerona, Thursday Afternoon, June 8, 1989*

Captain Frontera, of the Gerona Municipal Police, stood up after he finished the conversation with Madrid. He called for one of his inspectors and said:

"Come with me, I'll fill you in on the way."

He searched among his papers for the latest information about the horrifying murders. Regular reports had been distributed from Madrid for the last few months.

They left the building. Because the distance wasn't too far, they didn't use a car, but walked to the offices of Iberia. As they proceeded he made the necessary explanations to the inspector. As they entered the building, they were welcomed by the manager, bursting with curiosity about the purpose of their visit. Frontera began:

"Señor Jimenez, you were a controller in the tower of Tenerife when the crash happened, back in 1977, is that right?"

"Yes, unfortunately. It was horrible. I'll never forget it. Matias Oliver, the one who was recently killed in Sitges, was one of my colleagues at the time."

"He wasn't the only one, was he?"

"What do you mean?"

"There were two others."

"Yes, of course, I don't remember their names exactly, be cause we worked on rotating schedules."

"Jose Rodriguez and Pedro Planes."

"Yes, you may be right."

"Señor Jimenez, your ex-colleagues Rodriguez and Planes have also been murdered. Where you aware of that?"

"No I wasn't. But that's terrible. Why are you telling me this?"

"Don't you read newspapers?"

"Well, to be frank, I seldom pay much attention to that sort of reports and in any case, it never occurred to me that they could be people I knew. As you know, Rodriguez and Planes are not exactly unusual names. And Jose and Pedro are even more commonly used. How absolutely terrible. It never occurred to me that it could be them. Also, the papers never mentioned a connection between the murders and Tenerife, as far as I know."

"Yes, that's true, because they only discovered the connection today, in Madrid."

"So that means they've all three been killed?"

"Yes, by the same madman."

"Madre mia! But why?"

"We don't know that, yet, but all indications are that we are dealing with revenge, executed by a very disturbed person. Revenge, vendetta, aberration, delusion, you name it."

"Always the same killer?"

"Absolutely, no doubt at all."

"But ... that means ...," Jimenez hesitated, afraid to voice his conclusion, but Frontera continued the sentence:

"That you are more than likely the fourth victim on the list and also, that you are in danger of your life."

Jimenez looked at the two men, astonishment on his face, and stammered:

"B-but ... w-what can we do about it?"

"We will, of course, provide round the clock protection. Not just you, but also your family."

"How do you want to do that?"

"We'll discuss that now. As you'll understand, it is of prime importance that we catch the killer. I'll be honest: at this moment we don't have the slightest idea regarding his identity. We don't have a good enough description, and the only thing we have been able to establish at this point is, that for reasons of his own, he seems to have targeted the staff of the control tower that was on duty at the time of the crash in Tenerife. You're the last on the list."

"And I'll be bait."

"You could put it that way. We can only catch him with your cooperation."

"And if you're not on time?"

"We will be in time, we will take all possible and necessary precautions."

"All right, what do I have to do?"

"For now, we want you to act normally, just follow your daily patterns and routines. If we change that, the killer might become suspicious. We know from the previous cases that he is extremely careful and prepares the ground thoroughly. He'll know exactly what you do for a living, where you live and what you look like."

"Well, that's nice to know. Do you know if he's already in the neighborhood?"

"That's something else we don't know. Perhaps. But it can also take days, maybe weeks."

"I'll introduce you to the surveillance team, so you and your family will be able to recognize them. We'll also install a phone in your car. In addition I want to post somebody in your office on a permanent basis. He'll behave just like any other employee. It will also be important to inform the rest of the staff. After closing I would like to call them all together and speak with them. Do you have a guest room?"

"Yes, I do."

"We would like to use that as well. It will interfere a bit with your private life, but I think it's important to move a permanent guard into your house, as well. Even when you're not at home, I want one of my men on the premises. Although I'm convinced that your wife and children aren't in any danger, it's better to make sure."

The three of them discussed everything in detail and at eight o'clock, after closing, the office staff was also informed.

Meyer, who had parked across from the grey Renault 25 in the parking garage, had to wait until quarter past nine before he saw the familiar silhouette.

*56. *Amsterdam, Friday Morning, June 9, 1989*

At ten o'clock detectives De Berg and Freriks were seated opposite Commissaris Bakkenist of the Amsterdam Municipal Police. Three copies had been made of the long fax that had been received from Madrid. When the two detectives finished reading, Bakkenist asked:

"Well, what are your thoughts?".

"Obviously revenge, as suspected."

"By whom?"

"Relatives ... survivors."

"Were there survivors?"

"Yes, I think so, the two planes caught fire, but a number of people managed to escape."

"Where do you want us to start, sir?"

"KLM! They're bound to have all the information about the passengers, I'd say. There will be a lot of digging through files and paperwork, but there's bound to be a clue there, somewhere."

"Damages? Claims?" asked Freriks.

"Money is often a motive, but it's a little late for that. He would have acted sooner. No, it's something else, some sort of frustration, something that festered and grew out of proportions. The fact that the controllers are the victims, indicates that he must have decided that those are the guilty, the ones he holds responsible. It's not a matter of money. And the fact that it took twelve years to come this far, isn't too strange. Somebody can lose his family because of something like this, but life has to go on. A job, business, raising children, all things that tend to occupy you with the present, that will distract you. But suddenly everything is gone. The children have grown, early retirement, things for which you lacked the time before, now start to eat away at you. We know we're dealing with a middle aged man, probably some sort of pensioner, nothing left to do. Let's say he was forty five when the disaster happened. Still in the bloom of life. No, just because it took twelve years, knowing how those people died, I'm thinking of a delayed reaction, delayed shock if you will, of a disturbed person. Most probably we are dealing with a very nice, self-effacing sort of human being, somebody from whom you'd least expect it. And lonely, that's a certainty, I think, incredibly lonely."

"That doesn't make it any easier," said De Berg.

"Yes, you're right about that, but I just wanted to point out that we shouldn't waste too much time on financial motives. It's too late for that. He's related to one, or more of the people that perished. The fact that he's going after the controllers indicates that he's holding them responsible. He's punishing them."

"Yes, all right, but what, in heaven's name, is the connection to that blasted soccer match?"

"Yes, well, I don't know that either. Perhaps just a hint. Perhaps he's trying to tell us something, a sort of dare. Who knows. Let's just start with those passenger lists and the recipients of damage payments. That'll be the people most closely related to the victims. It seems logical that that's the only place where we'll be likely to find our suspect, a suspect who has lost touch with reality. The more I think about it, the more I'm convinced that he's somewhere in that group. What do we have up to this point? The whip, a white BX, a vague description and the fact that he's Dutch."

"You're right, sir." And then, addressing Freriks: "Come on, Pete, let's go to KLM."

Within half an hour they were at the headquarters of KLM, in the suburbs, between the city and the airport. A friendly, helpful man received them in a modern conference room. He listened to their story and their requests, but when they mentioned the list of recipients of damage claims, he pursed his lips thoughtfully and said:

"You must understand that this is a very confidential matter and I cannot decide that on my own. I will have to consult with management."

"We understand, but for strictly humane reasons, we'd urge you to do this very quickly, because at the moment there is a man in Spain who is certainly going to be dead, unless we can prevent it in time."

"How quickly will you need the information?"

"Now," said De Berg bluntly.

"I will ring the president for you," said the man and left the room.

"While you're at it, when he comes back, ask for two round-trips to Greece, will you, I'm planning a vacation," said Freriks.

"You won't have the time, dear boy, we're on an economy kick, don't you know?"

"I know, that's why I could use the round-trips. Besides, you're good at asking things."

"Get your wife to take a job as stewardess, then you can always travel for free."

"They don't have airplanes that old, any more."

There was a knock on the door and a girl in a white coat asked if the gentlemen would care for a cup of coffee. Yes, the gentlemen would care for some, thank you. While they were sipping their coffee, the friendly gentleman returned with a thick file tucked under one arm.

"Here it is, gentleman. The president asked me to impress upon you once more the confidentiality of the information I'm about to provide."

"Mister, in our headquarters there isn't even a roll of toilet paper that isn't confidential. We're used to that."

"The president also gave permission to take the file with you, provided you'd be good enough to sign a receipt."

He handed them a form to be signed which also contained a number of conditions for the use of the information in the file. De Berg read it through and then signed it.

Back in headquarters they spread the information on a large table and sat down opposite each other to sort through it. De Berg took the payment records of damage claims from KLM and Freriks concentrated on the print-out of Citroen BX owners from the DMV. De Berg mentioned the first name and Freriks checked it against his list. Fortunately the names were listed alphabetically on the DMV print-out. This was the real police work. It had nothing to do with the perception of the public. Most detecting was done this way. Checking, researching, just plain, boring dog's body work. No guns, no high-speed chases, no martial arts. That was but a small part, if any, of their work as detectives.

"Hurry up a little, will you, or are you still having problems with the alphabet?"

"Hey, if I knew my ABCs, I wouldn't have had to become a cop."

"You want coffee?"

"How do you spell that? With a 'c', or a 'k'?"

They drank their coffee and plowed on. After about an hour De Berg mentioned the name.

"Kellenbach, Janus Albertus and Maria Anna Kellenbach-Tromp, Sarphaty Park 135, 2nd floor, Amsterdam. Beneficiary: Jacques Izaak Meyer, born August 20, 1939, last known address, the same, also in Amsterdam."

Freriks turned the pages of the list of Citroen owners and recited the alphabet softly to himself.

"Aich ... I ... Jay ... Kay ... Ell ... Em ... Em-e-i ... Is that Meyer with an 'i' or with a 'y'?"

"With a Y."

"Here they are, wow, quite a few, Jacques Izaak you said?"

"Yes."

"Yes, I've got him, look, Jacques Izaak Meyer, born August 20, 1939."

They compared the information until Freriks said suddenly: "That's HIM!"

*57. Amsterdam, Friday Afternoon, June 9, 1989

It was already three o'clock before Bakkenist was finally able to get the Judge-Advocate on the phone. The facts, gathered by his two detectives, were spread out in front of him. It was absolutely certain. They had their man. The owner of the white Citroen from behind the Central Station, whose name coincided with one of the beneficiaries of the damage claims paid out by KLM for the loss of his foster parents. That was more than just coincidence. Anyway, a policeman didn't believe in coincidences. After a long conversation, both gentlemen thought it advisable to bring Meyer in for questioning. The results of that preliminary investigation would determine whether or not a formal arrest warrant would have to be issued. He had De Berg and Freriks report to him and gave them instructions to pick up Meyer for questioning.

De Berg and Freriks used an unmarked vehicle for their trip to Polderkerk. Before long they stood in front of Meyer's house, at 54 Butter Way, and rang the doorbell. There was no answer. Freriks tried to look inside, through the closed curtains, but couldn't see a thing.

"Let's look in the back," he said and walked along the row of houses, made a right turn and walked back along the narrow path between the backyards of the houses. They went through the gate of 54 and stopped in front of the kitchen door. That, too, was closed.

"He took a powder."

"Are you thinking what I am thinking?"

"Yes, I've an idea that this may be a dangerous absence for somebody."

"If it's really him, it's more than dangerous. It could be fatal."

"Ask the neighbors?"

"Might as well." they retraced their steps.

They rang the bell of number 52 and a lady opened the door. De Berg took the initiative.

"Good afternoon, ma'am, we're from the Amsterdam Police," he showed her his identification.

"We're looking for your neighbor, Mr. Meyer, in connection with an accident of one of his relatives."

"Mr. Meyer? I wouldn't know where he could be. He is a bit of a stranger. We know him by face, but that's really all. He's a bit of a loner, we just don't associate."

"Has he been gone long?"

"Well, I think at least a few days, because his car is gone."

"You haven't talked to him."

"No, we never talk. Frankly I think he's a bit of a creep."

"He lives alone?"

"Yes, you never see any visitors. Well, yes, maybe once a week, you sometimes see a lady come and visit. Not because I'm necessarily curious, but you can't help noticing sometimes. Also, the woman always drives up in an expensive BMW, at least, that's what my husband says, because I don't know a lot about cars. Anyway, a car like that, in this neighborhood, you notice that. But that's really all I know."

"Does he associate with anybody in the neighborhood?"

"I don't think so. He doesn't even greet people in the street. But, of course, you could ask on the other side, at 56."

"We'll do that, ma'am, thank you very much for your cooperation."

"Anytime, gentlemen."

They walked to the adjoining house on the other side, where they were greeted by a man. De Berg went through the same preliminary routine and the man answered:

"Mister, I've lived here seven years already and I have *never* exchanged one single solitary word with that Meyer already. I just don't know what sort of hermit that guy is already."

"What kind of man is it? How does he look?"

"A real gentleman, always in quality suits already. He must have plenty of money already, because I don't think he's got a job. Otherwise I can't tell you anything more about him already. I think he's just an arrogant bastard."

The man said good bye and closed the door.

"Bakkenist was right, a loner."

"I have the same feeling," answered Freriks. He paused and added: "Already."

"What next?"

"Call in." They got into the car and called headquarters. When they reached Bakkenist, De Berg said:

"He's not here and, according to a neighbor, he's been gone for days."

"I'm not too happy about that," answered the commissaris.

"I bet he's on the way to number four!"

"Search the premises?"

"Seems the smart thing to do, sir."

"Very well, you two stay there and I see what I can do about reinforcements to keep an eye on things. Perhaps the post in Polderkerk can help, then you two get back here and we can decide what to do next."

"Very good, sir."

"Well?" asked Freriks.

"You heard, wait for reinforcements for surveillance and then back to good old Amsterdam."

"Oh, wonderful, just in time for rush hour."

"Yep, that's for sure."

*58. Madrid, Friday Evening, June 9, 1989

Cortez came home, exhausted, around quarter to eight and lowered himself slowly into an easy chair in the living room. Half dazed he looked at the television screen without consciously seeing anything. His wife could see he'd had a hard day and didn't bother him with her usual household problems, small or large. She could see he was worried. She served him a glass of wine and asked if he felt like a snack, or anything else to eat, but he didn't feel like eating. She placed the wine in front of him and left him alone. She knew that he would fall asleep within minutes and then wake, about half an hour later, completely refreshed and restored to his former vigor. She went to the kitchen and set the table. The two children came in at almost the same time. Their son was 19 and the daughter was just 17. They were still in school. The daughter was still dressed in her school uniform, consisting of a plaid skirt and a grey blouse. It was a tense time for the children, they both faced final exams toward the end of the month. An hour later the family sat down to dinner.

To Cortez this was the most wonderful part of the day. There were too many evenings that he couldn't spend with them, so he enjoyed the nights that it was possible with increased pleasure. With a feeling of pride he listened to his children, Their achievements at school and the gossip about their friends. It was the burgeoning adulthood that touched him deeply, again and again. They had still some ways to go before they each had conquered their own square foot of space in the world. How many years of doubt and despair would they still have to face? Of course, everybody went through the same valley of emotions. It was the natural way, designed to be conquered, eventually, by the optimism and flexibility of youth. It had ever been thus. But when you looked at it from a distance, with the retrospective vision that came with age, it seemed such an insurmountable barrier, which always gave him a feeling of intense pity for all these youngsters. A feeling he was at some pains to disguise very carefully.

Just as his wife served the main course, the phone rang.

"I'll take it," he said and left the table.

"Don't make it too long!" warned his wife.

"No, no."

He picked up the receiver: "Digame!?"

"Amigo! Bakkenist, Amsterdam. How are you?"

"Ah, el comisario Holandes, do you have news for me?"

"Yes, and what kind of news! We've got him, Jaime!"

"Tell me."

Bakkenist gave a synopsis of the discoveries and when he was finished, Cortez said:

"And, did you arrest him?"

"No, that's why I'm calling you. He's been gone for several days. I'm afraid he's on the way to your jurisdiction."

"How long has he been gone?"

"We estimate about three days."

"Then he's here already."

"You should take that into account."

"I'll immediately warn Gerona!"

"Yes, I would do that. That's the reason I called you at home. As soon as we have a picture, we'll fax it to you and we'll keep you informed, of course."

"Thank you very much."

As soon as the connection was broken, he dialed another number, the home number of Frontera.

"Digame."

"Frontera?"

"Si."

"Cortez here. Listen, he's on the way."

"How do you know?"

"Warning from Amsterdam."

"Photo?"

"Is being prepared, tomorrow maybe."

"I'll alert them!"

"Keep me informed?"

"Of course! Will you come here?"

"Count on me."

Again the connection was broken.

59. Polderkerk, Saturday Morning, June 10, 1989

Armed with a search warrant they went again to Polderkerk. A locksmith and two technical people would meet them there.

"It was supposed to be my day off," said Freriks.

"My good man, sometimes you can be such a bore. You had a day off only four weeks ago!"

"Yes, of course, you're right. A most untoward remark of mine."

"Anyway, what else could you possible desire. A beautiful car under your behind, free of charge, you never have to get your hands dirty. You can hardly call it work. We're always off, you know that, don't you?"

"Oh, yes, and such a princely income."

"There you go ... how many can say the same."

"Oh, well, it's human nature to be ungrateful for the blessings bestowed on us."

"Human nature? Who are you kidding. Human nature isn't ungrateful. You're ungrateful. You wretch. Are you so happy at home?"

"Home, where's that?"

"That's where your bed is stored."

"What's a bed?"

They continued toward Polderkerk and a little later they stopped in front of Meyer's house. They walked through the little front garden and saw that the door was already open. Freriks looked with admiration at the lock, unblemished by the hands of the locksmith.

"Just look at that, nothing to see. That bird is a real magician."

"Yes," answered De Berg, taking a closer look at the lock. "He could make a lot more in another way. Working for our boss will never make him rich."

They entered. The technicians had donned rubber gloves and rattled around the house. De Berg and Freriks surveyed the living room and walked a bit aimlessly around.

"Found anything yet," he asked.

"We just got started," said one of the men.

"Let's start downstairs."

De Berg and Freriks also put on rubber gloves and looked at the wall combination, everything placed, arranged and displayed with millimetric precision. They opened a drawer and they found the contents so neatly arranged that it elicited a protesting remark from Freriks.

"Jesus Christ! What sort of nitpicker *is* this guy?"

"Yes, a nitpicker, we feel the same," answered one of the technicians.

"I've never seen anything like it in my entire life. Just look at the way all that stuff is put away!" he opened a number of drawers. "That guy doesn't do anything else but cleaning, all day long!"

"Yes, too bad we can't say the same about you," answered De Berg.

Carefully they searched everything, taking extreme care to replace everything exactly the way they found it. Freriks took a typewriter from a cupboard and placed it on the table. De Berg said:

"It's an Olivetti."

"You're thinking what I'm thinking?"

"Does anybody have a sheet of paper for me?"

"And a magnifying glass?" asked Freriks.

One of the technicians pulled a sheet from his briefcase. De Berg put it in the machine and struck the capital H several times. He took the paper out of the machine and looked at the letter through the magnifying glass. He bent closer, closed one eye and then straightened himself again. He handed the glass to Freriks.

"Take a look."

Freriks looked and while still studying the letter he said:

"It's him, no doubt about it."

"I thought so too, we'll confiscate this machine."

They found envelopes and writing paper in the same closet where the typewriter had been stored. They took out everything very carefully and looked at the stacks of paper. A large envelope was filled with glossy postcards, that fitted exactly in the smaller envelopes.

"And those, my man, are them. There's no other way."

"Do we have the original from Madrid at the office?"

"No we haven't got that, but there's no doubt about it. They're the same, measure this thing a moment, will you?"

The man did as he was asked and said: "Roughly four by seven inches. Eight and half by twenty centimeters exactly."

"It fits, take it away."

After searching the rooms downstairs, the kitchen and the hall, they went upstairs. As they entered the bedroom with the black leather bed spread, the pillows and the steel construction with chains, they halted, astonished. Freriks was the first to break the silence and said:

"I like it, although it's not my taste."

"Yes, well, that's IKEA for you."

They searched the bedroom and the other rooms. Then they found a locked door,

"Damn, why is this door locked?"

"I don't know, but it's got to be opened."

"What kind of lock is it?"

"Nothing special," said one of the technicians.

"Have we found any keys?"

"Yes, downstairs, there was a key ring in the hall."

"Let's try those first."

Freriks went downstairs and returned in short order with a ring full of keys. One by one they were tried until they found the one that fit. De Berg opened the door and stepped into the dark space.

"It's pitch black in here!" He searched for a switch and put the light on when he found it. They saw the wooden cross against the wall with the cuffs and the chains. And all the other accoutrements, neatly displayed, each in its own place. Sort by sort. Hooks and chains, sorted in order of size and length. The whips and *plumeaus* as trophies on the wall. The chrome and steel studs and pins and rivets, glistening against the shiny black leather. The harnesses, corsets, vests, pants and other strange and bizarre clothing and costumes.

It was again Freriks who first broke the silence:

"And this, my dears, is our hobby room."

"Goddamn," said De Berg, "that's sick!"

"But why? Don't you think it's nice and cozy? Yes, I would have done a lot more with color, but otherwise it's quite nice."

Although they were fully conscious of the seriousness of their task and they worked with care, the jokes and puns flew back and forth. Perhaps to break the tension created by the menacing surroundings.

"Here's something for your wife, Pete," said De Berg, holding up an unidentifiable harness, made of thin leather straps.

"It's not her size, I can see that from here."

From a drawer in a small cupboard, De Berg took some polishing rags and a small bottle of oil. He looked at it and said:

"We'll take that too."

*60. Gerona, Monday Night, June 12, 1989

At seven thirty Meyer drove his rented, white Ford Fiesta into the dim garage. He drove past all the cars on the first floor and when he couldn't find what he was looking for, he went to the next level. There he found the grey Renault. There was no free place in the immediate vicinity, but he figured that since he was at least an hour early, a slot was bound to open up in time. A slot that would give him a clear view of his target. He waited. He was sure of himself. He was confident that he had planned everything, as usual, to perfection and that all eventualities had been foreseen. This was the last one. At least for now. He wasn't too sure about that. Especially not after having been so occupied with Monique's problems at the office. It was just possible that he would have to pay some attention to the man who was making life so difficult for her. He couldn't prove it, but all signs showed that the man, Smet, was bent on destroying her. The man would be well advised to cease his nefarious activities, or he would be forced to take steps. He was determined that no outsider would ever again jeopardize his happiness. He would know how to find them all. All of those who stood in his way. Three times he had shown what he was capable of and tonight would be the fourth time. Then he wanted to concentrate on Monique, to hold her and to protect her, and if anybody dared to interfere with them, or harm Monique, like the man Smet, they would have to reckon with him, to their sorrow. It was no more than a matter of simple justice.

When you stole money, you were a thief. But if you stole someone's happiness you could not be prosecuted. And that was wrong. Because the theft of happiness was far worse. You were worse than a thief. Happiness could never be replaced, mere money could always be replaced. But he wasn't going to let his happiness be stolen, ever again. Perhaps he would even track down Frau Vollmer. That would be the crowning achievement of his task. Then life would really make sense again. How old could she be? Seventy? Eighty? It had to be possible to find her address. She wouldn't have changed her name. She was too much German for that. They were still so convinced of the protection of their environment that they seldom even considered it. It was almost impossible to associate shame, guilt and modesty with those people. A people that had shamelessly maintained the names of Dachau and Bergen-Belsen as if in the past they had been no more than holiday retreats, would not be concerned about changing the name of an individual. Dachau and Bergen-Belsen and all the others were again just friendly, German towns. You could even buy postcards from there. Frau Vollmer was just another nice old lady, always ready for a long talk, or a nice bit of gossip. But her name would not have changed, just her address. Because she had been able to leave the camp. Unlike his mother, who had stayed there, she had been able to leave.

He spotted a vacated slot near the grey Renault, started the car and parked again. His car and the car of his victim were separated by a thick concrete pillar. As if planned. A good sign. A sign from the guiding force he had felt so often on his previous missions. He took the whip from the plastic bag on the rear seat.

He stroked the beautiful leather. It felt soft and supple. He wrapped the tails around his hand and took the grip in his palm. Playfully he tested the weight on the inside of his other hand and felt himself to be strong. A man with a weapon stretched himself, increased his reach. It had ever been so. The farther one could reach, the more dangerous one became. History had first invented the dagger, then the spear, then the rifle and now the intercontinental missiles. But the basis of all was the hand. That held the dagger, pulled the trigger, or pushed the button.

At ten past eight the man entered the garage. Meyer carefully crawled out of his car and placed himself behind the pillar, between the two cars. A number of people walked through the garage and here and there a car was started. The sound of the engines sounded hollow in the concrete space and would easily muffle the sound of a falling body. Meyer looked around and saw no one in his immediate surroundings. That too, no doubt, was a providential circumstance supplied by the unnamed power that guided his quest. The power that had selected *him* for this task. The owner of the grey Renault approached his car, walked toward the driver's door, took out his key and bent forward to the lock. Just before he could open the door, Meyer appeared. Frightened, the man turned around. Meyer took a firmer grip on the handle of his whip and raised his arm. At that moment he heard a male voice that called:

"Alto, policia!"

A few cars down he saw a man between the cars, both hands on the roof of a car and a pistol, shiny in the reflection of the neon light, in his hands. Meyer ducked in reflex before the sound of the first shot screamed through the garage. He heard the impact of the bullet against the pillar. Then he heard the screaming voices of scared people, in panic because of the deafening sound of the shot, its volume increased by the echoing effect of the concrete walls. The bad lighting prevented him from seeing his attacker. He crawled between the cars until he reached a corner of the garage. People ran to their cars and left with screeching tires. In his corner he calmly reflected on the situation. Surprised, he realized that he had been located. Tracked down. They had been waiting for him, that was obvious. They had known he would be coming. But how? Nobody knew him. Not here. He had left no traces, he was certain of that. What had gone wrong? Or was it a coincidence that somebody from the police just happened to be there while he was trying to hit Jimenez? No, it was no coincidence. They knew who he was. He'd made a mistake somewhere. But where? And when?

He stood motionless and slowly the sounds in the garage faded away. He heard approaching sirens in the distance. They were going to block the area! That's why they had made no effort to catch him. They'd just called for assistance and were calmly waiting for him to make his move. They'd be blocking all exits and he'd be trapped like a rat. That thought made him shiver and tears moistened his eyes. He was lost! Where was that providence that had guided him so often before? He was startled when he felt something move near his legs. A small dog, a stray, sniffed at his shoes, looked up at him and barked. He made a soothing gesture and stroked the dog's head. The dog could betray him, he realized that all right. He squatted down and continued caressing the dog. The dog sat down as if it had finally found its master again. Suddenly Meyer felt the dog's collar. Of course, a man with a dog. Nobody paid that any mind. He took the rope, originally destined to tie up his victim, from his pocket and tied one end to the dog's collar. He stood up and walked calmly to the nearest exit. The dog pulled him forward, as dogs are supposed to do. A police car pulled up in front of the exit. He gave a friendly nod to the cops and crossed the street. Indeed, a man with a dog, nobody pays any attention to him.

*61. Amsterdam, Tuesday Morning, June 13, 1989

Monique had been in the office since nine. Late last night she had arrived from Singapore on a Singapore Airlines flight via Frankfurt. Jacques had not been home, but she was not worried about that. He told her before she left that he might go to Paris for a few days, to look at some museums. He'd probably be home tonight, or tomorrow. She looked at her watch and noted the time. Half past ten. She picked up a file, tucked it under her arm and walked down the corridor to Galen's office. She knocked.

He was clearly happy to see her when she came in. His face gleamed with satisfaction and he laughed as he came from behind his desk. He took her by the shoulders and kissed her on both cheeks.

"You did it, hot damn! I knew it. You've told them all where to get off!"

"Thank you, Edward."

"I'm so proud of you."

"I want to tell you that I will be forever grateful for what you've done for me during the last few weeks. Without your support I would not have been able to succeed."

"I always had faith in you."

"Listen, Edward, I saved Singapore for the company, but I want to confess something."

"Tell me."

"I say this with the greatest reluctance and I do not want you to think that I would ever hurt you personally. But I haven't saved Singapore out of love, or loyalty, for the company, but strictly to satisfy my own ego."

"Well, especially after all the weeks that are just behind you, I find that very understandable."

"You can tell your Board of Directors that the Singapore contracts have been signed."

She placed the folder in front of him. "And here is my expense account. I take it that my expenses will be reimbursed?"

"But why didn't you use the company credit card?"

"I didn't do that, this time, because if I had not been able to salvage the situation, I would have paid my own expenses."

"But why?"

"And here is another little surprise for you. The name that belongs to the numbered account in Luxembourg, and a copy of the deposit for fifty thousand dollars."

Galen read it and said, surprised:

"Well, I'll be damned, it's him! This is from Mr. Chen?"

"That's from Mr. Chen, yes. And these are copies of the offerings our competition made in Singapore. Compagnie Belgique d'Assurance in Brussels."

Astonished, he received another batch of papers from her and looked at them, speechless. Finally he uttered:

"Breughel, the villain!"

"Indeed, Edward, it was Breughel. Then, finally, you can tell your Board of Directors that I've resigned, effective immediately. Here is the letter."

Confused, Galen looked at the letter she placed in front of him.

"I hope, again, that you will not take this personally."

Without reading her letter, he sat back, looked at her and shook his head.

"But Monique, listen to me! You're not going to let yourself be chased away by that bunch of fossils, are you? I understand how you felt, and feel. But you weren't the only one. I too, was insulted."

"My dear Edward, I like you a lot, but my decision is final. I have been accused of fraud and treason and that's no joke!"

"The Board never accused you, Monique, that came from outside."

"I know that, but they also did nothing to contradict the accusations. That's enough for me."

"The gentlemen will most assuredly offer their apologies, I'm sure of it."

"For a value of half a billion, the gentlemen will say anything you, or I, want."

"Monique, please think about it for a while."

"Edward, here are the keys for the BMW and the papers. I took care of all finished and urgent matters. It's on my desk. I must leave the rest to you."

"Please listen," he tried to return the keys to her. "Please don't be hasty. Do it for me? Take a week off. Do what you like. Perhaps you'll change your mind."

"I'm sorry, Edward, I have decided."

She offered her hand, which he took between both of his, reluctant to let her go.

"I'll miss you, Edward." Resolutely she left the office.

She had brought a small suitcase to the office and now she placed it on the desk. She took out the contents of drawer after drawer and made her selections. Part of it went in her suitcase and part of it she replaced. She took some framed pictures off the wall and picked up some off her desk. She wiped away a tear and was angry with herself for not controlling her emotions.

There was a knock on the door and her secretary came in. Amazed she looked at Monique and asked:

"What are you doing?"

"I'm used to leave things in order."

She closed the suitcase, walked over to her secretary and kissed her.

"Thanks for everything, Irene," she said and walked quickly to the door.

"Where are you going?"

"Home!"

It was half past eleven when she left the building.

It was a warm day with a clear, blue sky and a gentle breeze.

*62. *Amsterdam, Tuesday Morning, June 13, 1989*

At eight in the morning he passed the border between Belgium and the Netherlands. Calmly he drove past Breda in the direction of Amsterdam. After the Utrecht Bridge he turned left and he was in front of her building ten minutes later. As he stepped out of the car he looked up at the seventh floor. She wasn't home, he was sure, and it would be better so. He crossed the lobby and took the elevator. As soon as he was in the apartment he sat down in the chair that, over the last few weeks, had tacitly been acknowledged as "his" chair. He looked around. How nice it was here, and how happy he had been. But he was empty, he couldn't think anymore. After a while, he didn't know how long, he stood up, took the framed pictures of his family and placed them on her small desk. Next he pulled the typewriter toward him and placed a sheet in the machine. He started to type:

"My dear, dearest sweetheart,

"Everything has been for nothing. My life, my love for you and everything I've done. In reality I am only a few months old. The months that I spent with you. But the bitterness that grew within me in that other time, the time before I knew you, has won and ruined everything.

"I've done it all wrong, my darling, and I've even involved you. When you read this letter you will probably know who I really am and who you have loved.

"I don't ask forgiveness, I only hope that you will not be disgusted with yourself. The man I was when I lived with you, was the man I could have been, if things had been different in my life. That was the strange, wonderful feeling I had whenever we were together. Only then did I realize it. It could always have been that way, if a person was created without memory. The hate that has always lived in me, has won and I am the loser. In the end they all won. Frau Vollmer and the other brutes from the camp and the four controllers in the tower at Tenerife. Three are dead and the fourth escaped me. No doubt, he'll be a hero! That's the way it always is. I cannot bear it any longer. None of them were interested in people. People were things that could be branded, tattooed, beaten, gassed, burned, or be burned. Everybody knows it. How the mass murders in Tenerife happened, however, is only known to me. Soccer is a cancerous growth that makes savages of millions of people and that prevents them from fulfilling their true destiny in life. What started as a simple game, has grown to the proportions of mass-hysteria that grows like a virus in their brains. All important aspects of life, such as responsibility, love, involvement, have been subjugated to worship of the leather ball. Also in the traffic-control tower of Tenerife, where the television set was fired up at five in the afternoon in order to watch a game played by twenty two unimportant little men.

"That was the sole interest of four grown-up men, who held the fate of 631 people in their hands. Among them was my Aunt Marie and my Uncle Jan. Those four men could have prevented the disaster, but their eyes were glued to the wrong screen. The man who burned the number 89219 in my Mother's arm, the woman who beat her to death, the men who forced my father to work in the quarry until he dropped and the killer who gassed my dear little sister, have all gone free. The four in the tower at Tenerife, who were so interested in the wrong screen, are the only ones I have been able to punish. At five o'clock the game started in Alicante and fourteen minutes later there was an explosion in Tenerife. I'm convinced that they were sorry not to have been able to follow the rest of the game.

"I have now told you everything. I don't ask you to forgive me. I'm only a few months old, the months I spent with you. Never before have I loved anybody the way I loved you. But you came too late in my life.

"Good bye, my dear, dearest one"

Meyer stood up, walked to the bathroom, undressed and took a shower. He shaved and used a blower to dry his sparse hair. He took the clothes he wanted to wear out of the closet. Dressed, he went to the refrigerator and took out a bottle of champagne. He placed the cooler on the table in the living room, took a champagne glass from the sideboard and opened the bottle. He poured and raised the glass to himself while he looked at the photos on the desk. He drained the glass. Then he stood up and opened the balcony doors, the curtains billowed in the light breeze. He looked at the clear, blue sky, stepped onto the balcony and looked downstairs one last time ...

In the lobby Monique pressed the button for the seventh floor.

* *Epilogue:*

As a result of Meyer's last letter, an independent panel of specialists investigated his allegations and came to the conclusion that Meyer was suffering from delusions. There was no television set in the traffic control tower of the Tenerife airport during the unfortunate crash. As of today, that is still strictly prohibited.

Jacques Meyer was buried in the Jewish Cemetery at Muiderberg. Two people attended: Monique and Uncle Gert.

Monique was completely vindicated by the Board of Directors and they offered their apologies. She accepted the apology, but refused to reaccept her position with the firm. She is now employed as the Division Manager for a firm in the same line of business.

Smet was requested to leave the firm at once. His wife has started divorce proceedings against him.

De Berg, Freriks and Bakkenist are still assigned to headquarters of the Amsterdam Municipal Police. Captain Cortez is still with the police in Madrid, in the same function.

Captain Adrover of Sitges suffered a heart attack on Wednesday, August 9, and survived. On September 1, of that same year, he took early retirement.

Frau Bullinger, nee Vollmer, is 74 years old and lives in Thurn. She's not aware that after 45 years she has been the cause of additional victims. She couldn't have cared less.

Son Vida, Thursday Night, October 26, 1989

About the Author:

Henk Elsink (ELSINCK) is a new star on the Dutch detective-thriller scene. His first book, "Tenerife!", received rave press reviews in the Netherlands. Among them: "A wonderful plot, well written." (De Volkskrant), "A successful first effort. A find!" (Het Parool) and "A jewel!" (Brabants Dagblad).

After a successful career as a stand-up comic and cabaretier, Elsinck retired as a star of radio, TV, stage and film and started to devote his time to the writing of books. He divides his time between Palma de Mallorca (Spain), Turkey and the Netherlands. He has written three books and a fourth is in progress.

Elsinck's books are as far-ranging as their author. His stories reach from Spain to Amsterdam, from Brunei to South America and from Italy to California. His books are genuine thrillers that will keep readers glued to the edge of their seats.

The author is a proven best-seller and the careful, authorized translations of his work, published by New Amsterdam Publishing should fascinate the English speaking world as it has the European reading public.

MURDER BY FAX

by Elsinck

Elsinck's second effort consists entirely of a series of Fax copies. An important businessman receives a fax from an organization calling itself "The Radical People's Front for Africa". It demands a contribution of $5 million to aid the struggle of the black population in South Africa. The reader follows the alleged motives and criminal goals of the so-called organization via a series of approximately 200 fax messages between various companies, police departments and other persons. All communication is by Fax and it will lead, eventually, to kidnapping and murder. Because of the unique structure, the book's tension is maintained from the first to the last fax. The reader also experiences the vicarious thrill of "reading someone else's mail". After his successful first book, *Tenerife!*, Elsinck now builds an engrossing and frightening picture of the uses and mis-uses of modern communication methods.

First American edition of this European Best-Seller.

ISBN 1 881164 52 7

From critical reviews of **Murder by Fax**:

... Riveting — Sustains tension and is totally believable — An original idea, well executed — Unorthodox — Engrossing and frightening — Well conceived, written and executed — Elsinck sustains his reputation as a major new writer of thrillers ...

CONFESSION OF A HIRED KILLER

by Elsinck

A dead man is found in a small house on the remote Greek island of Serifos. His sole legacy consists of an incomplete letter, still in the typewriter. An intensive investigation reveals that the man may well be an independent, hired killer. His "clients" apparently included the Mafia and the Cosa Nostra. The trail leads from the Mediterranean to Berkeley, California and with quick scene changes and a riveting style, Elsinck succeeds again in creating a high tempo and sustained tension. A carefully documented thriller which exposes the merciless methods of organized crime. In 1990 Elsinck burst on the scene with the much talked-about *Tenerife!* which was followed, in 1991, with *Murder by Fax*. His latest offering has all the elements of another best-seller.

First American edition of this European Best-Seller.

ISBN 1 881164 53 5

From critical reviews of **Confession of a Hired Killer**:

... Elsinck remains a valuable asset to the thriller genre. He is original, writes in a lively style and researches his material with painstaking care ...

DeKok and Murder on the Menu
Baantjer

On the back of a menu from the Amsterdam Hotel-Restaurant *De Poort van Eden* (Eden's Gate) is found the complete, signed confession of a murder. The perpetrator confesses to the killing of a named blackmailer. Inspector DeKok (Amsterdam Municipal Police, Homicide) and his assistant, Vledder, gain possession of the menu. They remember the unsolved murder of a man whose corpse, with three bullet holes in the chest, was found floating in the waters of the Prince's Canal. A year-old case which was almost immediately turned over to the Narcotics Division. At the time it was considered to be just one more gang-related incident. DeKok and Vledder follow the trail of the menu and soon more victims are found and DeKok and Vledder are in deadly danger themselves. Although the murder was committed in Amsterdam, the case brings them to Rotterdam and other, well-known Dutch cities such as Edam and Maastricht.

First American edition of this European Best-Seller.

ISBN 1 881164 31 4

DeKok and the Somber Nude
Baantjer

The oldest of the four men turned to DeKok: "You're from Homicide?" DeKok nodded. The man wiped the raindrops from his face, bent down and carefully lifted a corner of the canvas. Slowly the head became visible: a severed girl's head. DeKok felt the blood drain from his face. "Is that all you found?" he asked. "A little further," the man answered sadly, "is the rest." Spread out among the dirt and the refuse were the remaining parts of the body: both arms, the long, slender legs, the petite torso. There was no clothing.

First American edition of this European Best-Seller.

ISBN 1 881164 01 2

DeKok and the Dead Harlequin

Baantjer

Murder, double murder, is committed in a well-known Amsterdam hotel. During a nightly conversation with the murderer DeKok tries everything possible to prevent the murderer from giving himself up to the police. Risking the anger of superiors DeKok disappears in order to prevent the perpetrator from being found. But he is found, thanks to a six-year old girl who causes untold misery for her family by refusing to sleep. A respected citizen, head of an important Accounting Office is deadly serious when he asks for information from the police. He is planning to commit murder. He decides that DeKok, as an expert, is the best possible source to teach him how to commit the perfect crime.

First American edition of this European Best-Seller.

ISBN 1 881164 04 7

DeKok and the Sorrowing Tomcat
Baantjer

Peter Geffel (Cunning Pete) had to come to a bad end. Even his Mother thought so. Still young, he dies a violent death. Somewhere in the sand dunes that help protect the low lands of the Netherlands he is found by an early jogger, a dagger protruding from his back. The local police cannot find a clue. They inform other jurisdictions via the police telex. In the normal course of events, DeKok (Homicide) receives a copy of the notification. It is the start of a new adventure for DeKok and his inseparable side-kick, Vledder. Baantjer relates the events in his usual, laconic manner.

First American edition of this European Best-Seller.

ISBN 1 881164 05 5

Murder in Amsterdam
Baantjer

The two very first "DeKok" stories for the first time in a single volume. In these stories DeKok meets Vledder, his invaluable assistant, for the first time. The book contains two complete novels. In *DeKok and the Sunday Strangler*, DeKok is recalled from his vacation in the provinces and tasked to find the murderer of a prostitute. The young, "scientific" detectives are stumped. A second murder occurs, again on Sunday and under the same circumstances. No sign of a struggle, or any other kind of resistance. Because of a circumstantial meeting, with a "missionary" to the Red Light District, DeKok discovers how the murderer thinks. At the last moment DeKok is able to prevent a third murder. In *DeKok and the Corpse on Christmas Eve*, a patrolling constable notices a corpse floating in the Gentlemen's Canal. Autopsy reveals that she has been strangled and that she was pregnant. "Silent witnesses" from the purse of the murdered girl point to two men who played an important role in her life. The fiancee could not possibly have committed the murder, but who is the second man? In order to preserve his Christmas Holiday, DeKok wants to solve the case quickly.

First American edition of these European Best-Sellers in a single volume.

ISBN 1 881164 00 4

About Baantjer:

Albert Cornelis Baantjer (BAANTJER) is the most widely read author in the Netherlands. In a country with less than 15 million inhabitants he sold, in 1988, his millionth "DeKok" book. Todate more than 35 titles in his "DeKok" series have been written and more than 2.5 million copies have been sold. Baantjer can safely be considered a publishing phenomenon. In addition he has written other fiction and non-fiction and writes a daily column for a Dutch newspaper. It is for his "DeKok" books, however, that he is best known. *Every* year more than 70,000 Dutch people check a "Baantjer/DeKok" out of a library. The Dutch version of the Reader's Digest Condensed Books (called "Best Books" in Holland) has selected a Baantjer/DeKok book five (5) times for inclusion in its series of condensed books.

Baantjer writes about Detective-Inspector DeKok of the Amsterdam Municipal Police (Homicide). Baantjer is himself an ex-inspector of the Amsterdam Police and is able to give his fictional characters the depth and the personality of real characters encountered during his long police career. Many people in Holland sometimes confuse real-life Baantjer with fictional DeKok. The author has never before been translated.

This author is a proven best-seller and the careful, authorized translations of his work, published by New Amsterdam Publishing should fascinate the English speaking world as it has the Dutch reading public.